LOST HIGHWAY

A JOHN TYLER ACTION THRILLER (#3)

TOM FOWLER

For Lisa and Isabel.

And for my dad, who's the best mechanic I know.

1

———

Nothing in John Tyler's life prepared him for this.

He'd felt similarly before. Not ready. In over his head. The first time he went on a Special Operations raid in Afghanistan. When Lexi was born, and he held his baby daughter for the first time. While life with his daughter turned out well, Tyler didn't like feeling he wasn't ready. He made sure to put in the work and be prepared. It had kept him alive many times over the years. "How the hell does anyone own and run a business?" he wondered.

Lexi, filling her water bottle from the fridge, glanced at him. "With help, Dad."

"Smitty is helping."

"As much as you're letting him," Lexi said. She capped her bottle and pointed at the papers sitting in front of her father. "I know it's a lot to deal with. Don't you know anyone from the army who's a good accountant?"

"I did," Tyler said, "but he was a Braxton toady." Ryan Anderson had indeed been a savant when it came to numbers, but he couldn't escape the thrall of their corrupt former commander. "I shot him."

"Find another one, then." Lexi slung her backpack over her shoulder. "Try not to kill this one." She wore a light denim jacket over jeans whose tightness Tyler didn't appreciate. The red bookbag matched the ponytail holder in her dark brown hair. Despite living with his daughter full-time for less than two years, Tyler knew this wasn't an accident. He'd seen other bags on her back before, and they always coordinated with whatever hair accessory she chose. For a moment, Tyler wished his own problems were so simple. "I gotta go, Dad."

"Right," Tyler said, snapping out of his quick reverie. He glanced at the oven clock. Lexi's drive to the University of Maryland would get her to her first class right about on time. "Have a good day. Love you."

"Love you, too." She walked toward the door and turned before she got there. "Don't forget to meet with Cliff." Tyler waved his hand. "I mean it. You could use a distraction from being a new business owner."

"I guess." Having something take his mind off of everything would be welcome. The door shut as Lexi left for class. When he decided to open his own classic car repair business, Tyler never thought it would be so complicated. He didn't want to hire a lawyer on general principle, so he'd leaned on his old boss Smitty for advice. The buck stopped with the guy whose name was on the paperwork, however.

Tyler looked at the wall calendar pinned near the fridge. It was late February. He hoped to open in a week or so. Things went in fits and starts. A flurry of activity preceded a period where nothing seemed to happen. Tyler learned to hurry up and wait in the army, so he was used to it even if he didn't like the rhythm. Currently, the process languished in one of its many lulls. Cliff, one of Tyler's bosses when he worked in private security, wanted to know if he could handle a simple job for a few days. If nothing else, it would be a good distraction, and the extra money wouldn't hurt.

Tyler picked up his phone.

Farzaad Durrani looked around the empty room. It was the third he'd visited today, and he got the feeling it would also be the last. To his eyes, the listed measurements of twenty by thirty looked correct. Plenty of outlets lined the walls. A small bathroom opened off to the left. Durrani looked inside. Sink, tub, shower, but no escapable window. A door to the front and one out the back. Easy to guard and defend. All good so far.

His trusted associate Josef joined him. "I think this one may be right."

Durrani was diligent about hiring men from his homeland of Afghanistan. Josef, a Serbian mercenary, proved to be the sole exception. He stood out thanks to his blond hair and lean, angular face, but the man proved himself time and again. "I agree, my friend."

"The minimum time we can lease it for is three months," Josef said.

Durrani waved a hand. "Whatever they require. We won't need it more than a few days."

Josef walked the perimeter of the room. He, too, checked the outlets and walked into the bathroom. "Do we know what's behind the drywall?"

"Cinder blocks." Durrani rapped on the wall and nodded. "I think this place used to be industrial before they prettied it up. Business has been slow, though, so we're getting a pretty good deal."

"The second door?"

"Hallway to the back entrance and a small office."

Durrani shrugged. "Easy to keep locked . . . or guarded if we need to."

Josef's head swiveled as he took in the area. "I'm surprised we're mobilizing again so soon."

"I know," Durrani said. "I prefer to wait at least half a year before we work in an area again." He held up his index finger. "However, we have a unique and lucrative opportunity. It's been in the works for a while, but this is the right time and place. Make sure the men are ready and know what they're looking for."

"I will," Josef said with a nod.

"Have the usual crew deliver the supplies we'll need, too."

"It sounds like we're moving quicker than normal this time." Josef frowned. "Compressed timeframes can lead to mistakes. I'm concerned about some of the men being sloppy."

"Deal with it if it comes up," Durrani said. "We'll be able to hire their replacements several times over when this is finished."

"Maybe we can even take a few months off," Josef said. "Let the heat die down before we start working again."

Durrani clapped Josef on the back. It felt like slapping the wall again. "You will be able to enjoy yourself anywhere you want, my friend."

Josef's head bobbed slowly. "We'll start working on her security. I've heard they're down to one man but looking to bring in another." He paused. "I'm also concerned people might look for her."

"They will," Durrani said. "We won't be able to avoid it. It's one of the reasons we'll need to move quickly. A couple days might be all we get. I want to start acquisitions tonight."

"I'll make sure this room is ready," Josef said.

～

CLIFF ASKED Tyler to meet him at the offices of Patriot Security. Tyler considered it for a moment. It could be worth it to see the puzzled look on Danny's face. He made the expression often enough. In the end, Tyler decided the headquarters of his former employer wouldn't be the best place. He chose Rizzo's in the Little Italy neighborhood of Baltimore. He valeted his vintage Oldsmobile 442 and walked inside a few minutes before his reservation.

The maitre d' led him to a square table for two. Tyler took the seat facing the front door. Stairs to the second level and a hallway leading to the kitchen were off to his right. He could keep them in sight easily enough. At the appointed hour, Cliff strolled in. He was a tall light-complected black man whose wiry muscles looked unchanged from his active duty days. "Tyler," he said as he slipped his light jacket off. Tyler stood, and the two men shook hands.

"Good to see you, Cliff." Tyler touched the hair on his own forehead. "You're finally joining the rest of us in going gray, I see." Tyler would turn fifty-one in a couple months. Cliff was at least as old, but his short hair remained completely black the last time Tyler saw him.

"We've had a lot of turnover recently." Cliff nodded as the waiter filled their water glasses. "Danny doesn't make things easier, either."

"He never did." Danny's attitude and meddling in Tyler's work compelled him to leave the company about a year ago. Cliff had been a silent partner for a while. It sounded like he'd started taking a more active role. "Good to see you stepping up."

"Yeah." Cliff sighed. "I know I was less involved for a while. Had some stuff going on, you know?"

Tyler offered a congenial nod. He noticed his old boss no longer wore a wedding ring. "Everything good now?"

When the waiter returned, each man ordered. Cliff opted

for lasagna with meat sauce, and Tyler chose the veal parmesan. "I'm all right," Cliff said. "Don't worry about me. Patriot being short-handed is the reason I'm coming to you."

Tyler took a swig of his water. "Does Danny know we're having this conversation?"

"No. The potential client came to me directly. I didn't think we had anyone to spare . . . but then, I thought of you. This seems like something up your alley."

"How many people do I get to shoot?"

"Hopefully none," Cliff said.

"I'll pass, then," Tyler said.

Cliff grinned. "I know Danny gave you shit for the job in DC. Hell, I thought you played it right. You got the client back, killed a few drug dealers, and none of it landed on our doorstep. Worth a medal in my book. He couldn't get over it, though."

"What's the job?" Tyler asked. "I'm not really interested in rehashing the many failings of your comrade."

A different server dropped off two salads. Once he left, Cliff said, "It's a simple protection detail. You get to wear a suit, look menacing, glare at people . . . the whole nine yards. It'll probably last a few days."

"Who's the client?"

"You interested?"

"Interested enough to ask the basic questions," Tyler said. He poured some oil and vinegar on his salad and picked around the pepperocini. "Don't get your hopes up yet."

"Fair enough," Cliff said. "You ever hear of Alex Anne?"

"The singer?"

Cliff's eyed widened. "Wow. I figured you were way too old to know who she is."

"My daughter listens to her albums," Tyler said. "She's among the few modern acts Lexi actually likes."

"You've trapped her with your classic rock?"

Tyler smiled. "I can't help it if the girl inherited good taste in music from her dad."

"All right, so you know who she is," Cliff said. "She's got some local appearances and a concert this week. Kid's from the area, so they're expecting big crowds, media, and probably a few crazies here and there."

"I don't know, Cliff." Tyler swirled ice cubes around his water glass. "I'm working on opening my own car repair shop. It should be ready to go soon. There's a lot of stuff on my list right now."

Their waiter returned with the entrees, and he topped off their waters before leaving. "Businesses ain't cheap," Cliff said as he cut into his lasagna.

"Good," Tyler said, "because neither am I." He closed his eyes and inhaled the steam rising from his veal parmesan. The sauce smelled tangy with enough oregano to make it interesting. The meat was so tender he could cut it with only his fork. "If I do this, I'm going to need more than the normal Patriot rate."

"I had a feeling you'd want some good coin. The client's willing to pay well. They have a guy on the detail already but want another."

"You know much about him?"

Cliff shrugged. "Client says he's good at his job. I got the impression he's not very warm and fuzzy. They can't seem to keep a second man." Cliff spread his hands and smirked. "With some of the more charming aspects of your personality, I figured you'd fit right in."

Tyler pondered the offer as he ate the delicious veal. He could use the cash. All new businesses could, and while he didn't know much about being an entrepreneur, he knew money was a good thing to have in abundance. On the other hand, a few days protecting a pop singer would take him away from the shop at a crucial time. Maybe he could delegate some tasks to Smitty. In a pinch, he could ask his girl-friend Sara for some general management advice. It had been a few months since he'd seen any action, and hours of poring over spreadsheets made Tyler realize how much he missed it. Cuffing around a crazy fan would barely count. "I'll think about it," he said after a moment.

"I was hoping to leave with a yes," Cliff said.

"We might still get there. When do you need to know?"

"As soon as possible."

"You paying for dinner?"

Cliff frowned. "Why?"

"It's an extra tally mark in the *yes* column if you are," Tyler said.

"Patriot Security would love to buy your meal, then."

"Thanks." Tyler used the knife to push about half the remaining entree to the other side of the plate. He'd take it home for Lexi. "I'll let you know soon."

"Thanks," Cliff said. "It's just protection detail. You've done it a bunch of times. How hard could it be?"

Tyler knew the answer.

2

D urrani slapped a thin manila folder onto the table in front of Josef. The other man picked it up and opened it. "Not much here," he said. "Who's this guy?"

"The security detail," Durrani said. "A few others have come and gone over the last couple years. This man is the constant. Donnell Rodgers."

Josef frowned at the contents. "You looked over this already?" Durrani offered a small nod. "He doesn't seem like anything special. No military history . . . a few years with the Baltimore County police." Josef closed the folder and shrugged. "No wonder they're looking to bring in another man."

"Her father is cautious. I mentioned he's the constant, but he's never alone for long. Your intel is solid as usual. I expect them to have someone else in place before the concert."

"We could just grab her from her house," Josef said. "Even if this guy lives with them—"

"He does," Durrani interjected.

"Fine. Even so, he's one guy. The dad's not much. Shoot two guys and grab the girl. Easy."

Durrani shook his head. "In theory, perhaps. In practice, not so much." He slid another paper toward Josef, this one showing a picture of a nice house. "They have an excellent alarm system. Video. Multiple redundant backups. The dad is a major contributor to local police charities. Even if it only takes a couple minutes to do what you suggest, we would be on camera. There could be fans near her house hoping for a look at her. It's too big a risk."

"All right." Josef stood and walked the documents to the cross-cut shredder. It turned them into confetti. He learned years ago not to leave a paper trail. "You've obviously thought about this. I know you said you wanted to test her security. What's the plan?"

"She has two events before the concert," Durrani said. "Some appearance and album signing at a mall. It's a good venue to see what they've got. Make sure you have someone lined up. The other is her rehearsal. Her fan club members can get some tickets to see it."

"You're a member?"

"I am." Durrani smiled. "We'll need someone to go there as well. Think of it as the final rehearsal for us, too. You and I can wait in the garage."

"You must have a very wealthy buyer on the hook," Josef said.

"We will both be able to live the good life for a few months." Durrani already did, but he knew downtime and exotic destinations appealed to Josef. "There is always demand for the services we provide. In a couple years, there will be another pretty singer, and someone else will want to own her, too. Who are we to deny the wealthy men of the world the pleasures of a young woman?"

"Who indeed?" Josef echoed.

TYLER CHECKED his appearance in the mirror. At the repeated urging of Cliff, he agreed to meet with the potential client before making a decision. A perk of serving in the army was never needing to wonder about your wardrobe. Tyler missed those days. He'd never considered himself a fashion plate—something Lexi reminded him of from time to time—and he wondered how to dress. Would a suit be too formal? Would a shirt and pants be too casual? "Bah." Tyler undid his tie and tossed it onto the bed. He slipped the jacket on. If a navy blue suit and pressed white shirt weren't good enough for the client—tie or no tie—the hell with him.

The person interested in hiring him requested the meeting at a small conference room inside the Lord Baltimore Hotel. It was a nice place—not the high standards Tyler ascribed to a pop singer, but good enough. The historic nature of the building lent some extra cachet. It was also convenient to the Baltimore Arena. Short drives minimized security risks. Tyler arrived at the venue and secured a guest parking pass. A hotel staffer led him to the "breakout room," according to its signage. It offered no further explanation of what the hell a breakout room was.

Inside, a rectangular table offered comfortable seating for six. Audio conferencing equipment Tyler remembered from his army days sat atop it. A blank whiteboard hung on the otherwise barren walls. The client occupied the seat at the far end. He was about Tyler's age and twice his size. Beady brown eyes peered over glasses no longer big enough for his face. They may have fit well ten years and seventy pounds ago. He stuffed himself into a polo shirt one size too small and dress pants whose overworked button threatened to break free with every breath. He didn't stand when Tyler entered. "Jeff Wilkinson," he said from his seat.

"John Tyler." The two shook hands, and Tyler took a seat to Wilkinson's right facing the door.

"Tell me about yourself."

"I used to work for the company you hired," Tyler said. He inclined his head toward a leather portfolio. "Unless I've missed my guess, you have my file from Patriot in there."

Wilkinson sat there like he expected more. Tyler often left people feeling this way in conversations. They could learn to get over it. Eventually, Wilkinson said, "I do have your C.V. here."

He seemed like exactly the type to call it a C.V. Tyler wondered if he knew what the initials meant. The company provided a few pages detailing the qualifications of every person they sent into the field—a courtesy Cliff apparently extended to former operatives, as well. Tyler did a little research of his own. The porcine man at the head of the table was both Alex Anne's father and manager.

"Do you have anything to add to it?"

"I'm sure it's very complete," Tyler said.

"You were in the army for twenty-four years." Not a question.

"Yes."

Wilkinson tried to lean back in the chair but only made it a couple inches. "Your C.V. doesn't mention much about your experience."

"There are several good reasons."

Wilkinson frowned but continued. "And you worked for Patriot Security for eight years?"

"Eight years and two months," Tyler said. "But who's counting?"

"Why did you leave?" Wilkinson asked.

"You've dealt with Cliff so far, right?" The other man nodded. "His partner Danny is an asshole." Tyler shrugged. "I got tired of taking orders from him."

"How old are you, Mister Tyler? If you don't mind me asking."

"Fifty," he said. "I'll turn fifty-one in a couple months."

"I'm fifty-one," Wilkinson said. "I wouldn't hire myself to protect my daughter."

"Well, there are . . . a few differences between us."

"What are you saying?"

"I'm not sure of your ability to protect her," Tyler said.

"Are you implying I'm fat?"

"No, but I also don't need to, do I?" Wilkinson crossed his arms under his chest. "I'm not trying to be rude. We all have our limitations. Mine's probably in what people like to call soft skills. You're obviously concerned enough about your daughter to hire someone to protect her. It means you don't think you can do it yourself." Wilkinson didn't say anything. Tyler understood the power of silence. Normally, he was content to lapse into it and wait. Cliff wanted the favor, however, so he filled the conversational gap. "I'm extremely overqualified to be extra muscle for a teenaged girl, regardless of her profession or popularity. If my 'C.V' doesn't make it clear, nothing I say is going to help."

The client made a show of frowning, pursing his lips, grimacing, and any other expression he could summon to show how put out he was. Tyler offered nothing else. Eventually, the other man said, "You're very direct, aren't you?"

"Don't know any other way to be."

"I'm not sure Donnell is going to like you."

"Am I here to augment your daughter's security," Tyler said, "or win a popularity contest?"

"You shouldn't take Donnell lightly."

"I don't. I'm sure he's capable. You wouldn't hire a clown. The reality, however, is if he were doing a bang-up job on his own, you wouldn't need me."

"I have concerns," Wilkinson said. "My daughter is popular. A lot of it is great, but it comes with an ugly side, too. People always wanting to take her picture. Creepy fan emails and social media posts." He shuddered. Tyler wondered if people still sent good old-fashioned death threats in the mail. "Those have been on the rise recently. We haven't toured in well over a year, and it all starts soon. She has a couple appearances coming up, a concert at the Arena in two nights, and then we're on to Philadelphia and up into the northeast. I'd like you to stick around for a few days, maybe a week."

Tyler wondered what the appearances were. Celebrities needed attention. Some for a pathological reason, but their careers would wither on the vine without it. Proximity and accessibility to fans often clashed with good security practices. Tyler wondered where Wilkinson and Donnell fell when the topic came up for debate. He didn't relish the idea of leaving town now, but they could figure it out at the appropriate time. "Do you have a specific concern in Baltimore?"

Wilkinson shook his head. "No, but she's from Baltimore."

"So am I," Tyler said. "I'm not hiring extra security."

"You're not a popular singer."

"A relief to the ears of millions, I'm sure."

Wilkinson smiled for the first time in this sit-down. "If you'd like to come aboard, we'd love to have you."

"I'm thinking about it," Tyler said. "I want to know the chain of command, though. Would I work for you or Donnell?"

"Me." Wilkinson patted his chest a few times. "If you see something, I want you to act on it. I don't think Donnell will be a problem, but I'll address it with him if there's an issue." He paused. "What do you say?"

Tyler wanted to accept. On the off chance the job provided any excitement, he could use it. The money wouldn't hurt, either. Concerns about being away from the shop nagged at him. Tyler chided himself for being indecisive. Trying to open a business left him out of sorts. He could use the break, but he also needed to do the transaction through Cliff. Tyler stood. "I'll talk to Cliff, and we'll let you know tonight."

"What?" Wilkinson frowned. "Cliff told me—"

"I don't work for him anymore," Tyler said. "I'm a free agent. We'll let you know tonight. If it's not good enough, feel free to call another company."

The scowl continued a few seconds before Wilkinson nodded. "All right. I'll look forward to your answer, then."

Tyler left. He had a good feeling what the answer would be.

3

Lexi played the new Alex Anne album through her earbuds. She'd downloaded it on Spotify the day it came out, and it marked one of the few current albums in her library. Alex Anne's lyrics on this record employed a unique twist. She sang about love, lust, and the usual matters which infused popular music, but it came from the perspective of someone almost embarrassed to be rich and successful. She wanted to be an everyday girl and fall in love with an everyday boy. Though she'd never been wealthy, Lexi related on some level. The family moved a lot in her younger years—when her parents were still together—and Lexi's teen years were spent full of inconsistent friendships and accusations of being aloof. Maybe it was why she'd never been able to get into Katy Perry or Taylor Swift like so many of her classmates did.

"*I'd give up all this money to have you here tonight.*

"*I'd give up all this money just to make it right.*

"*I'd walk away from cameras and turn out every light.*

"*I'd give up all this money to have you here tonight.*"

She walked downstairs to find her dad working in the

kitchen. He wore an intense frown of concentration, a bit of a sneer at something not going quite right, and one brow slightly raised in confusion at what he was doing—his usual expression while cooking. For a man who only became a full-time parent less than two years ago, he was doing great, even if he didn't realize it. Lexi figured she ought to tell him sometime, but he'd never been big on sentimentality.

He smiled when he saw her, and his lips moved. She paused the music and popped her earbuds out. "I didn't think you'd be home yet. Didn't you have some meeting to go to?"

"Didn't take too long," her dad said. "Spent more time driving back and forth than I did at the sit-down."

"How did it go?"

He shrugged. "I said I'd talk to Cliff and let him know tonight."

Lexi sat as her father checked a skillet. She smelled chili powder and cumin. He was probably making tacos. Sure enough, chopped lettuce and tomatoes occupied bowls on the counter, along with a sealed bag of cheese and a package of shells. "You should do it, Dad."

"What?"

"The job," she said. "Whatever it is. You should take it."

"Trying to get rid of me?" he asked.

"Sort of." He shot her a curious look, so Lexi continued. "Ever since you stopped working at Smitty's, it feels like you've been a little . . . bored. Working on your taco recipe and waiting for a shop to open isn't your thing."

"I think we're finally coming up on the homestretch." He spooned steaming and seasoned ground beef out of the skillet and into a bowl.

Lexi stood and made three tacos, skipping lettuce and doubling down on cheese and tomatoes. She sat at the table and let the cheese melt into the meat. "I'm glad, but it doesn't matter. You've seemed a little . . . off for a while. Sara thinks you're a little lost. She mentioned something about tilting at a monster instead of a windmill, but I didn't get it."

Her dad stared ahead for a couple seconds. "You're talking to Sara?"

"Yes."

"Without me around?" Lexi bobbed her head. "There's no way this ends well for me, is there?"

She grinned. "Probably not. The daughter and the girl-friend are already talking about the male in our lives behind his back. I think your fate is sealed."

"For what it's worth, I think you're both right. Maybe I needed to hear someone else say it. There shouldn't be any rescuing or avenging involved, though." He talked as he assembled his own dinner. "Just standing around and making sure things don't get out of hand."

"What's the job?" Lexi asked.

"I'd be working on the protection detail for a singer." On his way to the table, he tried to suppress a grin. "You've heard of her. Alex Anne."

Lexi paused with a taco halfway to her mouth. "No way."

"Way." Her dad joined her at the table. "I haven't met her yet. So far, I've only talked to her father. He's also her manager."

"She's playing the Arena in a couple nights," Lexi said.

"I know. I'll be there if I take the job."

"Do you think you could get tickets?"

"I think I'd look like a jerk asking for a favor right away." Lexi frowned. "I'll see what I can do." He held up a finger to cut her off. "One ticket. Singular. Just you . . . before you mention nine other people you'd want to bring."

"Probably only two or three," Lexi said with a smile. "They'll have to settle for seeing it on Instagram."

"Will they post pictures of their middle fingers?" he asked.

"Nothing like that." She paused to enjoy a couple bites of

the taco. The beef could've used a little more spice, but the flavor was very good. "You're really going to do the job?"

"I'll call when we're finished eating."

"Good for you, Dad."

"I think it will be," he said.

TYLER CALLED Cliff to give him the news. "I knew you'd come around. Glad to have you back even if it's only for one gig."

"You haven't heard my rates yet."

The two came to an understanding quickly. Cliff insisted on calling Wilkinson, which Tyler understood. The company shouldn't give up a client's phone number to an independent contractor, which is what Tyler now was. A few minutes later, his phone rang, and a number he didn't recognize showed on the screen.

"I heard the good news," Wilkinson said. "Can you come back to the hotel? You need to meet Donnell and get up to speed on the schedule. I'll text you my room number." Tyler told him he'd be there as soon as he could. He hadn't changed clothes after the interview earlier. If they were good enough then, they must be now, too. Tyler fired up the 442 and drove back to the Lord Baltimore Hotel. With rush hour long past, the commute proved quick.

Knowing he'd joined Team Alex Anne, Tyler paid extra attention to every detail as he approached the old building. No doorman. Two revolving doors led into the lobby. Tasteful and expensive-looking furniture—mostly in black and gray — dominated the floor space. A baby grand piano sat in a corner. Tyler wondered what percentage of those walking by and fingering a brief tune really knew what they were doing. A mezzanine level overlooked the entryway and first floor. It could hold stalkers. Paparazzi. Drunk fans. Two staircases led down, and the one near the elevator posed an obvious vulnerability. Tyler rode up to Wilkinson's floor and knocked on the door.

A large black man answered the door. He was built like a football player, standing a good six-five and pushing three hundred pounds. He was a little heavier than Tyler's friend Leon Sharpe, now a captain in the Baltimore Police, and his full head of dark hair provided another key difference. Donnell scowled as his eyes scanned Tyler up and down. "You the new guy?"

"I am." Donnell jerked his head toward the interior. Tyler walked inside. The large man scanned the hallway before closing the door. "I wasn't followed," Tyler said.

"How do you know?"

"You see any bodies out there?"

"You army?" Donnell asked.

Tyler nodded. "Retired."

"You look retired."

"You want to see if I've lost a step, come at me."

"Won't be necessary," Wilkinson said. Tyler didn't look away from Donnell, who stood coiled and ready to strike. "Donnell, this is John Tyler. He'll be working with us for a few days."

Donnell relaxed, but his sour expression didn't improve. "You done this kind of work before?"

"No," Tyler said.

"What'd you do in the army, then?"

"Taught soldiers how to fix tanks and hummers and killed a lot of Taliban assholes."

"How many you kill?" Donnell said.

"The war kept right on going." Tyler shrugged. "I guess not enough."

Donnell grunted. Tyler finally took in the suite. The door opened into a sitting room which could have been lifted from a very nice house. The black and gray theme remained in place from the lobby. A sliding wooden door led to a king-sized bed, desk, and bathroom. "Alexandra's in the adjoining suite," Wilkinson said. "She's preparing for tomorrow. Probably posting on Instagram and TikTok. Her fans expect a certain number a day. You'll meet her tomorrow."

"We got an appearance in the morning," Donnell added. "Be ready." He scanned Tyler again. "You might want to wear a suit, too."

"I *am* wearing a suit," Tyler pointed out.

"Put a tie on, then."

Wilkinson waved his hand. "I don't care if you wear a tie. We'll be at White Marsh Mall at ten. Know where it is?" Tyler bobbed his head. "Good. Alexandra is doing a meet and greet in the food court." Tyler had been to the mall several times. He knew the area. A door from the parking lot. Foot traffic in both directions. People milling about the many eateries which ringed the ample seating space. Wide open and exposed. It seemed like a terrible place to put on an event. He must've frowned because Wilkinson asked, "You have some concerns?"

"It's a very open area," Tyler said. "Potential threats can come in at least three directions."

"We're mostly expecting fans. Alexandra hasn't performed around here for over a year."

"You selling tickets?"

"No."

"The public can come in, then," Tyler said. "People already at the mall who don't care about your daughter will gum up the works because they'll be attracted to the spectacle. Then, we have to consider the possibility of someone in the crowd wanting to do her harm."

"This is why I pay you and Donnell," Wilkinson said.

Donnell folded his arms. "You afraid of going to the mall?"

Tyler answered him with a question. "How many staircases come down from the mezzanine?"

"What?"

"Not a hard question if you're paying attention. How many staircases come down from the mezzanine?"

"What is this, a quiz?" Donnell asked, frowning. "I don't know."

"Two. One empties out right near the elevators. It's the biggest vulnerability I saw but not the only one."

"You thought a lot about this."

"I did," Tyler said. "The problem is I seem to be the only one."

"What's your point?"

"You need to be aware of threats before they happen," Tyler said. "Otherwise, it's too late. This thing at the food court is tomorrow, and I'm sure it's way too late to beg off now. I can't stop you from doing it, but I can make sure you're aware of the risks."

Donnell shook his head. "You paranoid or something?"

"You're not paranoid if they're really trying to kill you."

"We appreciate your perspective, Mister Tyler," Wilkinson said, his demeanor sincere. Donnell's face looked like his recent diet consisted solely of lemons. "I'm sure you and Donnell can handle White Marsh Mall tomorrow. I'll make sure management makes a security guard or two also available."

Tyler doubted the mall cops would be very useful, but he kept it to himself. He and Donnell could probably handle most situations which could reasonably come up. Wilkinson and his main security guy needed to think about these scenarios, though. They were probably lucky nothing happened to Alex Anne so far. "Am I meeting you at White Marsh?"

"Ten o'clock sharp," Donnell said. "Be on time."

"We just found the third thing I did in the army," Tyler said. "Show up early."

~

DURRANI INTERRUPTED Josef's late dinner with a question. "Are we good for tomorrow?"

The other man made a show of eating slowly before answering. "We are. We'll have someone there in the morning." He frowned. "He's not coming cheap, though. You want me to kill him when this is over?"

"No." Durrani shook his head. "We're getting a princely sum for the singer. We can incur a few expenses."

Josef shrugged. Durrani wondered if he would simply execute the paid confederate anyway. Josef never minded taking people out especially when it helped the bottom line. "All right. He knows he's there to test the security. He's already been arrested twice, so he's not worried about the cops taking him away."

"Good work," Durrani said.

"I know we're active again sooner than we expected," Josef said. "How are the acquisitions coming?"

"Off to a good start. I've also brought in Hajira. She's working on getting a few recruits."

"Mmm." Josef didn't like Hajira. He didn't care for operations with women, and Durrani gave up trying to convince him how useful she was. Josef grudgingly accepted it—he was a good employee, after all—but they rarely broached the subject, and the two had limited interactions.

"She'll find us a few," Durrani said. "She always does. Girls trust her."

Josef went back to his dinner. It looked like rice and some kind of meat. Durrani couldn't smell any spices. It fit Josef to eat a bland meal by himself. "We'll be good for tomorrow," the Serbian said after a moment, "but we can't keep her for long. She's too famous. Unlike a lot of our finds, people are going to notice she's missing."

"You worry about what the next day brings, my friend," Durrani said. "Like I told you, this end game has been in the works for months. I'll make sure we get away with our famous cargo and collect our money."

4

Tyler arrived at White Marsh Mall fifteen minutes early. He parked at the entrance near the food court and approached the doors. It was still a half-hour before the place officially opened. The only people inside would be employees and elderly folks who walked the floors for exercise. Two security guards milled about the interior. Wilkinson told one of them to let Tyler in when he banged on the glass. He walked up a few steps to where the event would soon take place.

A memory came to him. Tyler remembered the mall opening when he was about thirteen. He came with his mother shortly after. Most of the stores didn't interest him, but he'd never seen so many under one roof before. Foot traffic was heavy, and finding two chairs in the food court could have been the thirteenth labor of Heracles. He recalled a carousel taking up a lot of floor space back then. Of course, he wanted to ride it, and so did every kid there. It was gone now. Commerce marches on. Tyler smiled as he remembered he and his mother each leaving with a new pair of tennis shoes.

He paced around the center of the area. Workers had removed a bunch of tables and chairs to build a small stage and set up a long table for autographs and photos. Donnell chatted with a young woman Tyler recognized as Alex Anne from pictures he saw online. She was pretty in the classical sense of the word. Her medium brown hair hung past her shoulder blades. She wore a T-shirt, denim jacket, and tight jeans—a pair right out of the Lexi dress code. Tyler would need to get introduced to her at some point. For now, he concerned himself with where she would be meeting and greeting her fans.

Restaurants ringed the center area. Burger King. The obligatory Chinese joints. Other fast food chains. A few healthier options. The main entrance featured three doors. A few people already lined up outside. Once the place opened, mall patrons coming from any direction could access the food court from the other end. It was a logistical nightmare. Wilkinson should never have agreed to this. Donnell might have thought him paranoid, but Tyler had seen situations go pear-shaped simply because too many people were permitted access to the area. It only took one lunatic.

Fifteen minutes remained until the event started. Tyler checked the restroom hallway on the left side of the food court. It ended at an unalarmed exit door. He pushed it open. No one waited outside, and there was no handle or push bar to gain access. Tyler returned to the main area. He checked the far end. The food court took up the approximate middle of the building, so plenty of shops lined the mall in both directions and on both levels. An escalator, an elevator, and a staircase all provided incursion from the lower floor. It would be impossible to keep people away from this end.

Wilkinson approached wearing the smile of a man who didn't understand risk management. "What do you think?"

"I think you never should've come here," Tyler said. "There's too much access from too many places. You'd need a dozen people to do this operation properly."

"It's not an operation, Mister Tyler. Alexandra will sing a couple acoustic songs. Donnell will be on stage with her when she performs. I want you in front. Then, you'll both be around when she signs autographs and chats with her fans."

"Didn't you tell me there's a creepy component to her supporters?" Wilkinson frowned but nodded. "Do you really think none of those people are here today?"

"We have you and Donnell," Wilkinson said. "The mall's providing some security, and two county cops just arrived. I think we'll be fine."

"I hope so," Tyler said, but Wilkinson already walked away, leaving his anxious employee to patrol the perimeter a final time. The whole appearance was slated for an hour, and its start time coincided with the mall opening. People would come to see Alex Anne, but on a weekday, normal foot traffic would be minimal so early. Tyler hoped this all tipped the scales in favor of things going off without a hitch, but he doubted it.

As the witching hour approached, Donnell walked onto the stage. Alex Anne and her dad conferred for a minute as the main doors opened. People soon filled the area. Every seat Tyler could see was taken, and a crowd formed in front of the makeshift barrier separating the stage from the rest of the food court. A loud cheer went up as Alex Anne, carrying a tan acoustic guitar with a bunch of band stickers on it, strode onto the raised dais to perform.

She launched into a song Tyler had never heard, but he figured Lexi would know it by heart. If he didn't need to remain focused on the crowd, he would have recorded the audio for her. The pop stylings weren't his thing, but Tyler liked the way Alex Anne played the guitar. She didn't try to do too much with it. No flashy solos. No blistering fretwork which seemed out of place with the rest of the music. Simply solid strumming.

Tyler paced the barricade. As he moved down to the far end, some idiot shouted his love for Alex Anne thirty feet away. He was already running when the slender man hopped the railing, and before he could get onto the stage, Tyler lowered his shoulder and laid the guy out with a textbook tackle. Donnell stood in front of Alex Anne on the stage. The man who jumped the barrier lay woozy on the tiled floor. The two county cops hauled him to his feet, nodded their appreciation to Tyler, and led the fellow away in handcuffs.

"Sorry about that," Alex Anne said from the stage a moment later even though she had nothing to apologize for. "I'll start the song over." She seemed nonplussed by the interruption and threat to her safety. Maybe she dealt with this sort of thing often. Regardless, she redid the second song, performed a third, and ended the brief concert to cheers from the crowd. Alex Anne handed the guitar to her father, stepped down on the far end of the stage, and sat behind the long table.

Donnell and Tyler kept an eye on everyone, but no other threats emerged. On the whole, Tyler thought they were fortunate. There was only one lunatic, and he was a minor threat. He knew they might not be so lucky next time. Now, he only needed to convince Wilkinson of the fact.

"Did you play football in college?"

Alex Anne sat opposite Tyler. They all occupied her father's suite at the Lord Baltimore. She'd changed after the performance and now wore more normal jeans and a Gap hoodie. Her hair was pulled back into a ponytail. Lunch—in the form of sandwiches and chips from a nearby deli—covered most of the table. "No," Tyler said. "I went into the army right after high school."

"That was a pretty good tackle back there." She smiled, and Tyler saw her not as a pop star but as a young woman with a demanding job.

"Thanks. I've watched a lot of football over the years."

"You always knock people down with your shoulder?"

"Not usually," Tyler said. "It was the right call in the situation. Normally, I go for feet, knees, or elbows."

"F, K, E," Alex Anne said. She pointed at Tyler. "It almost spells fake."

"I guess it does."

"What's your name, new guy?" Alex Anne looked through the assorted items on the table, eventually grabbing a tuna sub.

"Tyler."

"That a first name?"

"No. I usually go by my last name."

Alex Anne unwrapped her meal. "Why?"

Tyler paused for a bite of his roast beef on rye. "Nobody calls you by your first name in the military."

"You're retired now, right?" He nodded. "Reclaim it."

"I got used to it over the years." Alex Anne chowed down on her sub, and Tyler gave her a minute to enjoy it. "My daughter's a big fan of yours." Donnell rolled his eyes on the other side of the room.

"Thanks." She smiled again. "How old is she?"

"Nineteen."

"I'll be nineteen in a few weeks," Alex Anne said. It was one more way she reminded Tyler of his own daughter. Lexi was a couple inches taller, had darker hair, and didn't dress to impress loonies who hopped over barricades—not normally, at least. Otherwise, they looked a fair bit alike. "I'm sure we can find a ticket to the concert, right, Dad?"

"Technically, it's sold out," Wilkinson said as he worked on his second sandwich.

Alex Anne waved a hand. "We'll figure something out. Tell your daughter she can come to the will-call window and pick it up. My dad will make all the details work." For his part, Wilkinson offered a small, noncommittal smile around a bite of food. "Thanks for what you did out there today."

"Glad to."

"I'm going to my room, Dad." Alex Anne stood and walked toward the door. "I'm sure we'll talk later."

Donnell stepped out into the hallway with her and returned after a moment. "She's good."

Wilkinson sat in the seat Alex Anne vacated. It groaned under his weight. "Thank you for your quick action today, Mister Tyler."

"It was one guy," Donnell said.

"Mobs start with one guy," Tyler said. "Put the first one down, and the rest lose their nerve."

"There was no 'rest.'"

"Maybe." Tyler shrugged. "I hope it was just one idiot. Either way, I'm glad we resolved it quickly and nothing else happened."

"Me, too," Wilkinson said. "Let's go over arrangements for the concert tomorrow after lunch."

"All right." Donnell still looked unhappy about the whole thing. Maybe he wanted the glory of saving Alex Anne. Maybe he was simply a prick. Whichever, Tyler didn't need to be around him more than another couple days. He could put up with it.

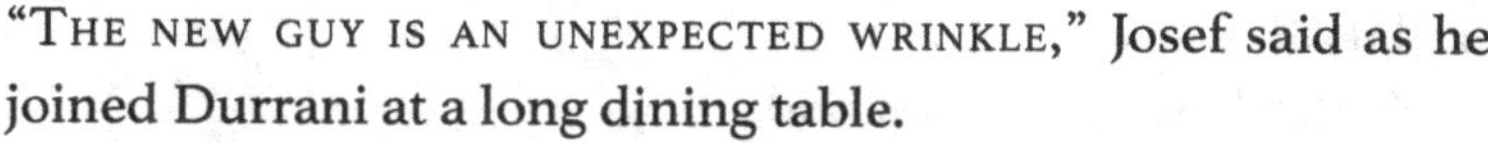

"The new guy is an unexpected wrinkle," Josef said as he joined Durrani at a long dining table.

"We'll know who he is soon enough."

"You seen his photo?" The older man shook his head. "Looks like ex-military."

"Lot of those around here," Durrani said. He picked up a chunk of bread and dipped it in hummus. "This state has so many bases. Army, Navy, the Naval Academy. There were probably two dozen former military men at the mall this morning."

"The rail jumper is out on bond." Josef eyed the bread. Durrani said nothing. He knew his employee wouldn't eat unless invited to. "I reminded him of his obligations and the price of not meeting them." He grunted. "Would've been simpler to kill him."

"Our goal is to get a truckload of girls out of this state. Let's not lose sight of it." Durrani finally gestured toward the plate, and Josef grabbed a chunk of pita. "We have a specific target in mind, but everything else we do can misdirect the police. Killing someone so soon would attract too much attention."

"Fine," Josef said around a mouthful of bread and dip.

Durrani took in a deep breath and released it slowly. He probably wouldn't forgive such crassness in a low-level employee, but Josef proved his loyalty and worth many times over. "Does the new man on the team change your plan for kidnapping the singer?"

"No." Josef put the pita down. "We'll have three guys waiting. Whether she has one or two with her won't really matter." He paused. "You know we have to kill them, right?"

"I wish there were an easier way." Durrani sighed. "The men who will be onsite have their instructions?" Josef's head bobbed. "It should buy us some time, then. I want to be wheels up twenty-four hours after the concert ends if we can pull it off."

"I think we can," Josef said.

"Let us hope you're right, my friend," Durrani said.

5

"**A**nd then the aliens took me into their ship."

Sara Morrison narrowed her eyes at Tyler, who nodded as if he'd been paying attention. They sat at a quiet table at Hunan Manor in Columbia. Sara enjoyed her dinner, while her date seemed preoccupied from the time he arrived at her house. "Tyler," she said, and he snapped out of his reverie.

"Sorry. I'm probably lousy company right now."

"You kind of are."

He looked down at his half-eaten General Tso's shrimp. "I guess I have a lot on my mind. Tomorrow night is the concert."

"How did today go?" Sara asked.

"Fine for the most part," Tyler said. "Some idiot hopped the railing in front of the autograph table, but I tackled him before he could get close. I don't think the dad takes these things seriously enough."

"You know I like you, right?"

Tyler grinned. "I should hope so."

"I say that because you might take them a little too seriously. Sometimes, one moron is just one moron. This singer . . . what's her name again?"

"Alex Anne."

"Alex Anne," Sara repeated. "She's been on tours before. Her father's been her manager the whole time, right?" Tyler nodded. "Nothing's happened. You said the other guy seems good. Maybe you'll be in for an easy few days."

"I could use them," Tyler said. "The shop's been chewing up a lot of my time. It's nice to have some work I know how to do."

Sara ate a bite of her Hunan beef before she answered. "You've been looking forward to opening the shop for a while now. Did something change?"

"No." Tyler paused. "Maybe." He swirled the water in his glass. "I've never been a business owner before. Never wanted to be. When the cartel burned Smitty's shop down, I felt terrible. Then, he didn't want to reopen, and it seemed like I needed to fill the void. I think I rushed into it."

"You can't get out of it now," Sara said. "Might as well make the best of it."

"I know." Tyler looked at his uneaten food. Maybe he'd be hungry later. He felt like he needed to paint. Stressful times made him want to sit at his easel and get it all out. It proved to be great therapy in many worse situations over the last several years. "Smitty tells me he's happy to help, and I've delegated some things to him along the way. I don't want to overburden him, though. This isn't going to be his shop."

"Take a few days. See how this job with Alex Anne is going and what demands the shop is going to place on your time. I've never opened a business before, either, but I know people who have. They say there's a lot of waiting."

"After twenty-four years in the army," Tyler said, "I'm an expert at waiting."

"Not all the time," Sara said, shooting him a wink. "I think this will be good for you. You probably needed to do something different, anyway. Get the knight-errant thing out of your system for a while and go back to running your business."

"Lexi told me I seemed a little lost."

"She's probably not wrong. You're retired, Tyler."

"Twice, in fact."

Sara grinned. "However many times, it's not always an easy transition. When you left the army, you had the security gig lined up, right?"

"More or less," Tyler said.

"When the shit hit the fan there, you didn't have anywhere to go. You found Smitty's. The cartel took it away. You probably were wandering around for a while. It's nothing to be ashamed of."

"Hopefully, you're right about this job. Maybe my knight-errant skills won't be needed."

Sara raised her glass of water, and Tyler clinked his against it. "Here's hoping. I think this will all resolve itself once your place opens."

"Got an old car you want to bring in?" Tyler asked.

"No," Sara said. "Just a middle-aged boyfriend who needs a kick in the ass every now and then."

"Can't help you there," Tyler said.

AFTER DINNER, Tyler drove into the city. The entire contingent was staying at the Lord Baltimore, and Wilkinson offered him a room, too. Tyler accepted. He figured Lexi would be happy to be rid of him for an evening, and the tone of her voice confirmed his suspicion. She got even more excited when she heard about the ticket which would be waiting for her at the will-call window, of course. For a girl who'd never been prone to screaming and squealing, Lexi did a lot of both when she got the good news.

Rather than go directly to the hotel, Tyler drove to the Arena first. It was a short jaunt between venues, but he wanted to cruise it himself. From the Arena garage, they would drive a short distance up Howard Street and make a right onto Baltimore Street. The traffic light represented a potential vulnerability. They'd be leaving after the show. Late at night . . . probably eleven. Traffic would be light. An attacker couldn't predict the color of the signal without some technological help, however, so an ambush may not materialize. The same was true at the next light at Hopkins Plaza.

The Charles Center Metro Station sat across the street from the hotel itself. It would be easy to hide an operative or two outside it. The SUV would need to slow down to pull in and then stop for everyone to get out. Plenty of time to dash across the road. Tyler parked near the hotel, walked around the block, and came up Howard from the concert venue. Driving the route was one thing. He wanted to see it from the street level.

His watch showed nine-thirty. About ninety minutes before they'd be making the trip tomorrow night. Tyler passed a few pedestrians on Howard who paid him no mind. On Baltimore Street, he walked past the Arena and several professional buildings. A few people milled about. None of them looked remarkable in any way. Odds were extremely high they were merely ordinary folks getting through life.

This was another vulnerability.

If an ambush at the first traffic light never happened, it would be easy to disguise shooters and kidnappers as everyday citizens elsewhere. Tyler saw it a lot in Afghanistan. Taliban operatives dressed like ordinary men to blend in, and the first sign something was amiss was an automatic weapon or suicide vest. By then, it was too late. Worse, they sometimes used children, who blended in even better due to an inherent lack of suspicion. If Alex Anne were the target of a sophisticated group, they could have a multi-pronged plan in place.

Tyler fetched his car, drove it up a narrow stretch of Hanover Street alongside the hotel, and checked in. The valet offered an appreciative nod as he approached. The man was probably happy to drive anything besides a boring midsize SUV. Tyler carried his two bags inside and scoped out the lobby. Nothing changed from his initial impression. With a reduced staff working at night, someone could easily hide in the mezzanine and wait for Alex Anne to go toward the elevators. A hotel with an underground garage and elevator service directly to the guest floors would have been a better call even if it were a little farther away. Security needed to trump convenience.

The amiable fellow behind the desk handed Tyler his keycard. The room wasn't on the same floor as everyone else's, but he was fine with something smaller and simpler. Once he set his luggage down, Tyler picked up the hotel phone and called everyone's rooms to check in. Only Donnell seemed annoyed by it.

AFTER THOROUGHLY INSPECTING his quarters and unpacking his suitcase, Tyler emptied his other bag. It held a travel easel and enough watercolor supplies for him to do a couple paintings if he needed. He'd surprised himself with how much he took to the therapeutic program. The idea of owning a travel easel—or knowing such a thing existed—would have seemed absurd to the man Tyler was a decade ago.

He picked up a brush, closed his eyes, and took a few deep breaths. Early on, he learned not to force a design. If he calmed himself and focused, his brain would tell his hand what to do. Tyler started with ribbons of black before switching colors. He drew a lone figure, added some clothes, and finished filling out the rest of the blacktop around him.

Forty minutes later, Tyler rinsed his brushes in the hotel's fancy sink. When he emerged from the bathroom, he stared at his handiwork. A man with his back to the frame stood in the middle of a road. It forked ahead of him. To the left was a square gray nondescript building with a small car waiting outside.

To the right lay a pile of bones and skulls.

The shrink who recommended this program to him cautioned him about trying to read too much into what he'd painted. "The subconscious mind works in mysterious ways," she told him. "It's kind of like trying to interpret dreams. We don't always know what to attach meaning to . . . or even how much." Tyler had seen more than most men, so his subconscious had more to process—or so the theory went. He figured the doctor's take was valid enough. Regardless, he couldn't help but give in to a simple analysis of this piece.

His classic car business and jobs like protecting pop singers were in opposite directions. Maybe his brain was telling him to pick one. "It's just one gig," Tyler whispered to the empty room. He'd never expected to take it . . . like he never thought he'd need to deal with a vengeful former commander or a ruthless drug cartel. A bunch of bodies later, here he stood. He didn't go out and seek trouble, but Tyler never walked away from it, either.

Maybe he needed to start.

6

Tyler took the elevator down to the lobby shortly before noon the next day. Wilkinson waited in a plush high-backed chair. Donnell and Alex Anne arrived a moment later. They all piled into a Suburban for the short drive to the Arena, and the new guy got stuck in the third row. "We should take two vehicles," Tyler said when the driver pulled away from the curb.

Wilkinson turned from his perch in the passenger's seat. "Why?"

"This is a single point of failure. A second SUV spreads out the risk. If the windows are tinted, attackers are unlikely to know who's riding in which."

"It ain't so big a deal," Donnell said. "We're going four blocks."

"I've seen a lot of bad shit happen in far less space."

"This ain't Afghanistan."

Tyler lapsed into silence. He wouldn't convince Donnell. The man didn't seem to like him or value his opinions. Maybe he felt threatened by having someone experienced come on board. Perhaps he simply enjoyed the status quo.

Tyler saw people get complacent over the years, and more often than not, it got them killed. "You served in Afghanistan?" Alex Anne said.

"Four tours."

"Was it hard to readjust when you came home?"

Very few people had asked this question. Tyler wished more people would. It would do a lot to help understanding of the issues many veterans faced when they tried to go back to their prior lives. "In a few ways, yes." The Braxton mess didn't help. His former colonel tainted Tyler's image of the army and people in power, but the subject would be a bit heavy for their short drive to the venue. "I've learned a lot about how to manage over the past ten years."

"Good." She smiled. "I don't think we have a second vehicle, Mister Tyler, but I appreciate your perspective."

"Thanks." At least someone did. Donnell dismissed his opinions, and Wilkinson didn't want to override his longtime security guy. It meant nothing would change unless something bad happened or Alex Anne pushed for it. The trip to the venue was a short jaunt, and they rode in silence for the rest of the brief duration. The SUV turned into the Arena garage, and the driver checked in with a security guard. They went to a section Tyler had never seen before. Only about forty spaces were marked off in this area. An elevator waited nearby.

"This is where performers park," Wilkinson said, answering Tyler's unasked question. "For bigger shows with a lot of people in the party, these spots can fill up."

"Just one guy guards it all?" Tyler asked.

"Usually, it's a three-person crew," Donnell said.

They all got out and took the elevator to the main level. From there, a short corridor situated away from the concourses and seating bowl led to the locker rooms and backstage area. Alex Anne's name appeared on a door in the form of a placard. Tyler frowned when she opened it without needing to unlock it. "There's always a guard or two around," Wilkinson offered. Tyler grunted. It didn't seem like enough. He tried to convince himself he wasn't being overly cautious.

After checking out the room for a few minutes, Alex Anne followed a narrow corridor to the fixed stage. The city built the Arena—originally dubbed the Baltimore Civic Center—about seven years before Tyler was born. He remembered thinking the stage was a mistake. It took up space which could be used for seats. Some hockey fans in the city thought it kept the NHL out of town because of the lowered capacity. Most of all, Tyler remembered thinking it was ugly, and despite a few name changes over time, Arena management couldn't make it look any better.

Donnell followed the pop star, and Tyler pulled up the rear. "We'll both be on stage tonight," the big man said. "The key is not to become part of the show. Nobody out there is paying to see you or me."

"Good thing," Tyler said.

Donnell grinned for the first time in all Tyler's interactions with him. Maybe the frost would thaw. "People on the sides . . ." He gestured to where the floor seats bumped up against the walls leading to the numbered sections. ". . . might see us. Obviously, if some asshole jumps the rail, we gotta do what we do."

"Does the building provide security?"

"Sure," Donnell said. "You'll see them in their yellow jackets." He shrugged. "They're all right. Might be some cops here earning overtime, too. Either way, we still gotta be vigilant." He pointed at Alex Anne, who stood at the front of the stage and surveyed the empty arena. "She's the one we're here for."

Tyler nodded. "Understood." He watched the young woman pace the front part of the platform. She was just about his daughter's age and already famous the world over.

Tyler spent most of his military career in the shadows. He didn't understand popularity. Alex Anne would sing, dance, change costumes, and put on a show for two hours. The seats would be filled with thousands of adoring fans . . . and probably a couple psychos. It was inevitable. Any time a pretty young woman dressed even a tiny bit provocatively, the nut jobs came out. Tyler wondered how long Alex Anne had been doing this. Recording. Touring. Spending months on the road in hotels. Did she finish high school? Was her father OK with her being as much of a commodity as a person in the eyes of many?

When Alex Anne smiled as she walked past, Tyler thought he saw happiness. For her sake, he hoped so.

JOSEF WALKED into Durrani's office. The boss sat behind his desk reading an actual newspaper. He was the only man Josef knew who didn't get his information from a phone or tablet. Josef had come to appreciate Durrani's old-school sensibilities over time. It was why he carried a file under his arm rather than sending it via email. "Tonight's the night," he said when the Afghan man looked above the tops of his glasses.

"Are we ready?"

"Every prong of the operation knows what to do. We'll grab the girl when the concert's over."

"And if she has both security guys with her?" Durrani asked.

"We'll deal with them," Josef said. "Our men will outnumber them." He smirked. "Besides, I think we have a way to separate them . . . to keep one occupied."

Durrani inclined his head toward the folder Josef still held under his arm. "What do you have there?"

"We know who the second guy is now." He tossed the

manila envelope onto the boss' uncluttered desk. "Ran a reverse image search from a picture at the mall." Durrani opened the file and recoiled. He stared at the first page with wide eyes, his hands gripping the edge of the desktop. "What? What is it?"

"I know this man," Durrani said in a breathless voice. He gaped unblinking at the photo of John Tyler. Josef had never seen the boss so spooked before. "We never knew his name for certain. I saw him a few times, though. He was probably the best killer the Americans had."

Josef frowned. "A sniper?"

"No." Durrani finally blinked, though he couldn't take his eyes from the image. "He went on raids. He and his team killed a lot of people I knew. Not just Taliban, either. We put a nice bounty on his head . . . for all the good it did. His men knew who financed us, too, and they went after them."

He probably meant opium dealers. "Life is presenting you a chance to get revenge," Josef said. "This is a good thing. We'll make a lot of money in the next few days, and you'll get to see an old enemy die."

"Yes." Durrani's head slowly bobbed, though his expression didn't change. The photo of John Tyler shocked him to the point he never looked through the man's file. There would be time for it later if Tyler survived the events of tonight. "Double-check your plan, Josef. Make sure everyone involved knows what they're doing." His finger tapped the picture. "This man is a complication. A wrench in the gears. One mistake, and he'll ruin everything."

"Everything will go according to plan," Josef assured him.

~

EVEN FROM BACKSTAGE, Tyler could hear the din of the crowd. The opening act—an all-male pop trio he'd never heard of—

finished their set. Everyone waited for the headliner with varying degrees of patience. Alex Anne's dressing room door remained closed. Her father milled about with what he called typical jitters before a show. Tyler hoped Alex Anne didn't inherit her nerves from her dad. Donnell patrolled the area while Tyler made sure the stage and the path to it remained clear. He looked out from the curtains. The far upper corners of seats were covered, but about twelve thousand people clamored for Alex Anne.

Five minutes later, she emerged wearing a white tank top, a red button-down shirt, a denim miniskirt which barely reached her legs, and her brown hair in pigtails. Alex Anne was an adult. She could dress how she wanted. When her career took off three years ago, however, she was technically a child. Someone would've needed to suggest her outfits, and her father was the obvious candidate. Tyler couldn't imagine asking Lexi to dress in such a way. The fact she would tell him to go suck a lemon was irrelevant.

The arena lights went down, and a roar came from the crowd. Phone cameras flashed throughout the floor seats. Colored bulbs pulsed from above the stage as Alex Anne walked through the curtain with her band. The floor shook with the noise from the stands. "It's good to be back in Baltimore," Alex Anne said, and somehow, the assembled fans shouted even louder. "You all know I'm from here, right?" Another roar indicated they did. She launched into a song Tyler heard Lexi play a few times. He never knew the names, but the words and music were familiar.

During his twenty-four years in the army, Tyler got exposed to many different types of tunes—most of it unwillingly. Small personal headphones weren't yet a thing when he left. He tended to think of younger artists as flighty, and he often found their songs shallow and not very serious. Alex Anne was different. Her lyrics carried realistic emotional meaning . . . plus an occasional drop of venom Tyler appreci-ated. He always felt the Beatles got better once Lennon grew bitter and acerbic toward the end of their run.

Music had to take a backseat, however. From his unobtrusive perch at the curtain, Tyler kept an eye on the crowd as Alex Anne hustled backstage for a costume change. The band played a quick instrumental until she re-emerged a couple minutes later. This time, she wore cutoff jeans, a midriff top, and an unbuttoned flannel shirt. The fans cheered their approval as the next song started, Alex Anne grabbed the mic, and launched into the first verse.

A few notes in, yellow-jacketed security guards moved to the left side of the stage. Arms went up, but some idiot hopped the rail and slithered between two members of the building staff. What was it with these people? Tyler sprinted from his spot as the maniac rushed the stage.

7

The height of the stage slowed the guy down a little. He couldn't simply jump onto it. This might have been the single good thing about its design. Tattooed forearms flexed as he put his hands down and spring onto the surface. None of the Arena guards managed to corral him. The band stopped playing abruptly, and a halted guitar note made Tyler wince as he closed in on the rail jumper. The slender blond fellow straightened up, spied Alex Anne, and took a step toward her.

Tyler lowered his shoulder and hammered the man in the midsection.

Another textbook tackle. The interloper let out a loud grunt as the collision drove him backward. He flew off the stage and landed hard on the concrete floor below. A roar went up from the fans in the floor sections. Tyler approached the edge and looked down. The guy held his head and looked woozy, but he was conscious. Now, of course, the venue's crack security force could handle him.

Donnell ushered Alex Anne behind the curtain and backstage as Tyler followed. The rest of the band joined them. An uncertain quiet descended on the crowd. Alex Anne sat in her dressing room flanked by her father and Donnell. All of them looked up when Tyler walked in. "Everyone all right?"

Alex Anne only offered a nod, but Wilkinson said, "Yes, thank you. I'm glad you took decisive action. We all are." Donnell made no gesture or noise to indicate his agreement.

Tyler didn't press it. "What happens now?" he asked.

"We decide if we'll continue the show." Wilkinson inclined his head toward his daughter. "It's her concert. Her choice."

Alex Anne ran fingers through her hair. "I want to go back out." Her knee bobbed up and down as if keeping the beat during an especially fast piece of music. She wrung her hands. "I haven't played here in about eighteen months. The show should go on."

"Take a few minutes," Tyler said. "You're clearly nervous." He moved his hand up and down in front of his chest. "Breathe in and out a few times. You've probably done hundreds of shows without a hitch. The asshole who hopped the barrier was an outlier. Don't give him space in your head."

"You have much practice making speeches?" Donnell asked after a snort.

"Sure. A bunch of times in Afghanistan before we kicked down doors and shot up the Taliban." He grinned. "How about you?"

"Thank you, Mister Tyler," Alex Anne said before Donnell could further the pissing contest. "I think it's helping." Her knee still bobbed but much slower. She turned to her father. "I want to finish the show. Will you have someone make the announcement?"

"Of course." Wilkinson took out his phone and walked into the corner to make a call. It wrapped up quickly. A few seconds later, Tyler heard the PA announcer tell the crowd the show would resume shortly. A fresh cheer reverberated through the building. "Let's clear the room." Tyler and Donnell left. They waited in silence as Wilkinson closed the door. A couple minutes later, father and daughter emerged.

Alex Anne patted Tyler's arm as she walked past. "Keep him around, Dad. I like him."

"I'll try," Wilkinson said. Tyler wondered if he would—and what answer he would give if asked.

Donnell shook his head and followed them toward the stage.

TYLER SCOWLED at the forms the mousy man put on the table before him. He sat in a small side office in the backstage area. "It's standard procedure in an incident like this, sir," the fellow said in a voice fitting his face and frame. The paperwork all carried official Arena letterhead.

"You have an SOP for someone jumping onto the stage and getting clobbered by private security?" Tyler said. It was an hour after the show ended. The crowd filed out a while ago. Alex Anne, Wilkinson, and Donnell were almost ready to leave. Tyler wanted to go with them to ensure she got in the SUV and to the hotel safely. Now it looked like they might leave without him.

"It covers incidents like these," the man said. "We do it for—"

"Insurance," Tyler broke in.

"Yes. I'm sorry, sir. We need you to fill it out."

Which meant the lawyers needed it filled out. Anything to deflect potential liability. A bunch of witnesses could corroborate everything Tyler said. This was pointless and unnecessary except to people in stuffed shirts earning hundreds of dollars an hour.

Wilkinson popped his head into the small room. "We're

headed to the hotel. I'm going ahead in an Uber. Donnell is taking Alexandra."

"If you wait," Tyler said, "I think it's best for us to go together as planned."

"It's a few blocks." The client frowned at the sheets. "Looks like you might be a while." Before Tyler could interject, Wilkinson continued. "Stay and finish it. We can't have trouble with the Arena. It's basically our home court." He turned and walked away.

Tyler sighed and looked at the paperwork. Security must have tackled some asshole at a past event who then claimed injury and sued. Now, the Arena management wanted to cover its collective ass. As usual, lawyers ruined everything.

Donnell appeared in the doorway. "I'm taking Alex to the hotel," he said.

"Wait a few minutes," Tyler said. Maybe Donnell would be willing to stick around. "I'll ride with you."

"I can take her by myself."

"I don't doubt you. But if I'm here for extra security, don't you think I should provide it?" With a two-person team, one could secure the lobby—especially the vulnerability posed by the mezzanine—while the other led the star inside. Flying solo, doing such double duty would be impossible. Tyler hoped Donnell would realize this.

"We'll be fine," the other man insisted. "Done this plenty of times. Ain't like Alex has never been on tour before."

Tyler glowered at the mousy man, who swallowed a lump in his throat and tried to smile around it. "Fine," he said. "If you want me to secure the hotel with you—"

"I told you we'll be good," Donnell said. He, too, turned and walked away.

"Do I really need to fill this out now?" Tyler said. "This is absurd. You're keeping me from my job."

"It would be an unresolved incident, sir," he said.

"So?"

"So it means future events Alex Anne might try to schedule here could be denied. We can't have unresolved incidents."

"Heaven forbid," Tyler said. No reaction. "You a lawyer?" The man shook his head. "Accountant?" He nodded. "Figures. Nothing good ever comes from you pricks being involved."

The bean counter didn't say anything. Tyler worked on the form as ordered. Donnell seemed capable. Getting Alex Anne into a vehicle should be easy. Even if leaving the Arena and the short drive to the Lord Baltimore went smoothly, the destination was a complicating factor. Fans. Paparazzi. Potential stalkers. The hotel would have its own security team, but they had hundreds of other guests and thousands of square feet to worry about. A second person would be an asset, and it matched how they went over it yesterday.

Still, Donnell had done this before. He was good at his job. Tyler could—and would—check on everyone later.

He concentrated on the paperwork.

ALEX ANNE FELT MUCH BETTER after a shower and a change of clothes. It would be her second-to-last of the night. At the hotel, she'd sleep in something more comfortable than her current jeans and hoodie. With her hair pulled back into a ponytail, no makeup on, and a baseball cap, she might even be lucky enough to go unrecognized for a night. Being a star was great and all, but there were times Alex Anne simply wanted to take a leisurely walk without people pointing or snapping pictures. Even her jaunts to the grocery store would end up on TMZ thanks to some random jerk with an iPhone.

After the trial runs of yesterday, it seemed weird to make the drive back to the hotel without Mister Tyler. She definitely thought of him as Mister, while Donnell was just Donnell. He was nice, in a distant, parental sort of way. And his shoulder tackle on the guy who jumped onstage was epic. For an older man, he could still move. His eyes were unnerving, though. They were dark brown, almost black. They were a killer's eyes, and Alex Anne tried to reconcile them with the man who seemed like a caring father. Maybe laying down his guns and embracing life as a parent had been one of the struggles he mentioned. She wondered if Mister Tyler thought about killing the idiot who made it to the stage. *That* would certainly make TMZ.

Donnell rode the elevator down with her. The Arena was good about giving performers a separate parking area in the garage. They enforced it with a large security patrol. Even now, over an hour after her concert ended, three men remained to make sure crazy fans didn't rush the cars. A few other vehicles were parked nearby, but Donnell, Alex Anne, and the three guards were the only people here. This was a nice change of pace. She'd been rushed by fans two or three hours after a show before. Not all venues offered the same protections to performers.

Their large black SUV awaited. One security guy stood on either side, while the third positioned himself about fifty feet away and made sure no one approached. Donnell opened the passenger's door for Alex Anne, then walked to the driver's side. "Good show tonight, miss," the guard on her side of the SUV said. He had a warm smile.

"Thank you," Alex Anne said. "You guys did a great job here."

"Much obliged."

Alex Anne looked across the SUV. A couple of strange muffled sounds went up, and then Donnell sagged to the concrete. Before she could ask what was going on, something sharp bit into her neck. It felt like a needle. Her hand shot to the area. She tried to run away, but it was too late. She already grew weak. Her vision swam. Her legs wobbled after only a few steps. The security guard caught Alex Anne as she fell. When she looked up at him, his warm face had grown cold and sinister.

Then, the blackness came.

8

———

Tyler looked over all the papers. He'd spent nearly an hour filling out information, writing a statement, and whatever else the lawyer who devised the forms required. Talking to the police—which covered much of the same ground, making the dead trees even more superfluous—consumed another fifteen minutes. They were quick and efficient. At a packed concert, plenty of people saw the idiot hop the rail. Thousands of witnesses could corroborate Tyler's story if necessary.

The accountant poked his head in the door. "Are you finished?"

"Yes."

"Great. You can leave it all there . . . including the pen."

Tyler turned it over in his fingers. It was nothing special. Better than a basic Bic, but the guy didn't give him some fancy fountain pen to write with. "How about I stick it in your eye?" The bean counter's only response was a loud gulp. Tyler left everything on the table as requested and shouldered his way past the mousy man on his way out of the room. He performed a quick check of the area, but as expected, everyone else already left.

He rode here in the Suburban, so Tyler would need to walk back to the hotel. He took the elevator down to the parking garage and confirmed the SUV was gone. One of the security guards waved as Tyler passed. He returned the gesture. Another walked the line of cars. Tyler didn't see the third and figured he was tending to something else with the concert over. He hoofed it through the exit. With the big event almost ninety minutes in the rearview by now, traffic returned to its normal late-night levels. Tyler passed more people milling about on Howard and Baltimore Streets than he did cars.

At the hotel, Tyler looked for the SUV parked nearby but didn't see it. The valets would have moved it somewhere, but he didn't see it any place on the short stretch of Hanover Street. He walked inside and saw no one in the lobby except the desk clerk. Tyler approached the young man, who looked to be in college and kept a couple textbooks to the side of the keyboard. "Did the Wilkinson party return yet?"

"I don't know." The kid shrugged. "I just came on like fifteen minutes ago."

"Did anyone come in?"

"You a cop or something?"

"I'm working security for the Wilkinsons," Tyler said. "I stayed behind at the venue, and now I want to make sure they've returned safely."

The clerk shook his head, and his long blond curls wagged. "Only people who came in were an older couple a few minutes before you."

Tyler grunted his thanks and headed for the elevator. He walked into his room and called Wilkinson, who picked up right away. "Alex Anne make it back OK?"

"I haven't heard from her."

"You don't sound concerned," Tyler said.

"Alexandra's from Baltimore. We haven't played here in well over a year. She doesn't get many chances to see her friends. Donnell probably drove her somewhere. It happens. She can be pretty persuasive when she wants a thing."

"It's not the protocol."

"Relax, Mister Tyler," Wilkinson said. "I appreciate your concern and your vigilance, but I'm sure everyone is fine."

"She go out after concerts a lot?"

"I guess. Sometimes."

"I'm going to call her room."

"I don't think it's necess—" Tyler cut Wilkinson off by hanging up. He dialed Alex Anne's room. It rang six times with no answer. He tried Donnell next. Same result. Tyler used his cell to call Donnell's. The line rang five times before going to voicemail. If the man were driving, he might not answer. Tyler tried not to be concerned. Donnell came across as a jerk, but he'd been in the business for a while. He was capable. Alex Anne trusted him. She was young and vulnerable, however, and he couldn't imagine being unconcerned if Lexi didn't turn up where she was supposed to be.

Tyler tried her room again. Same as before. He considered trying Wilkinson but knew he'd get an identical unconcerned answer. They were probably fine. Tyler's hyper vigilance saved his life many times as a soldier, but it wasn't always necessary in the civilian world. He changed out of his suit and got ready for bed.

~

DONNELL FELT CONSCIOUSNESS RETURN. Pain came with it. Memories trickled back as his brain tried to make sense of everything. He'd ridden down the elevator with Alex Anne. The security guys had already backed the SUV out and positioned it for an easy exit. Donnell walked to the driver's side where another guard waited. There was something in his hand. He got turned around, two muffled reports filled his ears, and the last thing Donnell remembered was sagging to the concrete and worrying about Alex Anne.

He felt his pockets, but everything was gone. Donnell took in his surroundings. He lay next to a dumpster in an alley somewhere. Whoever shot him probably thought they'd killed him, and this was a body dump. Using the side of the giant metal box, Donnell dragged himself into a seated position. Agony blazed along his side and back. The side hurt worse. His vest might have soaked one of the shots, but it felt like the other one got him good.

He wondered what happened to Alex Anne. Maybe the new guy was right. If they'd waited for him to fill out the paperwork, Donnell might not be sitting amid a bunch of old trash right now. He didn't like Tyler much and didn't think they needed him, but the man certainly seemed capable. No time to worry about it. Alex Anne was the concern. With Donnell down, she would make an easy mark.

Getting back to his feet brought a fresh hell with it, but Donnell fought to remain upright. He leaned on the dumpster. As he staggered away from it, he recognized the building to his right as the Baltimore Convention Center. They didn't move him very far. He looked at his wrist, but the bastards even took his watch. No way to know how much time passed. The Convention Center sat just south of the Arena. It was a quick and easy drive to get on the highway. Alex Anne could be in another state by now . . . if she were even still alive.

Donnell leaned against a sign to steady himself and tried to keep going. He stumbled to the left at the end of the alley, so he continued down Sharp Street. A couple of white college kids approached. Their happy faces turned to horror when they saw Donnell shambling toward them. "Help me," he croaked past his dry throat. They turned sharply to avoid him and dashed away. "Assholes." Donnell somehow stayed on his feet. He needed to get somewhere and tell someone to check on Alex Anne. Calling the cops would have been great, too, but he saw no payphones.

The sidewalk veered around grass and trees ahead. A short wall of brick topped by wrought iron enclosed a courtyard and a small building. Just past it, a steeple reached skyward. Donnell put his hands on the wall and used it to steady himself as he moved. He came to two black metal gates and pushed. They opened. He staggered toward the white wooden doors. The red stone walkway stretched about fifty feet, but it felt like a mile.

Two stairs led to the doors. Donnell tried the handle, but they were locked. He pounded on the wood. No response. Blackness crept in from the edges of his vision. A new wave of pain forced him to lean on the church wall. With the strength he had left, Donnell banged on the door again. His head grew light, and he sagged down the wall until he lay on the top step. He kicked the entryway a few times. Before he passed out, he thought he saw a shaft of light as someone opened up.

JOSEF CARRIED the unconscious Alex Anne over his shoulder. His large hand squeezed her butt as he navigated the chairs in the darkened room. It was a nice little perk of them coming in knocked out. A less scrupulous man would do worse. Even putting a light on didn't do much. The men already found eight girls, and they stirred as Josef set Alex Anne down on a metal chair. He used four short ropes to lash her wrists and ankles in place. One of the other girls shouted for help. "Quiet," Josef told her in a harsh tone. "No one is coming for you. Get used to it."

Alex Anne's face scrunched, and her breathing changed. She'd been out over an hour. Her eyes shot open, and she looked around. Confusion furrowed her brow. When she tried to move, she stared at the restraints keeping her in place. "What the hell?"

"Relax, girl," Josef said. "You won't be here more than a day or so."

"You kidnapped me?"

"Personally, no, but our organization brought you here."

Her wide eyes scanned the room. "What is this? Are you ransoming us off?"

Josef laughed. "No. Ransom is for idiots. We get paid a lot more to deliver you."

Her expression didn't change. The reality of her situation had to be setting in. "Where's Donnell?"

"Dead." Josef shrugged. "We expected two men, but it was easier with just the one. I heard he never saw it coming."

"You won't get away with this," Alex Anne said. "Mister Tyler will look for me. A lot of people will."

"Let them," Josef said. "No one will find you here." He locked eyes with each of the other girls. They looked a little younger than Alex Anne. Without her fame, the efforts to find them would be led by the incompetent police. "Pay attention. This room will fill up. Probably in a day. There will be eight or ten more of you. When it does, we're flying you all out of here. You'll be sold to the highest bidders." Josef leaned down and got in Alex Anne's face. "Someone is willing to pay a lot of money for you. He'll be on top of you in three days. Let your saviors spin their wheels. You're as good as dead."

Josef stood and left the room. He ignored the frightened chatter of the girls as he locked the door.

9

Thanks to her dad's old work laptop, Lexi felt she had a leg up in computer science. The machine's exhaustive suite of tools could carry out many functions—some of them even legal—and output screens would sometimes allow a behind-the-scenes look at how the process worked. This was different than trying to write something from scratch. Lexi chose C programming because it had been around for decades and served as the foundation for many platforms.

The first week of class served as an overview to object-oriented programming. Lexi learned a little in high school but still found the review useful. From there, students made their own very simple programs. They started with the standard of getting "Hello, world!" to display on the screen. From there, they worked on basic math functions and outputting those to the display, as well.

The instructor was a bookish man but had a knack for explaining how things worked. He wore thick glasses, was slender, and his skin tone suggested he rarely ventured into the sunlight. There were probably programmer stereotypes he fit pretty well. Still, he was a capable teacher, and his first test proved challenging. Lexi felt glad to escape with an A-minus.

She finished her latest program, compiled it, and found it worked as expected. Lexi emailed it to the teacher. The clock on the wall told her class was just about over. She packed her bag and headed for the door. In the hallway, a set of footsteps hurried behind her. Lexi gripped her keys in her pocket as one of the young men in her class drew even with her. "It's Alexis, right?"

"Lexi," she said.

"I'm Ahmed." She looked at him and remembered him joining the class after the semester started. He frowned a lot as he tried to catch up with the old work and keep up on new assignments. Ahmed had a classic Mediterranean complexion and dark wavy hair. His winter clothes hid what Lexi figured was a soccer player's physique, "You seem like you know what you're doing in there." When he smiled at her, she couldn't help offering one up in return.

"It's a one-oh-one class. I have a little experience. Later in the semester, it probably won't matter."

"It matters now, though," Ahmed said as they kept walking. "Look, I'm not trying to be a creep or anything. I was just hoping you could help me with some of this stuff. I started late, and I feel a little overwhelmed."

Lexi pondered it. It was gratifying to have someone ask for her help. While she'd never fancied herself a teacher, she knew the basics well enough. She didn't have a job, so time wasn't a concern. And Ahmed was handsome. She felt her cheeks flush when he flashed a hopeful grin at her. "All right," she said. "I'll see what I can do."

"Great!" Ahmed held up his hand, and Lexi gave him a high-five. "I'm sure I'll be able to do better now."

"I hope I can justify your optimism," she said.

TYLER WOKE up at seven the next morning. He remembered being annoyed with Wilkinson's insistence everything was okay with no evidence to support his conclusion. Despite Tyler's concern, he didn't want to call anyone this early. If Alex Anne and Donnell did in fact go visit some of her friends last night, they didn't need their phone to ring before sunrise. The whole thing left him feeling agitated, so Tyler changed into athletic clothes and made use of the hotel's gym.

He ran three miles on the treadmill, then gave the heavy bag a serious beating for the next fifteen minutes. His fists were red and sore by the end. Tyler polished off his bottle of water and returned to his room for a badly-needed shower. He slipped his watch on along with a clean set of clothes, and it showed five after eight. Definitely too early for Alex Anne and maybe Donnell, too. Tyler hedged his bets with a quick text to Wilkinson. He received an automated reply a few seconds later advising him business hours started at nine.

Tyler rolled his eyes and left the room to get breakfast. He checked the restaurant but didn't see anyone he cared about. Ten minutes later, he returned to his room with a carry-out order of bacon, eggs, toast, and two coffees. After finishing, Tyler called Wilkinson. A sleepy voice answered, "Tyler, it's before nine."

"I know. You can't become a warrant officer without being able to tell time. The army has standards." Wilkinson mumbled something incoherent and probably uncharitable. "Any word from your daughter or Donnell yet?"

"No, but I wouldn't think they'd be up yet. If they went out last night—"

"Big if," Tyler broke in.

"If they did," Wilkinson said, raising his voice, "I don't think we'll hear from them before ten."

"Why did you hire me, Wilkinson?"

"Because I'm concerned about my daughter's security as we start this tour."

"Yet here I am," Tyler said, "trying to get you to tune into the facts. She and Donnell didn't check in last night. They weren't reachable. I didn't see them downstairs. And despite all your precious concern, you're making up excuses for why they might not pick up their phones."

Wilkinson didn't answer for a few seconds. Tyler figured he was seething, especially considering he'd been ambushed awake. "Fine. Do what you want. Call them if you think it's the right decision." He hung up.

"Prick," Tyler muttered. Maybe he wouldn't stay on any longer than he needed to no matter what Alex Anne wanted. If he were going to get the runaround from some well-paid asshole, it might as well be a building inspector. Tyler first tried Alex Anne's room. No answer. He dialed Donnell's. Same result. Odds were long the third time would be the charm, but Tyler tried Donnell's mobile.

Straight to voicemail.

TYLER WAITED a few minutes before repeating the routine. He got the same results. Wilkinson needed to know, and it wouldn't be by phone this time. The hell with his attempts to make excuses. If Alex Anne and Donnell never returned last night, there were a few options, and they were all varying degrees of terrible. Tyler rode the elevator to the proper floor, got off, and pounded on Wilkinson's door.

"What the hell!" He answered a moment later, red-faced

and with his hair in disarray. An ill-fitting hotel robe covered his white T-shirt and black shorts.

Tyler walked in without waiting to be invited. "I tried both their rooms and Donnell's cell phone. Oh-for-three. I think your theory is unraveling. We need to take this seriously."

"For heaven's sake." Wilkinson stomped to the desk and picked up the phone. He pushed four buttons, held the receiver to his ear, and waited. After a few seconds, his brows knitted. "She always takes my calls. We have an understanding."

"Concerned yet?" Tyler asked.

"Give me a minute." Wilkinson walked into the bedroom area of the suite and retrieved his cell phone. He made two calls in quick succession, and neither got met with an answer. "This is strange. Both their cell phones go to voicemail."

"We need to check her room." Tyler jerked his heard toward the adjoining door. He'd never make Lexi get a room connected to his—no doubt to her great relief—but she also lacked Alex Anne's fame. It complicated many factors.

"Let me find the key." Rather than leave them in an easily accessible spot, Wilkinson needed to fish a wallet out of his crumpled pants beside the bed. All the little security failings added up. Even if Alex Anne were happily snoring next door, Tyler couldn't right all the wrongs in this organization. He could only do his best job for the time he remained on contract. The rest was up to the client.

Wilkinson finally dug the right keycard out of his wallet and unlocked the adjoining door. Tyler hustled into the room and looked around. It was a mirror of the other suite. The front area remained pristine. Tyler walked to the bedroom and found it empty. Two suitcases remained standing near the dresser. The comforter retained the perfect creases left on it by the housekeepers. Wilkinson followed him in. "She's not here," he said, stating the obvious with a tremor in his voice. "She's not in her room."

"She's never been here," Tyler said. "No one's slept in this bed."

"What do we do now?"

Maybe now, Wilkinson would take the situation seriously. "We presume your daughter and Donnell are missing."

10

"Donnell would protect her," Wilkinson insisted, jabbing a finger at Tyler. His face grew more red as he talked. "He's been committed to her safety for years."

"Then, where are they?" Tyler spread his hands. "Why can't we reach them? Why do their phones go right to voicemail?"

Wilkinson scowled, took a deep breath, and rubbed his face. "I don't know, dammit. I don't know."

"We have to treat them as disappeared," Tyler said.

"No." Wilkinson shook his head quickly enough to make his jowls jiggle. "Donnell would—"

"He's dead."

"What?" The crimson color drained from Wilkinson's face. "Why do you think so?"

"It's what I would do," Tyler said. "He's a capable guy. Taking him down is the first step in someone doing something to your daughter. If they grabbed her, there's no point in keeping him alive. He's big. Hard to move. Poses a threat if he wakes up." Tyler dropped his thumb to his forefinger like a kid shooting a pretend gun. "Killing him solves all those problems."

"He would protect her." This repeat lacked certainty.

"Bullets don't care about someone's determination."

"Oh, my god." Wilkinson whitened further. He covered his mouth with his fist and collapsed into a seated position on the bed. "She's gone. Someone took her."

"We need to work on who could've done it."

"This is a job for the cops." Wilkinson held his phone in a trembling hand. "They'll know what to do. They'll get the FBI involved. Alexandra's famous. People will want to find her."

"We don't know enough yet," Tyler said.

"What do you mean?"

"Have you gotten a ransom demand?"

"No," Wilkinson said in a quiet voice.

"Your daughter has been missing for a while . . . maybe since after the concert last night." Tyler recalled filling out the paperwork brought on by walloping the stage jumper. If he hadn't been ordered to do it, he could have accompanied Donnell and Alex Anne to the garage and then to the hotel. Things would've gone differently. There was no point legislating the past, however. Tyler needed to play the hand he was dealt no matter how bad it was. Soldiers sought solutions. The blame game was for flag officers. "You're looking at up to ten hours with no contact and no demands? Not good. I think whoever took her isn't interested in ransoming her back to you."

"Why else would someone take her?" Tyler stared at Wilkinson for several seconds. "No. No. I don't believe it."

"Trafficking groups operate all over the country," Tyler said. "They sell girls globally. Like you told me, your daughter is famous. She could've attracted the worst kind of attention."

Wilkinson spiked his phone onto the bed and ran his

hands through his hair. When he looked up again, his eyes were wet. "What do we do?"

"I want to investigate."

"You? You're not a cop. You never were."

"True," Tyler acknowledged. "I have a . . . different skill set. It might prove more useful in getting Alex Anne back alive. They won't want to keep her in one place for long."

"I'm going to have to call the cops soon," Wilkinson said. He fixed Tyler with his sad eyes. "Go. Find her. I don't care what you need to do or who you need to go through to get her back."

"Glad we're on the same page," Tyler said.

TYLER STEPPED out of the elevator when his cell rang. He expected it to be Wilkinson telling him he'd just gotten a ransom demand. Instead, Smitty's name displayed on the screen. Tyler rolled his eyes and answered as he crossed the lobby. "What's going on?"

"You might need to come to the shop."

"I can't right now."

"I thought whatever you were doing was easy," Smitty said.

"It was," Tyler said. "Things don't always stay simple, though, and this went pear-shaped last night. I'm not going to be able to swing by. What do you need?"

"The inspector's delaying again. I think we're getting the runaround."

"City guy?"

"No," Smitty said, "private. This is for all the interior stuff like the wiring and equipment. The city's already signed off on the exterior."

Tyler walked outside and headed up Baltimore Street

toward the Arena. "You ran a business for years. Ever have to deal with this?"

"I never had a problem. Whoever was supposed to show up did."

A car sped through the Sharp Street intersection, and Tyler waited for it to zoom past before crossing. "You talked to the guy. What do you think is going on?"

"Not sure," Smitty said. "Maybe he thinks he can shake an older guy down for more money."

"Text me his info," Tyler said. "When I have a few minutes, I'll call him and straighten it out."

"If you kill him, you'll have to find someone else."

It might need to happen. Tyler signed a contract and paid a deposit, though. This was a complication he didn't need right now. "Doesn't seem like a great loss either way."

Smitty let out a dry chuckle. "All right, boss. I'll send you his info. On the upside, have I told you how nice it is not to be the man in charge?"

"Only every time the tiniest little problem comes up," Tyler said. "Thanks, Smitty. There's no way I could be ready to open the shop without you."

"Remember this conversation when you're writing my bonus check," Smitty said and hung up.

Tyler pocketed his phone. He would deal with the troublesome inspector later. The investigation demanded his full attention. Every hour Alex Anne remained in the wind, her odds of returning safely diminished a little more.

ALEX ANNE FLEXED HER SHOULDERS. Hers arms ached from being bound to a chair. She'd gotten a brief reprieve when one of the captors led each girl to the bathroom in turn. They even got to eat a granola bar and drink water without being tied up. Once everyone finished the insufficient breakfast, however, the ropes went on again. Alex Anne considered fighting back even though the guy in the room carried a gun. None of the other girls had any fire in their eyes, however. They cringed, trembled, and obeyed. Probably just how the kidnappers liked it.

The big blond guy dragged another girl in. This one was conscious and protested the whole way. She spat in the man's face as he led her to a chair. That show of defiance earned her a hard punch to the midsection. She folded in half and gasped for breath. "Foolish girl," the guy said in an Eastern European accent. "You will learn to obey. If not now, then wherever you're going. Get used to it."

With the new girl lashed in place, Alex Anne figured three-fourths of the chairs were occupied. She'd seen three men coming in and out. The other seats filled up quickly. At this pace, they might be ready to leave tonight. Or tomorrow. Despite the fact the prisoners just got breakfast, Alex Anne didn't really know what time it was. The room featured no windows or a clock. Their captors took any phones or watches the captives owned.

Alex Anne missed her phone. She used it too much like most girls her age did, but it mattered for her career. Fans expected Instagram photos and stories, new tweets, and TikTok videos. By now, with a gap in her content, people would be wondering what happened. There would be a buzz on social media. She wondered if her father knew anything. Was Mister Tyler looking for her? She wished he'd been able to come with Donnell when they left the concert. If he were there, she thought events would've unfolded differently.

"People are going to look for me," Alex Anne said as the blond guy walked to the door. "For all of us. You can't just kidnap a room full of girls and expect no one to notice."

He stalked toward her, staring down as he approached.

With the light behind him, the man cast an imposing silhouette. "We don't care if anyone notices. They never do anything about it in time."

"You don't know who's searching for me."

The man's fist shot up from below his waist, and he backhanded Alex Anne across the face. Her head snapped to the side, and she almost tumbled over. The light-haired guy leaned down so far she could smell his foul breath. "Do you think we're incompetent? We know who he is, girl. Probably better than you do. If he noses around, we'll kill him . . . just like we did the other one."

Alex Anne cried—for herself and for Donnell—as the man stomped toward the exit.

11

Tyler walked into the Arena's attached parking garage. He made his way to the area reserved for performers and VIPs. It currently sat unused. Two guards with nothing better to do stood as he approached. One was white, the other black, and both looked like they stepped off the Ravens' practice field. The white guy held up a hand. "Area's closed."

"I work security for Alex Anne," Tyler said. The two men looked at each other and shrugged. "She put on a concert here last night." Recognition didn't dawn on their faces. Tyler wondered if they could write their own names without needing to practice for a few minutes first.

After several excruciating seconds, the black guard said, "Neither one of us worked here last night."

Tyler took a deep breath to compose himself. Pointing out they answered a question he didn't ask wouldn't get him anywhere. "Can you guys keep a secret?" They exchanged glances again. "I'm serious."

"Sure," the white one said. He stepped forward, and Tyler read his name on the lanyard hanging from his neck. O'Hara.

"All right," Tyler said. "After the concert last night, someone kidnapped Alex Anne."

"Jesus," O'Hara said. "Where did it happen?"

"I think right here."

"No way," the black fellow said. He moved close enough for Tyler to make out his name, too: Stephens.

Tyler gestured to the concrete. "While I was upstairs dealing with paperwork, another guy brought Alex Anne down here. He's big . . . bigger than either of you, in fact. No way he lets someone take her unless he gets shot." When the guards expressions remained vacant, Tyler filled in the gap. "It would explain why the floor is wet here. Maybe I didn't notice it on my way out last night. It was late, and I wanted to check on everyone at the hotel. Now, I think someone washed away the blood."

"I guess it's possible," O'Hara said.

"You told me you weren't working last night. Do you know who was?"

"No," Stephens said. "I was here until five. Three guys took over for me. Seemed like a lot to work this area on a concert night. It's usually only two." His slender brows furrowed. "Thing is . . . I didn't recognize any of them."

"No shit?" O'Hara broke in before Tyler could pose a similar follow-up.

"We don't work for the Arena. Our company does security for a lot of the venues in this area. Guys come and go sometimes, so maybe I wouldn't know one guy who came to relieve me. But all three?" He shook his head. "Seemed weird."

"But you let them take your place?" Tyler said.

"They had the authorization." Stephens shrugged. "I checked their IDs. Everything looked legit. Even called it in. I'm not giving my post to any three dicks who come walking up. The boss told me it was all good, though, so I left." His brows knitted. "Now, I wish I didn't."

Tyler couldn't find fault with how the man handled the situation. It conjured up memories of his own issues with commanders giving orders they shouldn't. "You did your due diligence," he said. "I'm gonna need to talk to your boss, though."

O'Hara snorted as he handed Tyler a business card. "Good luck. Prick barely tells us anything. Can't imagine he'd have five words for you."

Tyler smiled. "I can be very persuasive."

TYLER VISITED PREMIER COLISEUM SECURITY. They had no reason to talk to him, but his Army retiree ID got him past a fellow veteran at the front desk. Their headquarters looked like a small warehouse no one ever renovated to make it more inviting. One large entrance door and a smaller one at the back. Bare metal walls lacked any adornment. A few desks were arranged on the concrete floor. Only one was staffed. The manager's office was up a steel staircase and was the only thing above ground level. Tyler climbed and waited outside the door. A few minutes later, it opened. "Come in, Mister . . . Tyler, is it?"

"Yes." The man who invited him in had dark wavy hair and an olive complexion. He had on a pink button-down embroidered with the company logo, dark pants, and mirrored aviator sunglasses. Tyler guessed him about thirty. The time he'd spent working for Danny at Patriot Security soured him on young executives. Hopefully, this fellow was more competent than Tyler's former boss, but wearing ridiculous shades indoors didn't bode well.

"What can I do for you?" A nameplate on his uncluttered desk identified him as Nick Barberis.

"Your company manages security for the Arena, right?" He nodded. "Have any problems recently?"

Barberis shook his head. "Nope. Been pretty easy."

"How about the Convention Center?"

"All good there, too. Why are you asking? You work for someone who's trying to buy us out?"

"You keep good tabs on the Arena events?" Tyler persisted.

"What?" Barberis said. His brows pulled into a frown above the dark frames. "Of course I do. I know every event my guys work, even if I'm not there."

"You ever hear of Alex Anne?"

"What is this, Mister Tyler?"

"It's a simple question. You might try answering it."

"I never heard of her," Barberis said after a moment. Tyler didn't need to see his eyes to know he lied. "Who is she, your girlfriend?"

"She's a singer who played the Arena last night," Tyler said. "Big crowd. Probably a sellout." Barberis sighed. "I thought you knew all the events your guys worked."

"OK, so I heard of her. So what?"

"So no one's seen her since last night. The last place I know she was is your parking garage."

"You saying my guys kidnapped this girl?" Barberis slammed his hand down atop his desk.

Tyler fought the temptation to roll his eyes at the amateur intimidation attempt. "I'm saying some of your guys might have seen her. Maybe they saw someone else there, too . . . somebody who wasn't supposed to be there."

"Nobody said anything. Now, if you'll excuse me, I have work to do." Barberis looked down at some papers on his desk. Tyler saw the top of a bruise around his left eye in the gap between his face and the frames. He grabbed a stapler off the desk. "Hey, what are you doing?"

Tyler opened the stapler and whipped it down onto Barberis' right hand. He stifled a yell as the metal staple drove into his flesh. "You're not telling me everything," Tyler said. He lifted the office tool, and capitalizing on the other man's surprise, slammed it into his face. Another staple bit into his cheek.

"Ow, shit!"

A follow-up whack knocked the sunglasses off. Now Tyler saw the shiner in all its glory. He sat on the corner of the desk while Barberis touched his face and pulled back bloody fingers. "What happened to you?" Tyler said. "And don't feed me some line to try and make yourself look better. It's a little late."

Barberis blew out a long sigh. "Fine. Three guys came to see me yesterday. Said they wanted to work the Alex Anne detail. I told them to piss off. I had plenty of workers already."

"I guess they didn't take it very well."

"Not really," Barberis said. He let out a mirthless chuckle. "One guy was older . . . like fifty at least. He was the boss. The other two looked like they just came from the gym."

"And they ended up in the Arena garage after the concert."

"Yeah. We got into it a bit. I got the worse end of it." He pointed at his upper face even though a first grader could have made the connection. "The older guy gave me money, said they would take over for the night and to forget about it." He gestured to his eye again. "Every time I look in the mirror, I remember."

"You call the cops?"

"No. They warned me not to. Showed me a picture of my younger sister and . . . told me what they might do to her. She's eighteen. I ain't risking her life, and I ain't going to the cops now."

"Anyone can find a photo," Tyler said.

Barberis glared at him. "They also showed me a live video. Someone followed my wife. They threatened to do worse to her. I can't risk her life, either."

"I'm not asking you to," Tyler reassured him. "I want you to tell me everything you can about these guys. What did they look like?"

"Middle Eastern. Afghani, I would guess, but definitely from over there."

"Why?"

"The older one said something in Pashto."

"You speak it?" Tyler got up from the desk and went back to the chair.

"My grandfather was Afghani," Barberis said. "The rest of my family is Greek. I spoke and heard it a lot more growing up, but I can hold my own in Pashto."

Tyler expected him to continue. Maybe the staples in his face clouded his brain. "What did they say?"

"Something about getting more girls."

"Hell," Tyler said. Middle Eastern enforcers and wanting a few more girls didn't paint a good picture.

"What do you think?" Barberis said.

"All I know is they speak Pashto and kidnapped Alex Anne," Tyler said. He flashed back to the trafficking in persons training he'd been forced to endure during his Army days. These guys showed all the signs. With a famous captive, they wouldn't stick around long. Once the group got however many young women they wanted, they'd disappear.

"They gotta be holding the girls someplace."

"I know." Tyler stood and walked toward the door.

"They're local," Barberis added.

"How do you know?"

"I saw a Maryland plate on their car. Might be able to get the number from our cameras."

"Could've been a rental," Tyler said as he quietly simmered over Barberis' lack of backbone.

"How many rental BMWs you seen in a fleet? And this wasn't some bargain Three-series. This was a Five-forty. They ain't got them at Hertz."

"Good to know." Tyler jotted down his cell number on a Post-It note. "If you get the plate or happen to think of something else, can you call me?"

"What are you going to do?" Barberis asked.

"Find them."

"Then what?"

Tyler stared at Barberis and left without another word.

12

___

Tyler lingered outside the office and called Lexi, hoping she'd be home and able to help. "What's up, Dad?"

"Can you get the Patriot laptop?"

"Sure," she said. "Let me go downstairs. Did something happen after the concert?"

"You're home today?" Tyler asked, dodging the question.

"I'm smart about arranging my schedule. Three long days, but then two at home with no classes."

"I'm glad to hear you inherited more than just my good looks."

Lexi snorted. She definitely favored her mother in the appearance department, which could only be a good thing. "All right, I have the laptop. It's booting up now. What am I looking for?"

Tyler glanced around and pressed his back against the building. "I want you to run a plate first." Lexi's fingers tapped on keys over the cell connection. "Maryland tag . . . Bravo Sierra Golf four five two Echo."

"Got it," she said a few seconds later. "It's a ten-year-old Honda Civic owned by a man named Wallace Duncan."

A stolen plate, then. Maybe someone in the group really owned the Five series sedan. There would be a fair number of them registered in the state, but Tyler could circle back to it later. "Thanks," he said. "One more thing. I want you to see if there are any recent police reports about a man named Donnell Rodgers . . . with a D like the quarterback."

"What's going on, Dad?"

Another quick check showed no one in the vicinity. Tyler still lowered his voice out of habit. "I hope you enjoyed the concert, but it all went to hell after. I got stuck filling out papers because of the idiot who rushed the stage. Donnell left with Alex Anne. No one's seen either of them since."

"What!?" Lexi shrieked through the phone. "Do you mean she was—"

"Yes," Tyler said, cutting her off before she could mention a word like *kidnapped*. "Like I said, Donnell was with her. He's a capable guy, and he's big. There would only be one way to deal with him."

"I'm looking." She paused. "For God's sake, Dad. Why is nothing ever easy for you?"

"I've asked myself the same question most days since I turned eighteen . . . and I probably could've started sooner."

"I get no hits on the name," Lexi said. "No police reports. I can't get hospital records, but if someone brought in a shooting victim, don't they have to report it?"

"Yes," Tyler said. He wondered if Donnell's body simply hadn't been discovered yet. Barberis' comments implied a professional trafficking organization. They could be well-versed in hiding corpses, even large ones like Donnell's. "All right. Thanks, kiddo. I know I dropped a lot in your lap, but we can't have word of this getting out. You need to keep all this under your hat."

"Dad! You're asking a lot, you know."

"Good thing you always live up to my expectations. I'll let you know more when I can, but I'm obviously focused on this. Love you."

"Love you, too. Don't get shot." She clicked off before Tyler could answer. He slipped his phone back into his pocket. The traffickers shot Donnell. They wouldn't have another choice. In the aftermath, though, they couldn't leave his body at the Arena. A quick disposal would be the order. Drop it somewhere close and return to base with the high-value target. Tyler took off on the short jaunt to the Arena. He walked the perimeter and noticed nothing. Not even the SUV, which they would have needed to destroy or hide.

Premier Coliseum Security worked more places than the Arena, however. If the kidnappers were resourceful—Tyler presumed they were—they would know this. He set off for the Convention Center. It didn't take long to find a pool of blood in the alley. By itself, it wasn't a fatal amount, but considering Donnell would've also bled at the garage, he may not have survived. Where, then, was the body?

Tyler crouched at the area and studied the ground. A few feet away, a dot of brown marked the concrete. Another one landed not far beyond the first. The drops were exactly the color of dried blood. Tyler stood again and followed the trail, keeping slow so he could see which direction it headed. Donnell had made a left on Sharp Street.

Tyler did the same.

Durrani's cell phone rang. Gulraiz. "I'm tailing the other guy like you suggested," he said when the boss picked up.

"Good. I was hoping we could take out both when we

grabbed the girl. Keep an eye on him. He could be a problem." Durrani paused. He fully expected John Tyler to be a major concern. Why did he need to resurface now? "What's he doing?"

"Snooping mostly. I picked him up at the Arena. From there, he went to the security company."

"What about now?"

"He's walking," Gulraiz said. "An alley behind the Convention Center."

"Is there a body?" Durrani asked.

"No." Gulraiz dropped his voice to a whisper. "I can't get any closer, or he might see me. He's looking at something on the cement. I can't tell what it is."

"It's probably blood." Did someone move the big man's body? He shouldn't have survived the ambush. If he did, he might've ended up in the hospital. The police would start snooping around if this were the case. Good thing they'd be on the move with the girls soon.

"He's standing again. Coming my way. Hang on." The line went quiet. A moment later, Gulraiz said, "All right, I'm hiding behind a car. I don't think he saw me."

"You'd better be sure," Durrani said.

"He's walking away from me . . . kind of slow. It's like he's following something."

If there was a pool of blood in the alley, Tyler could have been tracking signs leading from it. "Stay on him." Where did the trail lead? Did the other guy survive? Could he identify the men who were there? Even if the other man lived, John Tyler couldn't. "New plan," Durrani added after a few seconds of contemplation. "Find somewhere inconspicuous and deal with him."

"You told us how much of a problem this guy was," Gulraiz said. "Now, you want me to deal with him alone?"

"You're a smart guy, Gulraiz. Look around. Choose a place

to ambush him. Just make sure he's dead. We don't want both of them surviving."

"I'll do it, boss." Durrani broke the connection. He couldn't share his man's optimism. Not where John Tyler was concerned.

THE GUY TAILING him was nowhere near good enough. Tyler picked him up in an SUV's driver's side mirror initially, then kept an eye on him using windows. The fellow never varied his pace. Never crossed to the other side of the street. He simply stayed about twenty feet behind and stared at his mark the entire time. If this guy indicated the quality of the traffickers' organization, Tyler liked the odds of getting Alex Anne back.

He kept an eye on the blood trail, but he couldn't follow it to its conclusion. Leading this asshole to it—and maybe to Donnell—would be a serious tactical error. If the big man survived, these men shouldn't know about it. Tyler thought the dots led near a church, but he kept walking past it. He continued on Sharp Street and waited to cross at Conway. The guy was still behind, though he looked awkward waiting amid a small crowd and trying not to be obvious.

When the light changed, Tyler crossed Conway. A branch of the Federal Reserve Bank lay on the right, and a bunch of row houses were on the left. There were plenty of alleys in what Tyler remembered as the Otterbein neighborhood. They could prove too visible, however. Alleys usually held things like parking pads so residents could actually keep their cars somewhere without competing with guests and tourists for coveted spots on the streets. Too many chances to run into someone.

As he approached Barre Street, Tyler spotted a house

badly damaged by fire. The windows were gone and replaced by plywood. An X made of yellow caution tape passed for the front door. Tyler made the left and neared the gutted home. He stopped, took his phone out, and acted like he engaged in a short conversation. His phone's screen showed the reflection of his pursuer waiting at the top of the street.

After a quick look revealed no nosy neighbors, Tyler slipped on a pair of thin black gloves, pushed the tape aside, and walked into the house. Much of the interior was charred. Paint bubbled and cracked. Someone must've taken the appliances out of the kitchen. Not a single wall hanging or piece of furniture remained. Whatever personal touches the residents bestowed upon their house vanished in the blaze. Tyler lingered in the kitchen. It offered an open but not massive space, and he would hear an intruder's footsteps on the bare wood floors.

A moment later, he heard footfalls approaching. "You don't need to try and be quiet," Tyler said. "You're a lousy tail, anyway."

A Middle Eastern man entered the kitchen. His right hand held a large hunting knife.

13

Slender and wiry, he stood a couple inches taller than Tyler, putting the guy at six feet even. "Want to tell me who you work for?" The man maintained his glare. Tyler repeated his question in Pashto. Recognition flickered in staring brown eyes but no further response. "Maybe what you're doing in Baltimore?" Tyler had a guess. Some former drug traders from Afghanistan fled the country when the Taliban fell. While a few maintained their old profession, others branched into alternate commodities—including girls. "Fine. Have it your way. We'll see if I can get you to talk before I kill you."

The knife came forward, and Tyler stepped to the side. He didn't like fighting people with blades. A trained opponent could be predictable. An amateur would swing wildly and hope for the best. Either way, one nick in the wrong place, and the fight would be over. The assailant took a backhand swipe after Tyler moved, but he was already out of range.

The attacker came at him again. This time, Tyler grabbed the knife wrist before the man could complete his swing.

Tyler shoved the man toward the counter and slammed his face onto the faux granite surface. Knocking the weapon from his hand was easy at this point. The assailant pushed Tyler away, frowned at the knife on the floor, and raised his fists. Tyler did the same. He blocked two quick punches, and when his foe moved closer, he drove his forehead down onto the bridge of the man's nose.

The crack sounded satisfying, and the Afghan man backed off a couple steps. He covered his face with his left hand. "Make it easy on yourself," Tyler said in Pashto. "You can still recover from a broken nose."

"I kill you, American dog," the guy said in accented English. He took his arm away and flexed his face a few times. After a quick lunge forward, he launched a roundhouse kick, which Tyler evaded by stepping back. The assailant tried a more conventional front kick. Tyler moved enough to trap the other man's leg between his side and arm. Reaching out and grabbing his opponent's belt, Tyler lifted the man a few inches and slammed him to the floor. A couple quick punches left his foe woozy.

Tyler grabbed the nearby knife, crouched over the fallen assailant, and held the blade above his chest. Just left of center, between the bottom two ribs, and angled toward the heart would do. He put the sharp point on the man's shirt and applied a little downward pressure. A spot of red showed through the fabric. "Time to talk."

"Piss off," the prone man said. He threw a punch, but Tyler blocked it with his forearm and then drove an elbow into the guy's face. Fresh blood ran from his already-injured nose, and he groaned around a few ragged breaths.

"I'm running out of patience." Tyler added a little more pressure. The tip of the knife disappeared into the man's flesh, and he grunted in pain as a fresh stream of blood poured forth. "Going between the ribs is pretty easy." Tyler moved the blade a little and scraped bone. "One more shove, and this knife goes into your heart."

"You Americans love to torture."

"I followed the rules of engagement when I was a soldier," Tyler said. "I'm not bound by any now. I still don't like torture . . ." He paused and shoved the blade a fraction of an inch farther in. ". . . but if I'm right about your group, you deserve what you get."

"Go to hell," the Afghan man said through gritted teeth. "I tell you nothing."

"Have it your way. I'll figure it all out, anyway." Tyler pushed down hard on the hilt, driving the knife between the ribs and into his heart. He stood and moved to the remains of the front door. No one took an interest in the place. Tyler took off his bloodied gloves and walked out of the house. No one else tailed him.

CONFIDENT NO ONE ELSE FOLLOWED, Tyler reacquired the blood trail near the United Methodist church. It stopped right before the stairs. Donnell must have staggered here. Did someone from the congregation take him in? He stepped up to the door, tested it, and found it locked. No services today, so probably no need to be open. Tyler knocked a few times and got no response. He lingered for a few minutes before leaving. Even if Donnell made it there, he would be in bad shape. If the church employed anyone who could care for him, they wouldn't want to move him.

Tyler walked back to the Lord Baltimore. As he entered the lobby, a pretty young clerk waved him to the desk and handed him a keycard. "From Mister Wilkinson," she said with a sincere smile. He took it while managing to hide the blood on his sleeves. It was nice to deal with someone who really liked her job. Tyler rode the elevator to Wilkinson's floor. He tried the card at the suite door, and it worked.

Wilkinson turned when Tyler entered. "You didn't find her yet."

"Didn't expect to so soon," Tyler said. He walked into the bathroom. It featured a long double vanity which looked nicer than any in his house. Tyler turned the water on and washed his hands and forearms.

Wilkinson came in. He must have seen the blood swirling in the drain. "What happened? Did you kill someone?"

Tyler shushed him and cleaned his gloves with the hand soap. When he'd finished and dried everything, he said, "Yes. Someone tailed me when I was out."

"You must be getting close, then," Wilkinson said.

"I think you've watched too many cop shows on TV." Tyler left the bathroom and sat at the desk. "Here's what I know for certain. The men who worked security in the garage last night aren't part of the company the Arena uses. Someone came and intimidated the boss to let them be there. He said the man in charge was Afghani. The guy who followed me today was, too."

Wilkinson sank onto the couch. "What's all this mean?"

"The Taliban had a fair number of supporters in Afghanistan," Tyler said. "Some of them were opium traders. It's very common over there. Once the Taliban fell, a bunch of their members and backers fled the country. Some ended up here. They still knew how to run a trading business, but they didn't have an abundant supply of drugs on hand. So they turned to moving . . . other things."

"Like girls," Wilkinson said with a voice full of dread.

Tyler nodded. "In some cases, yes. The demand is high in certain parts of the world. The army used to make us watch trafficking awareness videos every year. I know more about it than I would care to, but it seems useful right now."

Wilkinson stood and paced in front of the couch. "Do we go to the cops now?"

"They won't be able to do much," Tyler said. "If the operation just started, there may not even be any reported kidnappings yet. These guys are pros. The one tailing me wasn't very good at it, but then again, I'm a hard mark. He probably could have followed an average person for miles. They'll have a facility we can't trace back to them, and I'm sure transportation is already lined up. When you grab someone famous, you can't linger too long. People start asking questions."

"Alexandra's social media is already abuzz," Wilkinson said. "Fans are wondering why she hasn't posted a picture or video since right after the concert." He paused. "If local police can't help, what about the FBI?"

"You might have better luck with them." Tyler shrugged. "Any law enforcement operation is a bureaucracy. They can only mobilize and move so fast. I'm one man. I can decide and act much quicker."

"Like you said, though . . . you're only one man."

"I think Donnell might be alive." Tyler held up a hand when Wilkinson wanted to talk. "If he is, he's probably in a bad way. I don't think we're going to get anything out of him in time, but it might be worth a try."

"I think it is." Wilkinson plopped down on the coach, which groaned in protest. "I'm nervous, Mister Tyler. You might be very good, but with Donnell out, you're a team of one."

Tyler stood. "I've already figured out we're looking at Afghani traffickers. I want to keep digging into it."

"I'm not going to stop you," Wilkinson said, "but I can't wait very long."

"Understood," Tyler said.

~

Durrani glared at his ringing cell phone. He should've received an update a while ago. This probably meant bad news. "Not good, boss," Josef said when Durrani picked up. "I found Gulraiz."

"I presume he's dead."

"Yes. Looks like he got into a fight and then someone stabbed him. It was professional. Between the bottom two ribs and into the heart."

"You're saying it's something John Tyler could've done?" Durrani asked.

"I think so, yes."

Durrani shook his head. He never should've told Gulraiz to follow Tyler. The man was good at rounding up girls and keeping them in line, but he'd barely been a soldier. He was overmatched against someone like Tyler, who continued to plague Durrani to this day. There were other ways to deal with him, however. "All right, Josef. You handle it. I'm going to try another way of keeping Tyler off our backs." He hung up and looked over the short dossier on John Tyler Josef prepared.

Since leaving Special Operations and retiring from the army, Tyler worked in private security for about eight years. Afterwards, he got a job as a classic car mechanic. He also lived with his very pretty daughter. Durrani studied her photo. She recently turned nineteen. For an American girl, such an age probably meant she'd taken several lovers already. No matter. Her height and good looks would fetch a nice price even if she'd squandered her purity. He called his nephew. "Yes, Uncle?"

"Have you made contact with the daughter?" Durrani asked.

"Yes. She's friendly. I think she likes me."

"Good. I knew you could do it. We can use this. Things

need to speed up, though. Her father is meddling in our plans. When will you see her again?"

"Probably not until tomorrow," the young man said.

"May not be good enough," Durrani said. "Try to see her today. You want her to like you, to trust you. Get her in bed if you can. She's an American girl . . . it probably won't be too difficult."

"What if I can't?"

"Either way, bring her to me. We could use her. If nothing else, her presence will keep her father in line."

"She's not the type to come quietly," Durrani's nephew said.

Durrani sighed. "Pity for her, then. If you can't get her to come with you—willingly or not—then you need to kill her." Silence filled the line. "Did you hear me?"

"Yes, Uncle. I'll do it."

"Make sure of it," Durrani said. He broke the connection, stared at Tyler's picture on his desk, and seethed. "I hope your daughter is worth it to you."

14

There was no clock on the wall.

Alex Anne remembered her father telling her casinos did this so that high rollers couldn't look up from their chips to figure out what time it was. Her kidnappers did the same. The only light entering the room streamed in when the door opened, and it was always the same magnitude. It came from the hallway or rooms beyond. Without the sun or a clock, Alex Anne had no idea what time it was or how long she'd been bound to this chair.

She heard her own rapid pulse in her ears. How many selfies did she take in yoga pants after finishing a session? She'd practiced mindful breathing and meditation enough to make them easy, but here and now, they were a struggle. Alex Anne couldn't help hearing other girls in the confined space when she closed her eyes. No amount of breathing and attempts to clear her mind could force the sounds away.

"You're Alex Anne."

She tried to tune the voice out, too. A couple minutes of breathing helped get her racing heart under control. Alex Anne opened her eyes to see another girl staring at her. She had raven black hair pulled into a ponytail, and the clothes she wore suggested she got snatched on her way to or from the gym. The girl must have been cold. "I'm right, aren't I?" she asked again, keeping her voice low.

"No," Alex Anne said.

"Bullshit." The other young woman scooted a few inches closer. "My younger brother's like . . . obsessed with you. I've seen enough of your pictures and videos."

Alex Anne let out a long sigh. "Yeah. Fine. You're right. Not that it matters right now."

"It could. People will look for you."

"You think they're going to find us here?" Alex Anne wanted to know. She wondered about Donnell, who collapsed like he'd been shot before pain bit at her neck. What about Mister Tyler? He seemed like the type to pursue her kidnappers, but would he find them in time? Would her father even let him? He'd probably turned everything over to the cops by now.

"I think you might be our best shot. Don't worry . . . I won't narc on you to these other girls. They might recognize you on their own, though."

It was an ever-present danger everywhere she went. Alex Anne had always been more concerned about creepy middle-aged men recognizing her than girls her own age. At some point, she drew the wrong kind of attention from someone. Why were all these other young women here, then? Wouldn't it be smarter to grab one famous person and make an escape? "You know my name," Alex Anne said. "What's yours?"

"Emily."

"Nice to meet you, Emily. I really wish it were under better circumstances."

"Me, too," Emily said. She paused and looked around. "Everyone here is scared. They keep bringing in new girls.

Once all the seats are full, I think things are going to get worse for us."

"Let's hope someone is trying to find us, then," Alex Anne said. "Everyone here has a family."

"But not a security detail," Emily pointed out.

A lot of good it did me, Alex Anne thought, but she kept it to herself. She needed to hope Donnell survived, and Mister Tyler took up the hunt.

~

LEXI SAT at a coffee shop near the College Park campus. While she crammed her full load of classes into as few days as possible, her schedule still contained gaps. It made her spend the equivalent of a workday at or near the university. "Good practice for when you have a job," her dad told her, and she couldn't disagree. An employer wouldn't leave her an hour to do as she pleased, of course, so she figured to enjoy these respites while she could.

While college offered many perks over high school, math was a requirement at both. Lexi liked math on some level, but she didn't care for the way most people taught it. Instead, she found videos presenting the same material in shorter, more digestible chunks. Too bad the University of Maryland would never adopt ten-minute remote classes. She was into her second such video when she felt someone standing beside her. Lexi slipped off her headphones and looked up.

Ahmed waited in line. He must not have seen her. "Hi, Ahmed," she said.

He looked down astonished, and then recognition spread over his face. His smile forced color to rush to Lexi's cheeks. She wasn't used to the feeling, but she liked it. It had been a while since a boy made her blush. "Lexi, what a surprise. I just stopped in before my next class."

"Me, too." She glanced at her watch. "I've got about a half-hour."

The line moved up, and someone behind Ahmed muttered. "I'll catch you in a few minutes." He advanced a couple steps. Lexi slipped her headphones back on and resumed playback. She could have taken calculus, but she wanted to review algebra first. The higher math could come later. She'd need some of it for computer science classes, anyway. A few minutes later, Ahmed stood behind the chair opposite her. She muted the playback and invited him to sit.

"You come here often?" she asked. The line made her cringe inwardly.

Ahmed didn't seem to notice or mind. His expression never changed. Maybe he grew up somewhere her question didn't serve as a cheesy pickup line. "I've been here a few times. If you make a habit out of it, I might have to stop by more often."

She grinned. "I suppose I could arrange it."

"Great." He paused a beat. "Thanks for the email you sent. You have a knack for explaining things well. It helped a lot. I still feel behind, but maybe I'm on the way to digging out."

"Just don't ask me to pick up a shovel," Lexi said.

Ahmed glanced around the coffee shop. "Do you want to go out tomorrow night?"

She willed herself not to blush again. "Like . . . on a date?"

"Exactly like a date," he said. His knee bobbed up and down as the corners of his mouth turned up.

"Kind of odd on a school night," Lexi said. "Why not wait until the weekend?"

"I have to help my uncle move." Ahmed rolled his eyes. "It'll be a process, and I'm sure I'll end up tired. Tomorrow night would really be better. If you can, of course. I hope your mom doesn't make you do your homework."

"My dad would be the one to worry about. He's cool about

classes and me going out, though." She smiled. "Sure. Why not?"

"Great." Ahmed's expression mirrored hers. "I need to get back on campus, but I'll text you later, OK?"

"Sounds good." Lexi saw her own happy face reflected in her laptop screen as Ahmed walked out. She hadn't been on a date since moving in with her dad. Not because he forbade it or scared boys away—though she imagined he'd be quite good at it if he wanted to. While changing schools, making new friends, keeping up with the old ones, and wondering what the hell was going on with her mom, Lexi always felt like she carried a lot on her plate. Then, the Braxton mess happened, and she got kidnapped by men working for her dad's former commander.

It had been a hell of a year and a half. Having something to look forward to felt good.

~

A PAINFUL FOG enveloped Donnell's world.

As he awoke, he realized he was lying face up. When he opened his eyes, nothing looked familiar. He lay on a bed in a small, nondescript room. An IV fluid bag hung off a stand to his left. He didn't see any monitors or fancy equipment. This couldn't be a hospital. He searched his hazy memory to try and piece together where he ended up. It took a minute of intense thought to get his mind to recall what happened.

The concert ended. Some idiot rushed the stage, and the new guy got forced to fill out some paperwork about it. It kept him from making the trip with them like they'd planned. Donnell and Alex Anne took the elevator to the garage. Then, he ran into a wall. Nothing concrete came to him. He saw himself staggering down a street somewhere and coming to a gate. "Where the hell am I?" he muttered past his dry throat.

"Far from Hell, I hope," a voice said from nearby. Donnell rolled his head to the side. A slender white man who looked to be in his fifties stood in the doorway. He wore a pair of black dress pants and a thin gray sweater over a white button-down. His brown hair thinned on top. "We were worried about you."

"Where am I?"

The man entered the room, filled a cup with water, and handed it to Donnell. "You don't remember?"

Donnell gulped the water down and shook his head. "It's not coming to me."

"You're in a room at the Old Otterbein United Methodist Church," the stranger said. "You came to our door, and you were badly injured."

"Who are you?"

"I'm the pastor . . . Glen Crimmins."

"You call the cops?" Donnell wanted to know.

Crimmins shook his head. "We try not to if we can avoid it. A hospital would for a man in your situation, but we don't have to play by the same rules. You're fortunate. We've helped a few refugees in the past, and our deacon used to be an air force medic. I didn't think we'd need to use this makeshift infirmary again, but . . ." He spread his hands.

"I'm grateful." Donnell winced. He'd be more grateful for some morphine, but he doubted a church stocked such powerful drugs. "What did you mean when you said a man in my situation?"

"You've been shot." Crimmins refilled the cup and handed it back to Donnell. "Twice in the back. Luckily, you were wearing a vest, but these must have been large-caliber bullets. You took solid hits, and one of them got through." The pastor pointed to Donnell's ruined Kevlar draped over a chair. Blood covered the inside of it. "It saved your life. I'm no doctor, but I don't think you would have been able to make it here if you'd taken the full force of those slugs."

Donnell closed his eyes and tried to remember. *You've been shot . . . twice in the back.* He and Alex Anne got off the elevator. The SUV waited nearby. Three security guys did, too. Alex Anne walked around to the passenger's side. They'd done this a bunch of times. It was always a short drive from the venue to the hotel. A man stood in front of Donnell. He heard another approach from the rear.

He couldn't recall anything else.

"What is it?" Crimmins stared down, concern knitting his brows. "Are you remembering something?"

"I think so," Donnell said. "I'm pretty sure someone's in worse trouble than I am."

15

Tyler drove back home. Wilkinson seemed annoyed to see him go, but the man perked up at the mention of the erstwhile Patriot Security laptop's capabilities. A few former red team guys put them together for the company. Tyler didn't understand everything the machine did, but he always found it impressive. Lexi had become quite adept at using it for all manners of things. Patriot employees used the devices to gather information, run background checks, and speed things up in doing an end-around of law enforcement. When Tyler left the company, he never returned the equipment, and recent conversations with Cliff revealed they didn't much care.

At his house, Tyler grabbed the bag holding the laptop. He then went to his basement, pulled some cash from a secret room, and left again. Lexi must have still been at college. She did three long days a week, which struck Tyler as the smart way to go about it, especially when the campus lay a good forty-five minutes from home in traffic. He drove back downtown, parked at the hotel, and took the elevator to Wilkinson's floor.

The suite was now packed.

Tyler muttered a curse under his breath as several sets of eyes focused on him when he walked in. He recognized two right away: Captain Leon Sharpe and Sergeant Rich Ferguson of the Baltimore Police Department. So much for not calling the cops. "Tyler," Sharpe said as he approached. "Why am I not surprised to see you here?"

"I kind of have the same question." Tyler felt conspicuous with the laptop bag slung over his shoulder. He didn't want to draw any further attention to it by setting it down, but standing around with it would be both awkward and uncomfortable. In the end, he opted for dropping it onto a chair.

Sharpe's eyes followed it, but he didn't mention it. "Wilkinson told us he had a couple guys working for him."

"Right now," Tyler said, "it's just me. The other guy is MIA."

"Funny you should mention him," Ferguson added as he sidled up to his boss. "We were hoping you might be able to tell us what happened to Donnell Rodgers."

"Wish I could help you, Sergeant."

"It's lieutenant, now."

"Congratulations," Tyler said.

"Thanks," Ferguson replied, though his smile suggested he doubted Tyler's sincerity. "I'm not sure I believe you about your desire to help, though. You seem to like doing things your own way."

"I followed orders, consulted manuals, and felt beholden to codes long enough." Tyler shrugged. "It's easier when you stop giving a damn about those things."

"I guess I'm not quite there yet." Ferguson took a seat. He, too, noticed the computer bag. "Can you take us through what happened?"

"Sure." Sharpe wandered off and directed a couple of uniformed officers. "Donnell and I worked security for the concert last night. A moron rushed the stage, and I dealt with it. After the show, some asshole at the Arena made me fill out paperwork."

"I sympathize," Ferguson said with the hint of a smile and a quick glance toward the captain.

"We'd planned on both escorting Alex Anne back to the garage and the hotel. It's a short trip, but they brought me on for a reason. Instead, Donnell insisted on taking her by himself while I was stuck signing forms. By the time I finished, they'd already left, so I walked back to the hotel. I couldn't reach Donnell or Alex Anne. It seemed odd to me, but Wilkinson said he might have taken her to visit friends."

"You didn't push it?" Ferguson asked.

"I might've mentioned it more than once," Tyler said. "There's only so much you can do when the boss isn't interested in your opinion." Wilkinson frowned, and Tyler wondered if the man could hear him. A lot of people milled about, but this wasn't a massive suite. "This morning, when they were still unreachable, I raised the alarm."

Ferguson bobbed his head slowly. "I'll be honest . . . we just started here, so we don't know much yet. No one has seen Mister Rodgers since the concert ended. I wish we knew something about him, but we just don't." He trailed off as if expecting Tyler to fill the gap, which didn't happen. "We'll have people look for him, too, but we want to focus on Alex Anne. She's more of a high-value target. Other than the guy rushing the stage, have you come across any threats?"

"Someone hopped the rail at a signing," Tyler said. "Kind of a similar thing. I handled him, too."

"You think they could be related?"

Tyler spread his hands. "I don't see how. Two idiots did the same thing. Alex Anne has a lot of fans. Not all of them are nice, well-adjusted people."

"All right." Ferguson removed a business card from his

wallet and slid it across the table. Tyler went to grab it, but Ferguson kept is finger pressed down on it. "You get a lead, come across something, whatever . . . you call me. I don't want to hear about any more of your vigilante behavior. I can't stop you from looking around, but when it comes to getting Alex Anne back, let's leave it to the professionals."

"Sure, Lieutenant," Tyler said. "Let me know when they get here." Ferguson rolled his eyes as Tyler snatched the card and put it into his pocket. He wanted to follow up on the possible lead with Donnell and the church, but slipping out with such a large police presence would be complicated. He sat and waited for about a half-hour before they finally rounded up their people, packed all their bags, and left.

"I know what you're going to say," Wilkinson said as he closed and locked the suite door.

"You did the right thing," Tyler said.

Wilkinson's jaw hung open a couple seconds before he answered. "Not the response I expected."

"I'm not going to work with them." Tyler moved the laptop back to the table. "You need to cover all your bases, though, and focus on getting your daughter back. I think I'm pretty damn good, but like you pointed out earlier, I'm also one guy. Relying on me isn't enough."

"Good." Wilkinson nodded. "I'm glad you understand."

Tyler unzipped the laptop bag, slid a stack of cash out as unobtrusively as possible, and stood. "Sure. Now, I'm going to get back to work."

"Where are you going?"

"I think I might know where Donnell is . . . or at least where he visited."

"You could have told the police!" Wilkinson gestured toward the door as if they were still out there.

"You're not paying me to hand things over to them," Tyler said. "You're paying me to find Alex Anne. Now, if you don't mind, I'm going to see if I can learn what happened to Donnell. If he's alive, I hope he might be able to tell us something."

"Why do you need the cash?" Wilkinson demanded. "Where is he?"

"A place which thrives on donations," Tyler said.

JOSEF HAD NEVER FELT comfortable around women. He figured the unease and indifference allowed him to work for Durrani. His mother kept the family going but seldom offered much attention to her children. Josef left as soon as he could, fell into the military life, and spent most of his time around men. His relationships with women over the years were usually brief, rarely fulfilling, and often violent.

With Durrani distracted by the specter of John Tyler, Josef said he would take a turn in the field. This would be his first try to grab a girl. He knew the type they were looking for: pretty, under eighteen, and gullible enough to drive off with a stranger. If the latter turned out to be untrue, Josef counted on his ability to muscle a brat into the SUV.

He strolled down Baltimore Street in an area of the city referred to as "The Block." People more familiar with the neighborhood said it shrank over the years, and the police presence was more frequent now than in the past. Still, prostitutes walked the streets, and lap dances in the clubs always came with the promise of something more if the price was right.

Josef was about to head into a club when a young woman stepped out from an alley. "Hey, mister. Looking for a good time?" He eyed her up and down. The longer they worked the streets, the more likely hookers would get into drugs and other bad habits, which diminished their beauty. This one must have been a fresh-faced recruit. She was probably sixteen but could pass for older. Bright green eyes were the best feature of a pretty face.

From farther into the alley, a man approached, and the girl frowned as he stood behind her. "She asked you a question, friend." He was white, probably in his twenties, and large but paunchy. Cuffing a bunch of underage girls around would be easy for a man like this.

"I'm interested," Josef said. The man beckoned him deeper into the shadows, and they all walked about twenty feet.

"What do you want?" the pimp said. "She'll do anything." The young woman winced. Prying her away from this guy might be easier than Josef thought.

"I've had a long couple days," he said. "My boss is kind of a jerk. I want it all."

"Where you from?"

"Doesn't matter." Josef flashed some cash. "My money is American."

"You got someplace we can go, Mister?" the girl asked.

Josef answered her with a question. "Do you want to get rid of this man?"

Her pimp responded for her. "What the hell are you talking about?" For her part, the young woman regarded Josef with wide eyes.

"I wasn't asking you," Josef said. He watched the other man's movements. He'd try a show of force to keep his hold on his property. Sure enough, the guy reached for his waistband. His bulk slowed him a critical instant, however. Before he even closed his hand around the pistol's grip, Josef held a knife. He shoved the pimp into the wall and stabbed him rapidly in his ample midsection over and over. After a final thrust to the chest, Josef let the dying man slide down the brick to the cracked concrete.

To her credit, the young hooker didn't run. She looked between Josef and her former pimp a few times. "Do I work for you now?"

Josef moved a trash can to conceal the body from people walking along the sidewalk past the alley. "No," he said. "You don't need to work for anyone else again. My employer and I have something much better in mind."

"What do I need to do?"

Josef swept his arm toward the street. "Just come for a ride with me."

EARLIER, what looked like a blood trail led Tyler from the area behind the Convention Center to a United Methodist church. He went on foot again to see if anything else turned up. He found no new evidence. The house of worship was a dead end—hopefully not for Donnell. Tyler approached again and banged on the large wooden door. It made an impressive sound, and he imagined the echo inside. No one answered.

Tyler tried again. He scanned the street and found no one nearby. "I'm looking for someone," he called, his face near the mahogany-colored wood. "I think he may have come here. He was pretty badly hurt." No reply. Tyler gave it a few more good raps. "I'm not with the cops. He and I work together, and if he's here, I need to see him. Please."

Silence served as the only response. Tyler kept his ear against the door, and he thought he heard footsteps clattering against the floor inside. A moment later, someone answered. "What's the man's name you're looking for?"

"Donnell. Donnell Rodgers."

"How do I know you don't mean to harm him?"

"Your door isn't bulletproof," Tyler said. "If I wanted to hurt Donnell, you'd already be dead."

Another minute passed before the deadbolt opened. The large door moved inward a few inches, and a man's thin face appeared in the opening. "No one's ever mentioned shooting me through my door before."

"I could probably find some more vulnerabilities," Tyler said, "but I'm more interested in finding Donnell. Is he here?"

"We're not a hospital, Mister . . .?"

"Tyler. John Tyler. I know you're not, but I followed what looked like drops of blood to the sidewalk out there." He pointed behind himself. "In my experience, churches tend to help people and not go to the police."

The door opened a little farther, and the slender man bade Tyler enter with a jerk of his head. Once Tyler stepped inside, he locked up again. He was clad in the kind of clothes Tyler would expect a priest to wear when not in the official getup. He'd never known one—including army chaplains— who kicked around in a T-shirt and jeans. Some amount of gravitas came with the job. "You're putting me in a bad spot, Mister Tyler. I don't want to advertise the fact we can patch up people we find shot on our stoop."

Tyler made a locking motion over his lips. "Mum's the word, Father."

"Pastor," the man said. "We're not Catholic. Glen Crimmins."

"Pleased to meet you." Tyler held up a stack of bills. When he shut down a drug cartel operating in Maryland a few months ago, Tyler kept some of their clean money for his troubles. He planned to use it to pay for Lexi's college. A few thousand to the Old Otterbein United Methodist Church would be for a good cause, however. "I have a donation. I told you I wouldn't say anything, and I presume you won't, either. Whatever you did for Donnell wasn't free. I'm sure you need supplies . . . and while you might not be Catholic, I've never known any church to refuse a good-faith contribution."

Crimmins offered a small smile and took the five thousand. "I'll tell the bishop we had a generous anonymous gift. Follow me." The pastor led Tyler out of the church proper, along a couple hallways, and down a short flight of stairs to a nondescript door marked *Storage.* "At one point, it really did hold supplies. We decided to help some refugees a few years ago, and . . . well, you'll see. It's not much, but we do what we can." He paused and lowered his voice. "Donnell doesn't remember everything. I get the feeling someone's in trouble. You're right about churches not wanting to call the cops, but I can't ignore someone in danger."

"Let me talk to him," Tyler said. "We work together. I'm already looking into everything."

The door swung in. Donnell lay in a bed, his feet hanging over the far end. Shelves lined the opposite wall. An IV bag did its job near the bed, but Tyler saw no other medical equipment. He wondered how they'd managed to take care of an injured person. When Donnell didn't move, Tyler thought the man was asleep. His head turned, though, and his eyes narrowed in recognition. "Huh. You found me. Maybe you're pretty good after all."

16

"**G**ood to see you're alive," Tyler said. He stepped into the room, and Pastor Crimmins followed.

"So are we," the holy man offered. "Donnell came here in bad shape. It was touch and go for a while, but your friend is tough."

"I'm glad you were able to help him." Tyler gestured around the small area. "This isn't exactly a hospital-grade setup, though."

"You're concerned. It's fair. Our deacon used to be a medic in the air force. When he came to the church, he said he'd seen enough killing, and it was time to work in a more positive direction." Crimmins let the comment hang in the air.

"Good for him," Tyler said.

"This room was never designed for emergency surgery." Crimmins pointed to the IV stand. "We bought it because we saw a lot of dehydrated people. I never expected to be hanging actual medicine from it."

Donnell scrunched his face. Tyler wondered what kind of pain pharmaceuticals a church carried on hand. It would be hard for them to obtain controlled substances like morphine without raising some questions. A bottle of Tylenol might not be enough for gunshot wounds, but what else could they do? Tyler pushed those concerns aside. "Let's get down to business. Donnell, what do you remember from last night?"

"You looking for Alex Anne?" he asked. His voice sounded strained, and the pastor filled a cup of water and handed it to him.

"I'm trying. Wilkinson's already involved the police. I can't blame him, but I'm still going to do what I can. If I'm able to get her back and . . . handle the situation, so much the better."

"It sounds like our patient's memory has improved," Crimmins said.

Donnell nodded. "It's coming back to me."

"It also sounds like we're dealing with a kidnapping."

"We are," Tyler said. "The police are already in on it."

"Why not simply leave it to them?"

Tyler ignored the pastor's question. "You two went to the garage. What happened?"

"The SUV was pretty close," Donnell said. "Three security guys were there. I didn't recognize them, but it's been a while since we did an event there. Two were definitely Middle Eastern. Both had the right complexions, and I heard an accent when one talked. The other one looked American . . . white."

"You know who shot you?"

"No." Donnell's head moved a fraction side-to-side. "Alex Anne walked around the SUV. I was about to open the driver's door. One of the detail stood in front of me, but another must have moved behind me. I kind of felt it, y'know? Then, I guess he shot me. I don't really remember." His eyes took on a faraway look. "Next thing I know, I'm lying in an alley somewhere. Bunch of blood around me. Everything hurt. I got up and started walking. Guess I made it here."

"Good thing you did," Tyler said. He wondered about the American man. It seemed unlike an Afghan group to work with outsiders. Times change, however, and trafficking girls was bound to be different than moving drugs. "I'll keep working." He turned to the pastor. "Can he leave here?"

"No," Crimmins said. "Not for several days. At some point, he'll need to rehabilitate from his injuries, which is well beyond what we can do. We're already stretching our capabilities keeping him here."

"I understand. I might need to see him again while this all shakes out."

"Come anytime," Donnell said. "I don't know what I can do from this bed, but if it helps get Alex Anne back, I'll damn well try."

Crimmins bobbed his head in assent. "Whenever you need to come back, we'll be here. It goes without saying we'd appreciate being kept out of anything official."

"You and me both, Pastor," Tyler said.

RICH FERGUSON SAT behind the desk in his office. He still needed to hang a decoration or two and fill the bookshelf. Even with the room remaining incomplete, it still felt a little weird to have a space to himself. During his time as a sergeant, his desk butted against his partner's. Paul King got the promotion to fill Rich's old rank, and he deserved it. For his part, Rich still struggled with not taking an active role in homicide investigations. He needed to manage the cops in the bullpen and pitch in where he could—sometimes on high-profile kidnapping cases.

A knock at his door shook Rich from his brief reverie.

Captain Sharpe took up most of the frame and blotted the light from the rest of the squad room. "Can I come in?" Even at conversational volume, the man's voice boomed with authority.

"I don't think I'm allowed to say no," Rich said.

"You are." Sharpe grinned. "Might not look so good in your eval at the end of the year." He sank onto Rich's guest chair, which squeaked in protest at the muscular man's bulk. "What do you think of the kidnapping case?"

"Looks like a red ball from the start."

"It is," Sharpe said. "It's why we're using you and Homicide. We want the best on it."

Rich leaned back and shook his head. "I don't know, Captain. We have people out chasing down the tiniest of leads. I'm trying to manage it all while not letting them know how hopeless I think the whole mess is."

"You're probably right. Famous people with protection details don't get snatched up by some random prick. It's an operation. Professional. My guess is they've done this before . . . here and maybe in other parts of the country, too."

"You think we need the feds?" Rich asked.

Sharpe folded his hands over his barrel chest. "What do you think of Tyler?"

"Not as much as you." Rich frowned. "I know you two served together, but he's a wild card. We can tell him to leave things alone, and he won't. He's going to poke and prod and smash, and in the end, we have to hope we find a missing girl. Or maybe a bunch of them."

"You know you could've been describing your cousin there, right?"

Rich realized it, though the comparison didn't improve his mood. C.T. also played fast and loose, but he'd shown willingness to hand things over to the BPD when the time came. Tyler didn't strike Rich as the type to cede control. "What's your point, Captain?"

"I've been in this department a long time," Sharpe said. "Seen a lot of turnover, new policies, new commissioners . . . all of it. Lots of situations change. The only constant is we're a big organization. I'm proud of the work we do, but it's hard for us to do delicate work at speed. You might call Tyler a wild card, and I won't argue. C.T. has done some things we can't. You and I might question the way he goes about some stuff, but I give him rope because he comes through. Tyler's the same. He's one guy. He can pivot faster than we can."

"We'll just have to deal with a trail of dead bodies," Rich said.

Sharpe spread his hands. "If we're dealing with professional traffickers, I won't mourn them. You shouldn't, either."

Rich sat up and looked at his phone, hopeful for a text or call from one of the teams in the field. "We're going to keep doing things the way we do them. Maybe your friend gets there first. Good for him if he does. I'm not letting up, though."

"I don't want you to," Sharpe said. "You keep a handle on everything. Update me when you feel you need to. Let me worry about Tyler."

"What if he gets in the way?" Rich said.

Sharpe stood, and the light dimmed again. "We're the police. We'll handle it like we always do."

DURRANI'S PHONE trilled in an unusual tone. He glanced at the screen. A video call request. He almost never accepted these, but his wealthy client wanted an update. Declining could damage the relationship. He tapped the green button. A palatial background filled the small screen. "Do you have positive news, Farzaad? When do I get the girl I'm paying for?"

"We have her already."

"Why is she not already here, then? I hoped to have her tied to a bed by now."

Durrani stared at the client. He was an overweight man born into wealth who managed to be smart enough to add to it over time. The Jordanian enjoyed all the trappings of the good life, and those who crossed him had a bad habit of disappearing. "You are not our only customer," Durrani said in as respectful a tone as he could. The reward for Alex Anne would probably exceed what they got for all the other girls combined, even docking some money for her lack of purity. It would happen to several of the others, as well. Durrani never figured out why Americans hated sex and prostitution yet raised their daughters to be whores.

"I am paying you the most, yes?"

"We're managing risk. Spread out a bunch of girls disappearing, and the police can't cover them all. Abduct one famous person, and you get the full weight of the department."

The Jordanian waved a hand. The man probably kept local officials in his back pocket. A police investigation wouldn't threaten him, so he didn't understand the line Durrani walked. "I hope I can expect her soon, at least."

"Absolutely," Durrani said. "It'll take time to get there, but she'll be yours in a couple days at most."

"She'd better be," the client said, and Durrani's screen went dark.

Durrani called Hajira, who answered right away. "Tell me where we stand," he said.

"This might be the easiest it's ever been," she said in a Nigerian-accented voice. "I've got four right now. One of the men is keeping an eye on them."

"Only an eye?"

"I think so," Hajira said, "but I can't help who you hire."

Durrani did the math in his head. The chairs were filling up. They'd have a lot of girls to take to auction after delivering Alex Anne to her new owner. "Very good," he said. "I knew I could count on you. See if you can work a couple more but bring the ones you have tonight. I want to be wheels up within twenty-four hours."

17

The walk back to the Lord Baltimore Hotel afforded Tyler time to think about the situation. He'd managed to track down Donnell, but the man couldn't tell him much. Part of the security force being Middle Eastern wasn't a revelation. Tyler dealt with an Afghan attacker, and Barberis told him three such men paid him a visit. No new information. It proved hard not to think of his visit to the church as wasted time. He didn't have a single lead on where Alex Anne could be.

Wherever she was, her captors wouldn't keep her there long. Even if they didn't know the cops were now on the hunt, they'd need to move quickly. Law enforcement involvement became inevitable when dealing with someone famous. Why Alex Anne? The world was lousy with pretty girls singing pop songs. Did something about her make her a more inviting target? Tyler had nothing to go on, so he needed to start at the beginning.

He crossed the lobby and rode the elevator to Wilkinson's floor. No one else was in the suite. The client sat at the desk, rubbing his forehead. "Anything?" he said without taking his hands away.

"Donnell's alive." Tyler sank onto a corner of the bed. "Probably lucky he is. If his fortune holds, he'll stay on the good side of the dirt. He couldn't tell me anything helpful, though."

"What are we going to do?" Wilkinson's eyes looked red and puffy. "Alexandra's out there somewhere, but no one knows where. I had to call the police, but I don't know if they'll be able to do anything." His voice cracked near the end, and he lapsed into silence.

"I want to start at the beginning of everything," Tyler said. "Lots of girls around your daughter's age do the same thing she does. Why her?"

Wilkinson's head wagged side-to-side. "I've asked myself the same question. Of course, I think she's remarkable. I always have. But in the grand scheme of things . . . like you say, other girls are doing pretty much similar acts. How remarkable are any of them, really?"

"I know I've harped on a few vulnerabilities I've seen, but you went years without an incident. Did anything change?"

"I don't think so."

"No particularly credible threats?" Tyler asked.

"We always get some," Wilkinson said. "It's part of the business, especially for an attractive young woman. I forward any really bad ones to the FBI."

"Any arrests?"

"No."

So much for the vengeful stalker angle. It probably didn't mesh with the likely involvement of Afghan traffickers, anyway. "What about friends? The people who say they like you the best are sometimes the most jealous of success."

Wilkinson frowned. "You think one of Alexandra's friends might have sold her out?"

"It's happened before," Tyler said.

"I'm sure it has, but I don't think it did here." A long sigh strained Wilkinson's belt. "Mister Tyler, I appreciate you sticking this out and trying to help. You're not an investigator, though. I'd love to see a miracle, but I can't expect one."

"What about her mother?"

"What?"

"Alex Anne's mother," Tyler said. "I've never seen her or even read anything about her."

Wilkinson waved a hand. "She's not involved in our lives. Hasn't been for years, really."

"She might want a cut of the money."

"No. She comes from a wealthy family." He shook his head. "I haven't spoken to her in a few months, and I doubt Alexandra has, either. I used to think it was a shame, but it's clearly the way her mother wants things. How can you not want your daughter to pursue a singing career?"

Because you're concerned about the trappings of fame, Tyler thought, but he kept it to himself. "Humor me," he said. "Like you pointed out, I'm no investigator. I kick in doors and shoot people, and sometimes, I even learn things doing it. What's her mother's name?"

"Amanda," Wilkinson said. "Amanda Painter. She lives in Delaware."

"And she's not involved with . . . anything?" He waved a hand.

"She is. Sort of." He paused. "Amanda has always fancied herself as a communications and social media expert. She decided she would handle the fan club. Maybe it was a way of getting involved even though she still barely talked to Alexandra. She managed the Double-A Songbirds."

"Dreadful name," Tyler said with a grimace.

"Yes," Wilkinson said. "I think Alexandra came up with it when she was twelve. We've never changed it."

Tyler stood and grabbed his computer bag. He fired up the Patriot laptop. Lexi's proficiency with it dwarfed his, but he could do the basics like chase down a name. Amanda Painter lived in a town called Kitts Hummock, which Tyler had never even seen a sign for during his trips through the nearby small state. He didn't even know what a hummock was. The Delaware map showed it on the water, which would inflate home values. "I'm going to finish this in my room," he said as he collected his things.

"All right," Wilkinson replied with a faraway look in his eyes.

A couple minutes later, Tyler resumed his search. He tried the home and mobile numbers for Amanda Painter. Both went to voicemail. He cursed his lack of proficiency with this laptop. The things it could do would land the operator in trouble even in lawless countries, but none of the power did Tyler any good if he couldn't tap into it. He came across a program of dubious legality to find her credit cards and recent charges. The program was amazing; Tyler only needed to type in some information, and it quickly spat out results. For a woman who bought something multiple times every day, Amanda Painter had been silent for the last two.

A perk of being in the army for twenty-four years was knowing a lot of people. Many of Tyler's fellow soldiers who left the service went into law enforcement. He remembered one—Musa Sadozai—caught grief sometimes for being born an Afghan Muslim and fighting with the United States Army. He took the taunts much better than Tyler would have. When Musa didn't re-up, he mentioned going to Delaware to be a cop. Tyler didn't have his number, but he found it easily enough via the laptop. "Been a while," Musa said after they re-introduced themselves,

"It has, and I wish this were a social call, but I'm pretty jammed up. You know a town called Kitts Hummock?"

"Sure . . . and before you ask, I know what a hummock is, too."

Tyler grinned. "You're smarter than me, then."

"Never in doubt. You need something in Kitts Hummock?"

"Yes," Tyler said.

"You want the Kent County Police, then. I'm state."

"But I'm calling you, and time might be a factor. There's a woman who lives there. I'm worried about her." He didn't want to go into all the details and hoped Musa would play ball despite the lack of info.

"I suppose I can help you out," Musa said. "What's her name?"

"Amanda Painter. She's been off the grid for a couple days. Can you do a welfare check?"

"You got an address?" Thanks to his computer, Tyler did, and he rattled it off. "You think she's in trouble?" Musa asked as a follow-up.

"Maybe," Tyler said. "Her daughter is. It's . . . kind of complicated."

"I wish you had something more for me."

"All I know for now. Remember, I'm not the intelligent one here."

"Yeah, yeah," Musa said. "All right. I'll look into this and let you know what I find."

"Thanks, Musa." They both hung up. Tyler hated waiting when he knew Alex Anne's future was on a clock. He used the laptop to see if he could uncover anything about trafficking groups operating in the area while keeping his phone close at hand.

~

HER DAD WASN'T around when Lexi arrived home. She set her heavy bookbag down and texted him. *Everything all right? You going to make it for dinner?* What a weird situation. He joined the small security detail for Alex Anne, and then the girl went missing after her first major event. Lexi knew her dad blamed himself even if he didn't come out and say it. He always took failures hard, and his therapeutic painting program helped.

Her phone buzzed as he replied. *I'm still here. No update, but it's still bad. I'll be careful. Love you.* Lexi fired off a quick response and turned her attention to her homework. She'd been getting a lot more of it this semester than the first. Maybe the courses were a little harder now, but they didn't feel any more challenging. Professors always liked piling up the busywork. At least it felt useful in her software development class—she needed the practice. Writing an essay was a total yawner by contrast.

Even though she'd been eating a lot of it recently, Lexi ordered a couple pizzas for delivery. Maybe her dad would make it home later and be able to enjoy some. She listened to music until the driver arrived, ate alone at the kitchen table, and then returned to her room to get serious about homework. Might as well start with an essay. If she got something she disliked out of the way first, the rest could only be better.

Lexi was a few minutes into some research when her mobile buzzed again. She figured it was her dad. Ahmed's name popping up surprised her, but she smiled and opened the message. It was a cute bitmoji of him holding a bouquet of flowers. *Hope your evening is going well.*

Cheesy but effective. Lexi smiled and jotted off a reply. *A little better now, thanks.*

A minute later, he texted again. *Looking forward to tomorrow night? I know I am.*

I am. I have a date booked. He's cute and funny in a sort of cheesy way.

A laughing bitmoji appeared on her screen. *I'll take it. See you tomorrow.*

Lexi grinned, set her phone down, and returned to the grind of her homework.

~

TYLER WISHED he were better with the laptop. Having Lexi with him would help, but she shouldered a heavier workload this semester. If he didn't make much progress, he might need to call her, anyway. When his phone pulsed on the desk, he hoped it was his daughter. Instead, the number he recently dialed for Musa filled the screen. Tyler figured it was bad news—this whole situation had been nothing but—but he answered anyway. "Your woman is dead," Musa told him.

Of course. Tyler pinched the bridge of his nose. "Let me guess . . . she didn't go in her sleep."

"Her throat was cut ear-to-ear. She bled out in her bed."

"You see the scene?" Tyler asked.

"No," Musa said. "I asked a couple locals to check it out. They told me, and they sent pictures. After talking with the coroner, my guess is someone made her suffer. It wasn't one quick slash. She had a few broken ribs, too. It means—"

"Someone stomped on her chest," Tyler said. He'd heard reports of the Taliban brutalizing and killing people—almost always women—like this, but he'd never seen it, himself. Despite what Jeff Wilkinson told him, Tyler wondered what role Amanda Painter played in her daughter's life and career. If she'd been relegated to fan club manager all this time, why was she dead? "Your locals know how long ago it happened?"

"Their best guess is about two days. They'll know more once she gets the full workup."

The estimate lined up with Amanda Painter's online activity stopping. "Thanks, Musa. You . . . back on the straight and narrow?"

"Yes," he said. "No booze for me. Haven't touched it since I left the army. I like it here. I mostly work the highways and teach shooting. I've been able to get back to my roots."

"In a lot of ways," Tyler said, "you're the opposite of most soldiers I know."

"I probably always will be," Musa said. "Good to hear from you, Tippy. Don't be a stranger."

Tyler grinned at the old special operations nickname. "I'll try. Take care, Musa." He ended the call. His old unit mate confirmed the worst: Amanda Painter was dead. The big questions remaining were who killed her, and how much did she tell her murderers before they cut her throat? Wilkinson could say her involvement remained minimal, but she was Alex Anne's mother. Even when Rachel went to jail, Lexi wanted to talk to her mom. Tyler always encouraged her to. Maybe Wilkinson put his foot down, and if he did, it could have made Alex Anne want to talk to Amanda even more.

At least the news focused his searches on the old Patriot laptop. When he knew whom or what he searched for, Tyler could get some decent results. He dug into Amanda Painter some more. She owned a private art gallery and curated it herself, using the two degrees she earned. It struck Tyler as a vain rich person's job. He couldn't find any connections between her and Alex Anne or her and Wilkinson. Amanda maintained a social media presence, focusing on Instagram for her business. She knew how to snap good photos of paintings and sculptures.

Her other accounts offered a few more personal insights. About seven months ago, Amanda Painter met a man she described as well-traveled and retired early. She began dating him shortly after. Tyler used a program on the laptop to scour her connections, posts, and overall online footprint. A hit came back on her boyfriend: Farzaad Durrani.

Tyler knew the name.

18

In Afghanistan, the army maintained files on the Taliban as well as their most fervent supporters—both idealogical and financial. Durrani fell into both camps. He'd been an opium trader the Afghan government could never catch, and he was glad to funnel money to the Taliban when they came into power. Tyler wished he could access some of those old records now. They detailed Durrani's opium business. He settled for what he could find with the laptop. It would gather open source and unclassified intelligence, at least.

About a decade ago, Durrani fled Afghanistan. He landed in Turkey for a few months and then came to America. Without easy access to an abundant supply, he couldn't maintain his drug trade. Instead, he turned to girls. Old habits died hard. He'd been investigated a few times and even detained twice, but nothing ever stuck. The man enjoyed a clean arrest record, and his money probably convinced some people to look the other way.

His laptop offered more information. The BMW 5 Series Barberis saw was a cash purchase about a year ago. Tyler checked Durrani's known associates. Software gleaned this data from various social media sites, public records searches, résumés posted online, and other sources Tyler didn't know or understand. Not as if he understood social networks much, either. Mostly, people posted pictures of their food and cats, or they overshared personal details of their lives, and they did both for the fleeting approval of strangers. Lexi tried to get him into it, but he wouldn't bite. None of it was useful except to someone gathering information.

The list of associates was small. Durrani didn't have a big web presence. Nothing on Facebook, Twitter, or Instagram. His LinkedIn page saw infrequent updates. Other than Amanda Painter, most of the names belonged to other Afghan men. For a few years, Durrani had owned a home in the ritzy Fallston area of Harford County. It was a good choice for a home base. Close enough to Delaware to visit his girlfriend. Near enough to major cities like Baltimore, Philadelphia, and Washington to ensure a steady supply of girls for his creepy clients. A big enough house to hide certain aspects of the operation if he needed to. Further, the county sheriff was an elected position, and campaign contributions could always help in a pinch.

Tyler grabbed his keys, collected his car, and got on I-95 headed north. He lived in a pretty nice area of Baltimore, but it paled in comparison to some of the streets of Fallston. Tyler's house would have fit twice over in some of these mansions, and his yard would have made a nice place for the landscaper to store his equipment to work on the rest of the estate. Sculpted hedges and manicured lawns edged up to the pristine sidewalks. Tyler wondered if the neighborhood watch busted people for having a few leaves or blades of grass out of place. They wouldn't have much else to do.

Durrrani lived at the end of a cul-de-sac. His house was massive, like all the others on the road, with a three-car garage, brick front, and white shutters. Other than color choices, not much separated the homes stylistically. Visit the model, punch out your cookie cutter, and move in six months later. The joys of suburbia, where you were as unique as everyone else. It reminded Tyler of Talbot Lakes in Bel Air. Trading the drug kingpin he killed a few months ago for a trafficker didn't represent much of an upgrade, but this area managed to be even swankier.

Most mansions showed only an occasional light in the windows. It was early evening. One man walked a small dog, but Tyler didn't see any other activity. He tried Durrani's landline, but it rang without a machine picking up. The trip turned out to be a dead end. The clock ticked for Alex Anne, and this wasn't a productive way to use whatever time she had left. Tyler left Fallston and hurried back to Baltimore.

～

FEAR GRIPPED ALEX ANNE, and she fought for calm. The dreadful room which had been her world for the past who-knew-how-many hours was filling up. Only five spots remained unoccupied after the men lashed two wailing blonde girls to their chairs. When all the seats were taken, what then? Were they getting on a plane? Would this be one of those sick auctions she'd seen in movies before?

Alex Anne shuddered, and only some practiced deep breathing kept her gorge down. She looked around the room. The men kept it dark most of the time, and her eyes had adjusted. Every other girl shook, cried, or fought against her restraints. Fear and desperation thickened the air. Her cell-mates were all young—probably none older than seventeen. In addition to being a celebrity, Alex Anne was also the oldest captive in the room.

She figured this made her a leader, but what good would

it do? The guys who came in and out were tall, broad, and carried guns. They'd all manhandled a few girls on the way in so far. Even if all got themselves free, they wouldn't stand a chance. The guards would mow them down, clean up the blood and bodies, and collect more girls to fill the room again. She wondered if this ever happened before.

A young redhead scrutinized Alex Anne. "I know you," she whispered.

Alex Anne shook her head. "I don't think so."

"I do." Her green eyes scanned her surroundings. "Judging by the way everyone else is looking at you, I don't think I'm the only one."

"Fine." Alex Anne sighed. "I'm who you think I am."

"How the hell did they get you?" the girl asked.

"After my concert." Alex Anne thought of Donnell and Mister Tyler again. They were probably her last hope. One was dead, and the other one could've joined him by now. "They had a plan."

"Anyone looking for you?"

"I certainly hope so," Alex Anne said.

"They'd better hurry up."

To accentuate her point, one of the men stormed in the room and hollered at the girls to be quiet. "We'll gag you if we have to!" He looked foreign, probably Middle Eastern like the rest, and he spoke in an accented voice.

The other girl was right. Anyone looking for Alex Anne—or any of the missing young women—needed to work quickly.

~

TYLER DROVE through a McDonald's on the way back from Fallston. He'd eaten at many all across the world. They were consistent, and he admired the trait. A chicken sandwich here was the same overseas. Tyler took his with fries, and while he normally eschewed dessert, he washed everything down with a chocolate shake. The extra calories and energy would help if the next chance to eat didn't happen for hours.

At the hotel, Tyler parked his car and headed to Wilkinson's suite. The client wasn't alone. Two Maryland state troopers talked with him, and they eyed Tyler in the well-practiced wary way cops always made look so easy. "There he is now," Wilkinson said, and Tyler's hopes of avoiding much of a chat with the police flew out the window. The pair —a short, wide woman and a much taller man —approached.

"I'm Captain Norton," he said. He wore his blond hair short. The buzz cut suggested former military, though it was also popular in law enforcement. Less for a criminal to grab in a fight. "This is Trooper Meadows." The woman bobbed her head, and her short, dark hair didn't move. "Mister Wilkinson tells us you're on the security detail."

"I'm pretty new," Tyler told him.

"You worked with a man named Donnell Rodgers?"

"'Worked with' is a little generous. I only started a few days ago, and I don't think he was keen to have me around."

"You know what happened to him?" Meadows asked.

"I presume he's dead," Tyler said. "I think we're dealing with pros, and leaving someone like him alive is a big risk."

"You don't seem too broken up about it."

"Like I mentioned, he didn't seem too eager to work with me. Besides, crying into my cereal doesn't get me any closer to finding Alex Anne."

The two troopers exchanged a look. "We'll handle looking for her," Norton said.

"Might want to get on with it, then." Tyler tapped his watch. "She might not have long."

"Did you report what happened, sir?" Meadows said.

"The Baltimore police were already here. I hope you're not going to trip over one another."

Norton crossed his arms. "We don't need a lone wolf, Mister Tyler. Leave this to the professionals."

Tyler grunted but didn't offer any further reply. It didn't deter the captain. "You seem like the type who struggles to let things go. Find out anything already?" When Tyler remained silent, Norton frowned. "I need to know."

Decision time. Norton rose to a high rank, and he wouldn't get there without being trustworthy. Still, one mistake or easy tip-off, and the traffickers would be in the wind with all their victims. Finding Alex Anne was the chief concern, and it came before Tyler's standards, his pride, or any concerns he harbored over police tactics. "Fine." He told the pair about Durrani.

"We'll get this guy," Norton said.

"I went to his house." Tyler shrugged. "No one home."

"He'll turn up. When he does, we'll be there."

"Not if I'm there first."

"Thanks for what you've done so far," Norton said, "but we've got it from here."

Tyler showed a thin smile. "Have a good day, Captain."

When the two troopers filed out, Wilkinson asked, "You're going to stay on this?"

"I'll see it through to the end."

"Tell me something, Mister Tyler. Your C.V. was vague, and you didn't exactly clarify it in our interview. What exactly did you do in the army?"

Tyler blew out a deep breath. "I went in as a Ninety-One Bravo . . . a wheeled vehicle mechanic. Mostly, I worked on Jeeps and Hummers. I was always a good shot. My father was in the navy and taught me about guns when I was a kid. It didn't take long for the army to realize I'd be good at . . . certain special operations work."

'You were a Green Beret?"

"I was."

"Did you . . . kill many people?"

"Not enough to end the war," Tyler said. "Didn't keep count. Let's say I took care of my share."

"You think you can find my daughter?" Wilkinson said.

Despite not being a trained investigator, Tyler had tangled with men like Durrani before. They were never as infallible or invincible as they appeared at first blush. "I do."

Wilkinson's face darkened even as an overhead light gleamed in his eye. "Will you kill the men who took her?"

"Leave the bloodlust to me, Mister Wilkinson," Tyler said. "My conscience can handle it."

19

─────

Sara Morrison dreaded the alarm on her phone. She rubbed sleep from her eyes as she tapped the screen and turned off the noise. The combination of her distance from the Pentagon and a desire to get to work early meant she rose at 0430 most mornings. She'd be out the door forty-five minutes later, and if traffic didn't betray her, sitting at her desk around six. Applying some makeup in the car helped. Sara grew quite adept at it over the years.

As she heated oatmeal in the microwave, Sara unlocked her phone and checked the news feed. Something always happened overnight, and she knew better than to go in blind. The microwave beeped as she scrolled through the usual foreign policy news. A regional headline at the bottom of the page caught her eye.

LOCAL SINGER MISSING

"Shit," Sara breathed into the empty kitchen as she opened the article.

BALTIMORE, MD.—Popular singer Alexandra Wilkinson, who performs under the stage name Alex Anne, is missing after a recent concert at the Royal Farms Arena.

Her disappearance is considered suspicious according to an anonymous source. The whereabouts of Wilkinson's bodyguard is also unknown. Calls and emails to Jeff Wilkinson, her manager and father, were not returned.

Anyone with information about Alex Anne should contact the Baltimore Police Department immediately.

Despite the hour, Sara texted John Tyler. He'd been tight-lipped since joining the singer's security detail. His reticence was nothing new of course, but Sara needed to know he was all right. *Just heard about Alex Anne. You all right? Please let me know.* Sara reheated her oatmeal and ate it at the counter. Her phone vibrated a couple minutes later.

Tyler replied. *Didn't know it was in the news. Probably not a good thing. I'm fine. Trying to find her before the worst happens.*

As usual, Tyler didn't have anything else to say. He was the least talkative of any boyfriend Sara ever had. She found it refreshing sometimes and frustrating in occasions like these. Still, Tyler was who he was. She couldn't change him, and if she did, he wouldn't be the same man anymore. Rather than harp on his communication skills, she sent a short reply. *Just be careful. Do you know anything yet? I probably can't help, but let me know if you think I can.*

She didn't expect Tyler to respond, but he did. *Just a name. Durrani. Met him before.* It sounded Afghan, which provided the context for where Tyler would've encountered this mystery man. Maybe Sara could help, after all.

The unexpected story meant Sara finished her breakfast later than normal. She rushed through getting dressed, left her house at five-twenty, and drove toward the Pentagon.

Hopefully, it would be a quiet day. She wanted to do a little research, and she worked in the best place in the world for it.

TYLER'S PHONE BUZZED AGAIN. He figured it was Sara sending another text, but a different number displayed on the screen. Leon Sharpe. *Meet me for breakfast. The restaurant in your hotel, 25 minutes.* Tyler checked the time—0505. He hadn't slept long or well last night, and even lying down to get some rest made him feel like he betrayed Alex Anne. What if her kidnappers moved her in the night? What if Tyler could have found them? He'd turned these dreary scenarios over in his mind for a good twenty minutes before he finally drifted off. In the end, he knew he'd be of more use to her if he caught a few hours of shut-eye.

Twenty-five minutes gave him time to shower and get dressed. He put on black pants and a matching sweater. Outside his room, a folded copy of the *Baltimore Sun* waited. Tyler picked it up and flipped through it on the elevator. He hit the lobby at 5:29 and saw Leon Sharpe already in the restaurant. One worker milled about and scowled at the captain. "Leon. This place open yet?"

"Not for another half-hour, no. Good thing I know the manager."

Tyler inclined his head toward the disgruntled employee. "I think he's going to spit in your eggs."

"Better check yours, too," Sharpe said. "I ordered you the same thing."

"Great." Tyler pulled out a chair and sat. "I hope you also told them to get moving on the coffee."

"They know we're in a hurry."

"Speaking of which." Tyler tossed the paper onto the table and jabbed his finger at the article about Alex Anne.

"You've got a leak somewhere. Whoever blabbed to the paper might get these girls killed."

Sharpe scowled at the headline. "I know. It's why I wanted to talk to you this morning. I don't think this will affect the timeline."

"Bad guys read the paper, too, Leon."

"Someone has to." Sharpe paused as the stringy-haired server dropped off a pot of coffee, two mugs, and a dish of assorted creamers. The captain poured them each a full mug and added a pack of sugar to his own. "I wanted you to know the state cops are going to be looking into this, too. I'm fine to let you do your own thing more or less, but I don't think you'll get the same from them."

"They came by last night," Tyler said. "A captain named Norton and another trooper. They didn't seem receptive to the idea of me shooting a bunch of assholes."

"Their involvement is inevitable, but we've been looking into this, too. Whoever these guys are, they're pretty savvy. Our tech people found a Facebook post they used to try and lure girls." Sharpe shook his large head. "It was probably successful. We've seen a few teenaged girls reported missing within the past twelve hours."

Tyler paused with the mug of coffee halfway to his mouth. "Facebook? I'd think traffickers used the dark web."

Sharpe smirked. "You gonna sit there and tell me you know what the dark web is?"

"Not really," Tyler admitted. "I just figure it's even more lawless than the regular one."

"You're not wrong. They do use it, but so do we, and they know it. A lot more traffic comes across social media every day. Easier to blend in with the noise."

Tyler sipped the coffee. Acceptable. A touch weak. He'd need at least three cups but probably didn't have time. "Were your people able to figure out who made the post?"

The same waiter returned before Sharpe could answer. He set a plate of scrambled eggs, sausage, home fries, and toast in front of each of them. "Enjoy your breakfast," he muttered before walking away again.

"The profile doesn't exist anymore," Sharpe said. "They're going to try and find out who it belongs to, but no one is optimistic. People are too good at this stuff nowadays."

Tyler inspected his food for loogies before eating some eggs. "So the police leaked a story which could accelerate the timeframe, and they don't know anything more about the men responsible. Do I have it right?"

"A little uncharitable," Sharpe said.

"Just like before," Tyler said, "I'm not wrong."

Sharpe ate half a piece of toast in one massive bite before answering. "I don't know who's responsible for it. Even if it was us, I doubt it'll have any effect on things. If these guys are pros, they know the cops are going to get involved at some point. They figure they're not going to get caught."

"How long do you think we have?"

"Not long." Sharpe shook his head. "They've already nabbed someone famous. Can't stick around much. Considering the other few missing girls . . . my guess is a day. Maybe two if you're feeling optimistic."

"I almost never feel optimistic," Tyler said.

"Me, either," the captain said. "Plan on finding her today or not at all."

Tyler slipped his phone from his pocket and sent Sharpe a very short text. *Farzaad Durrani.*

"Who the hell is this?" Sharpe asked as he looked at his screen.

"A name I came across in my short investigation." Tyler held up his hand before Sharpe could say anything—probably reminding him he wasn't an investigator. "I know it from back in the day in Afghanistan. He was an opium trader then. My guess is he's moved on to girls."

"Jesus Christ."

"I've been to his house," Tyler said. "Nobody was home, and I doubt you'll catch him there."

"It's not like you to share information so willingly," Sharpe said with a studious frown.

"It's also not like me to be at ground zero for a damn trafficking operation." Tyler turned up his hands. "Here we are. All hands on deck."

The captain nodded his large head. "All hands on deck."

20

Sara stared at the blinking cursor. She sat in a SCIF—a secure compartmented information facility—where cleared folks could access, store, and discuss top secret information. The Pentagon was full of them, and she'd probably been inside most. Her presence attracted attention, though. Sara was a senior official, and people like her usually sent a junior staffer to do most of the boring keyboard work. She waited for a few rubberneckers to clear out before she got down to work.

After a few minutes, only a Marine staff sergeant remained, and he was on the other side of the room. Four rows of cubicles flanked a central aisle. At the front of the SCIF, an unoccupied breakout room held a long table, a dozen chairs, and a bunch of video teleconferencing equipment. Sara entered the name Durrani and waited for results. They populated right away. She sifted through the results. Tyler didn't give her anything else, so she needed to narrow data on her own. The most promising short summary belonged to Farzaad Durrani, identified as a former Taliban supporter who fled Afghanistan.

Sara clicked his name, and the various reports the military and intelligence community collected on Durrani downloaded. They'd amassed quite a bit. The man had been one of the principal backers of the Taliban's initial rise to power, both in terms of money and ideology. Durrani hated women, which ran counter to traditional Afghan society. His mother had been educated and probably tried to teach him better. Sara saw communications where he explicitly supported the plan to attack and burn down schools for girls. Of all the crimes the Taliban committed, their crusade against women was the most insidious.

With his favored regime installed, Durrani amassed more wealth as an opium trader. When the military began cracking down on major Taliban backers, Durrani increased his security force and continued operating with abandon. His financial support increased. Maybe he figured it would make him a marked man, and he simply didn't care. Or he thought his men and the Taliban would protect him. In reality, a bunch of Green Berets under the command of Colonel Leo Braxton destroyed Durrani's compound, killed his men, freed his servants, and burned his drugs. The man himself managed to escape.

While the military lost track of him, various intelligence agencies kept him on their radar. Durrani fled to Turkey where some of his family lived. A flag went up about six months after his arrival, questioning his finances and wondering if he trafficked in persons. Later, the man came to the US, set himself up as a consultant in imports and exports, and managed to avoid the serious scrutiny of law enforcement.

While much of Durrani's history remained classified, enough was freely available to allow a resourceful man like Tyler to pull much of it together. Sara went after known associates. Someone like Durrani would want ideological fealty. Many of the people in his network—alive or dead—also hailed from Afghanistan. A few came from Turkey. The outlier was Josef Mitrovic, a former Serbian soldier turned mercenary. His history suggested a malleable philosophy based on who wrote the checks.

Sara copied and pasted a bunch of information into a blank document. She didn't want to take the risk of printing and delivering it to Tyler. A routine search when leaving work could turn it up, and even if all the data were unclassified, she'd have to answer some questions. She'd settle for writing notes and committing them to memory. Sara looked up. The SCIF's other occupant finished his work. "Sergeant . . . can I have your opinion on something?"

The man walked closer. He looked to be in his mid-thirties, and his lean, angular face begged to ask a question. Instead, he offered a dutiful nod and a simple, "Ma'am."

"Have you been deployed?"

"Yes, ma'am. Afghanistan and Iraq, one time each."

"Good." She gestured to the screen. "I need to put together an unclassified report. Obviously, I never spent the kind of time over there you did. Could you review what I have here?"

"I can't imagine I know more than you, ma'am," he said, "but I'd be glad to."

He spent a couple minutes scanning everything, opening a couple other reports, and checking Sara's Word document. When he finished, he said, "Looks good to me, ma'am. I don't see any classified or sensitive data."

"Thank you, Sergeant." He gave her a quick smile and nod before he turned on his heel and left. Sara read over her list a few times, carried the paper to a shredder, and dropped it in. She'd remember, and she'd tell Tyler what she could. Sara walked back to her temporary desk, signed out, and locked the SCIF on her way out.

ALL DURRANI'S plans were coming together. The room of girls neared capacity. They'd secured their high-value target. He'd gotten wind the police were investigating, but they wouldn't find anything. Even if his name somehow got out, none of it could be linked to him, and they'd find a nice but unoccupied house in Fallston for their troubles.

John Tyler remained his only lingering concern.

The man had a habit for showing up, smashing things, and leaving again. He'd seen it firsthand in Afghanistan. Durrani's drug network should have been off the Americans' radar. A unit rolled in, however, shot a bunch of his foot soldiers, confiscated his money, and burned all his product. Durrani managed to slip away before the shooting started, but the occupation forces cost him millions of dollars plus a few men.

Now, he could have some measure of payback. He called his nephew Ahmed, who picked up in a sleepy voice. "Wake up. You have work to do today." Ahmed mumbled something incoherent. "Sleep on your own time. You didn't bring me Tyler's daughter last night."

"I know, Uncle. I didn't have a chance."

"Will it be done today?"

"Yes," Ahmed said. "I'll see her later."

"So she likes you?" Durrani asked. "Ah, Ahmed. I remember when the thought of talking to a girl would paralyze you."

"Lexi's easy to talk to."

Durrani frowned. Was Ahmed getting attached already? "Remember the work, my naïve nephew. She is a means to an end. If you want a girlfriend, find one in another class. I'm sure they're all full of American whores."

"I remember," Ahmed said with a sigh.

"Good. I don't care what you do. Have sex with her if you want. She'll probably try to get you in bed, anyway. Just bring her here by tonight."

"What if she doesn't want to come along?"

"Kill her," Durrani said, a little annoyed he needed to answer the question. Didn't he already tell Ahmed this? "Make sure you get pictures, too. Whether you screw her or kill her, I want photos. They'll keep her father out of our operation."

"You sound very afraid of him," Ahmed said.

Durrani ended the call. Ahmed knew his role, and he was reliable. John Tyler's precious daughter was no different than any other American girl. Durrani would have pictures in hand to prove it later. Then, he could finally be rid of Tyler once and for all.

21

Lexi's phone buzzed with a text toward the end of her last morning class. Once dismissed and outside the room, she checked her phone. Ahmed wanted to know where to meet her. Lexi replied and suggested they meet inside the student union building. She already headed in that direction, and she opened the main door two minutes after sending the text. Despite telling herself she wasn't anxious, she paced the floor until Ahmed approached a short while later. He smiled when he saw her. "Ready?"

"Sure. Where are we off to?"

"How about a matinee?" he said. "The movie theater a few minutes away has a good rate for students."

"We'll need lunch later," Lexi said. "I'm hungry."

"Me, too." Ahmed gave her a thumbs-up. He wiped his hand on the pocket of his jeans. As they walked, he kept a white-knuckle grip on the straps of his bookbag.

"You all right? You seem a little nervous."

"Oh." Ahmed took his hands off the straps. "First date jitters, I guess."

She grinned and grabbed his hand. "It's all good." Hopefully, he wouldn't feel hers trembling. They walked to a nearby parking lot and got into Ahmed's car, a Toyota Corolla. Lexi resisted frowning when she saw the automatic gear selector. They drove off campus and a couple miles down Route One. Ahmed didn't speed much even with light traffic. It felt like an excruciating pace. Lexi's grandfather drove faster. If they went on any more dates, she resolved to be the driver.

The theater looked like it began its life as a different business. The building was long and squat. The place showed second-run movies on their four screens. Lexi and Ahmed picked their film. He bought the tickets, though she insisted on paying for the popcorn and drinks. The squat nature of the building revealed itself in the lack of stadium seating. They snagged a couple of seats near the front. Lexi tried the popcorn. It was mediocre even by movie theater standards, but hunger compelled her to keep eating.

Before the opening credits ended, Ahmed slipped his arm around her. He didn't even do the ridiculous and obvious stretch first. Maybe he recovered from his earlier bout of nerves. Halfway through the runtime, Lexi nestled into him, and he gave her shoulder a squeeze. When the movie ended, they walked out hand-in-hand.

College Park featured many diners, fast casual, and other inexpensive restaurants to lure in students on budgets. Ahmed selected The Hungry Terp, and they grabbed a table inside. Like most diners, the menu was a dozen pages long. Lexi felt hungry again, so she opted for a burger and fries. Ahmed got the same. The place wasn't crowded, so their food came out quickly. About a half-hour later, Ahmed paid the bill, and they walked back outside into the cool early afternoon air.

"You have more classes today?" Ahmed asked as they got back into his car.

Lexi nodded. "One more. It starts in about an hour."

Ahmed flashed a nervous grin. "I live close to here. Want to wait it out at my place?"

"Smooth," Lexi said, though she couldn't resist a smile. "I'll be on campus again tonight . . . working on a project in the mainframe lab."

"Mainframe?" Ahmed frowned. "Seriously?"

"I had the same reaction." Lexi shrugged. "It's useful when you're still learning programming, though."

"Maybe I could see you afterward?"

Lexi leaned across the console, put fingertips on Ahmed's face, and kissed him. When he went for another, she didn't object, but she pulled back after the second. They would have time for more kisses later. "You know where it is, right?"

He squeezed her hand. "I do. I'll see you tonight."

RICH FERGUSON STARED at his screen and wanted something to change.

Four girls reported missing. All of them between fifteen and eighteen. This represented a huge outlier. Baltimore earned its reputation for shootings, stabbings, and murder, but missing persons of this age group were rare. Rich knew the odds of finding them alive diminished by the hour. In his experience, a teenager disappearing rarely ended well. They turned up dead far more often than not.

This was why Captain Sharpe wanted the homicide team on it. Rich served as a lieutenant for the city's best investigators. He'd seen more than his share of corpses in his tenure as a cop, and he glimpsed a few more before in his ten years in the army. Thinking of his service time pulled John Tyler to mind. Rich frowned and shook his head. The man probably meant well, but in his limited dealings with Tyler, Rich thought he was a man who couldn't let things go. He'd say he didn't want trouble, but people ended up dead around him in alarming numbers.

Rich looked at the name Sharpe gave him. Farzaad Durrani. He'd already uncovered the basics. Fifty-five years old. Originally from Kandahar, Afghanistan. Fingered by the US intelligence community as an ardent supporter—in terms of both money and ideology—of the Taliban. Some information remained classified, but the freely available data showed Durrani fled his home country almost a decade ago and landed in America a few months later. He'd raised no red flags since. The man listed himself as a business consultant, paid his taxes, and owned a nice house.

Nothing untoward jumped out at Rich. He recalled working with his cousin C.T. to bust up a trafficking ring a few years ago. They were Chinese, but the hours of training Rich endured in this area taught him tactics didn't differ much around the world. He dug deeper into Durrani's life. The Baltimore Police Department identified few known associates. Most were other men from Afghanistan. None were criminals. If Durrani were the mastermind Sharpe suspected, he'd been clever and careful.

A credit card receipt from two days ago showed Durrani bought food in Baltimore. Later the same night, pop singer Alex Anne went missing, and her bodyguard vanished along with her. The poor man was probably dead. Rich wondered how many more girls vanished afterward. The BPD took four official reports. There were bound to be some unreported. He checked additional jurisdictions in Maryland and identified three more.

Rich considered correlating times Durrani established a known presence in Maryland with coincidental disappearances. He could even expand it to search surounding states, though he'd need help. A warrant would be the first step, and he directed Sergeant Paul King to apply for one. For a national check, he'd need to bring in the FBI, a line Sharpe didn't want to cross. Rich knew someone at the Bureau and thought him trustworthy, but he didn't like the idea of defying the captain.

His desk phone rang, and Rich picked it up. "I suppose congratulations are in order," the man on the opposite end said. Rich recognized the voice—Casey Norton, also a captain but with the Maryland State Police.

"You might want to wait a couple days." Rich leaned back in his moderately comfortable chair. "What can I do for you?"

"I hear you're involved in the Alex Anne investigation."

"She did disappear from the city," Rich said.

"I'm on it, too. Even got a name."

"Durrani," Rich said. "We're looking into him. I want to try and see if he's involved in anything going back a while."

"Who put you onto him?" Norton asked.

"Captain Sharpe."

Norton grunted. "Every time I hear his name, I'm surprised he hasn't been put out to pasture yet."

"He gets results," Rich said, and he heard the defensiveness in his own tone.

"Sure. And the hell with how it actually happens. Kicking in doors and beating people up doesn't work anymore. Be careful hitching your wagon to his horse. He might steer you straight off a cliff, and I won't be able to offer you a job if he does."

Rich already turned Norton down once about a year ago. "If you want to work together," he said, "I'm all for it. I've seen cases of girls disappearing from other jurisdictions. Having the staties involved would help."

"See you soon," Norton said and hung up.

Rich glanced at the clock mounted on the wall above his old metal filing cabinet. He figured Alex Anne and the remaining girls would be gone by this time tomorrow, and probably even sooner. "Drive fast," he said to the empty line before replacing the handset.

NOT KNOWING how long she'd been held captive rankled Alex Anne. It had been at least a few hours at the bare minimum. She figured more like a day. By now, plenty of people would know she was missing. The same would be true for many of the fifteen other girls in chairs around her. Whoever abducted them all would be dodging the police. Alex Anne's many fans would be wondering why she hadn't posted any updates. No pictures. No videos. The last time she took twelve hours off from social media, she returned to a near revolution. Would the TikTok army be able to get anything done?

The heavy lock drew back, and the door swung open again. This time, Alex Anne saw the faint vestiges of light. It must have been daytime. The last few times the men brought in more prisoners, it remained dark beyond their room. The big blond guy and a shorter swarthy man shoved a weeping young woman into the room. She kept crying after they lashed her to the chair, so the blond gagged her. "What's going on?" Alex Anne said, and all eyes in the room shot to her.

"Quiet," the tall man said.

"We should know." A few nods went up around the room, but Alex Anne was the only one to find her voice. She figured she was the oldest. Leadership—or whatever passed for it in a situation like this—fell to her. Her heart raced in her chest as both men glowered at her.

"You don't need to know anything." The light-haired

man's accent sounded different from the rest. Probably Eastern European. "Sit there and be quiet."

Despite her pulse thundering in her ears, Alex Anne persisted. "What's going to happen when all these chairs are full?"

Both men moved closer to her. The shorter one leaned down. His breath smelled rotten, but Alex Anne fought the urge to wrinkle her nose. She wouldn't give him the satisfaction. "You'll be moved soon. Then, we go to the airport, and we leave this country." He stood and looked around the room. "Forever for you. I hope you said goodbye to the people who love you. You'll never see any of them again." He glanced at his watch as a panicked murmur rose in the room. "Won't be long now. Everything will be in progress by tonight."

The two men left. The rest of the girls talked among themselves—a few yelling and sobbing about what future awaited them. Alex Anne clung to the hope that Mister Tyler would find her and save her, but it grew harder to hang onto with each passing hour.

Especially because they didn't have many left.

22

For maybe the first time in his life, Tyler wished he were a trained investigator. He'd given Durrani's name to both the state and Baltimore police, so even if he kept hitting his head against a brick wall, they might make some progress. Tyler wanted to be out there looking for her, but he didn't know where to start. The knife-wielding guy didn't tell him anything. Donnell got shot without seeing much. Durrani represented his only real lead.

The man and his cronies tortured and murdered Alex Anne's mother—a fact neither the girl nor her father knew yet. They would need to, but Tyler wanted to concentrate on finding Durrani. He remembered Wilkinson saying his ex-wife had always been wealthy. Durrani may have been running a long con—get close to Amanda Painter to learn all he can about her famous daughter. Then, when he'd gotten what he needed, she became a loose end.

A loose end with a lot of money.

Durrani owned a nice house and car, but Tyler could never pin down the source of his money beyond some nebulous consulting work he claimed to do. His real fortune fell apart when he fled Afghanistan. Maybe he used Amanda for more than simply intel about her daughter. Tyler's old Patriot laptop zeroed in on the late Ms. Painter's bank accounts and credit cards with alarming ease. Her American Express showed a recent transaction for a large truck rental. She'd been dead at the time, so Durrani was using her wealth post-mortem to keep his operation going.

Tyler walked to Wilkinson's suite. "I have bad news and potential good news," he said when the client looked at him hopefully.

"I don't know how much more bad news I can handle." Wilkinson rubbed his forehead. "All right. Lay it on me."

"Alex Anne's mother is dead. Murdered, in fact, and I think the guy who's responsible for the kidnappings did it."

"My god." Wilkinson closed his eyes, and Tyler thought the man mouthed a silent prayer. "Did she suffer?"

"I'm afraid so," Tyler said. He hoped Wilkinson wouldn't push him for the details. "I know you weren't close, but she's your daughter's mother. I'm sorry."

"Poor Amanda. We'd been estranged for years, but I never …" He trailed off, shaking his head.

Tyler continued. "The one bit of potential good news is the man who killed her is using her credit card."

"You can track it?"

"With my laptop, yes," he said. "Durrani recently rented a large truck. It could be to move a lot of things, but my suspicion is he's going to fill it with all the girls he's kidnapped."

"Do you know where?" Wilkinson asked.

"There's an address on the rental. Seems legit. I'm going to check it out."

"Bring my daughter back, Mister Tyler."

As he left the suite, Tyler hoped he could live up to the client's instructions.

~

Casey Norton walked into Rich's office about forty minutes after their phone call ended. He wore his tan state trooper uniform, only his shoulder bars and hat identifying him as a captain. "You ditching the suit?" Rich asked as the tall man dropped onto a guest chair.

"I'm a man of the people," Norton said.

Rich snorted. "Like hell."

"I wear the uniform a couple days a week." Norton shrugged. "I think it's good for morale when troopers see their bosses dressed like they are."

The captain's words hung in the air, and Rich wondered if it was a gentle barb. He wore a suit, and he'd done so ever since he broke into the plainclothes ranks from being a uniformed sergeant. "A few minutes before you arrived, I got approval to go through Durrani's past purchases and history." Rich turned his monitor so Norton could see it. "So far, I've correlated several of his transactions to the disappearances of girls under eighteen in the last two years."

Norton's blue eyes scanned the documents. "Impressive." He paused, and Rich had a feeling a hammer would drop. "Can I play devil's advocate for a minute?"

"Considering what this guy is involved in," Rich said, "it's an accurate title."

Norton spread his hands. "Still . . . we need to make sure everything is lined up before arresting someone. Durrani lives in Maryland, right?"

Rich bobbed his head. "Fallston."

"And all these young ladies disappeared from somewhere in the state?" Rich nodded again. "All right. What's unusual about a Maryland resident buying things in his home state?"

"Nothing." Rich frowned. "Look, this asshole moves around. He's got plenty of hotel stays outside our borders. I'm willing to bet there would be a similar number of girls missing from those places during the times he was there."

"Maybe." Norton steepled his fingers. "I believe you. You're good at what you do, and I think you're on to something, especially if we can correlate his visits elsewhere to disappearances. The problem is I think a lot of this could be chalked up as coincidence. I know it's not something we really believe in, but answer a question for me. How many young females are reported missing in those states on a normal day?"

"I don't know," Rich admitted.

"Durrani's lawyer will. If you want to make your case, you're going to need to show things went well above the baseline while this prick was in town. Even then, you might be in for a long day."

Rich stared at his screen. He could get the numbers for Maryland easily, and the other states' info would be in the FBI's databases. Not too hard to find. Again, Rich contemplated reaching out to a colleague in the FBI who worked out of the Baltimore field office. Sharpe wanted him to hold off. The ticking clock dictated a different course of action.

SOMETIME LATER, the men brought food. Two of them carried bags, and the older guy Alex Anne figured was the boss supervised everything. He walked the length of the room, stopping at each row to scrutinize the girls. His expression never changed much. One of the lackeys untied Alex Anne's wrists and dropped two granola bars and a bottle of water in her lap. Her ankles remained bound to the chair. She shook out her arms, glad to be able to move them again. The rest of her body felt stiff.

"This is it?" one of the prisoners said. Alex Anne didn't

know her name. She'd arrived recently. Her green eyes flashed with defiance as she looked at the paltry food and drink.

"Eat it," the man said. "Keep your strength up. Stop complaining."

"Who are you people?" She struggled against the ropes holding her ankles in place. "Why are we all here? This is bullshit! You can't treat us like this."

The large guard backhanded her across the face. The girl's head snapped to the side, and she toppled over in her chair, which fell with her as her ankles were still bound to it. She glowered up at the man who struck her. Alex Anne thought she was either very brave or very foolish.

"Enough," the older man said as he approached. He bent a little to address the fallen captive. "Quiet, girl. I can have someone else in your chair quickly." He reached out and touched her face, forcing her to jerk her head away. "Someone prettier than you."

"Screw you, you old creep," she said. Another girl shushed her, but she started to say something else before the big guy picked her up, chair and all. "Put me down!"

"Make an example," the boss instructed his hired hand. "You and Pazir take her into the hall and have your way with her."

Both men smiled like wolves as they cut the shrieking girl's remaining bonds and carried her out of the room. The door slammed shut, but her petrified voice still carried. Alex Anne watched, waiting for it to open again. Maybe this was just a show of power. They wouldn't really go through with something so horrible.

When the poor soul kept screaming, Alex Anne realized she was wrong.

They would go through with it. Sounds of the men striking the young woman—and soon doing far worse to her

—carried into the room. Her wails didn't stop for at least thirty minutes. Alex Anne shook in her chair. She couldn't even think about eating her meager snack. The rest of the captives watched the door with wide eyes. The older man paced the room, a satisfied smile on his face.

The screams in the hallway ended when a gunshot rang out. Several girls in the room yelled in fear. Alex Anne stayed quiet only because she couldn't find her voice. One of the guards walked back in, tucking his shirt back into his jeans as he did. "Now, there are two empty chairs I need to fill," the older man said. "Let this be a lesson to all of you. Every single one of you is replaceable. If you want to end up like her, it's your choice." He nodded at the larger guy, who took up a post in the center of the room. "Eat your food and drink your water."

Alex Anne twisted the cap off the bottle. Her trembling hands caused a little liquid to spill. They were all replaceable. She wondered if this extended to her. She didn't recognize any of the others, though most knew who she was. Someone specifically wanted her. Was she expendable, too? Alex Anne decided not to find out as she sipped her water and sobbed.

Tyler eased the 442 into the parking lot. The address used to rent the truck resolved to a derelict industrial park in Jessup. It sat a few minutes—and several tax brackets—from nearby Columbia. A glorified strip mall stared back at him, nary a business sign to be found amid its light siding and dark windows. None of the places looked to be in use, though a couple of cars dotted the blacktop. The unit Tyler wanted lay at the far end. He left his car a few doors down and got out. Despite the need for urgency, Tyler retrieved a bullet-resistant vest and snap gun from the trunk. He slipped the Kevlar on over his T-shirt and put the lock breaker in his pocket.

There was no activity along the front of the row. Tyler padded around back, surveying the scene from behind an overgrown hedge which waited for spring to bloom. All quiet. He crept closer, but it soon became obvious no one laid in wait back here, either. At the front door, Tyler noticed a camera mounted high. He wondered if anyone still watched. The snap gun got him past the lock in a few seconds. He let himself in, closing the door quietly as he moved on.

The lights were off. Tyler flipped the switch, and they came on. A good sign. He stood in a small lobby. It was devoid of furniture, though the impressions of a desk and a few chairs remained in the thin carpet. Double doors led to the rest of the facility. Tyler walked through. He tried the light switch, but nothing happened. The old fluorescents he saw overhead were missing their bulbs. Some illumination came in through two windows on the left side, but the room remained no brighter than twilight.

Looking around the area, Tyler didn't see any way to keep a bunch of girls here. High ceilings helped make the room look large, but it was probably two hundred feet long and at least fifty wide. Metal shelves, all but a couple empty, covered the floor in neat rows. Three desks around the center of the room broke up the storage monotony. Tyler checked a large cardboard box remaining on one of the shelves. It held only cobwebs. The lone door in or out was the one he'd already come through.

This must have been a dead end. Durrani couldn't have rented this facility for any practical reason. It was certainly big enough to keep a crowd of captives, and the fact no one seemed to use any of the adjacent places helped. The configuration was all wrong, however. Did Durrani list this place and then not decide to use it? Maybe he did it to throw law enforcement off his trail if they made the Amanda Painter connection.

Tyler neared the desks when he heard footsteps behind him.

A burly American man strode in. His eyes narrowed on Tyler, and he raised his pistol. Tyler felt exposed and dashed for whatever cover a metal rack offered. It turned out to be good enough when a bullet dinged off it. He drew his M11, crouched, and leaned out. Two rounds thundered into the shooter's chest. He stumbled back a step, dropped his gun, and collapsed. Another pair of men—both Middle Eastern—scampered in and took up positions behind the racks. "Looking for anybody?" one of them yelled.

"Stick your head out, and I'll show you," Tyler said. They took cover at the end of adjacent rows. Probably eighty feet away. Tyler could plug them easily if they moved into the open, but too much steel screened his potential shots. Unlike the first idiot, these two seemed smart enough to get in good positions first. A loud metallic crash drew Tyler's attention. It came from the far end where the two recent arrivals stood. Another followed. Then a third.

They'd pushed the racks over, and they were all collapsing domino-style toward Tyler.

He couldn't run back toward the entrance because two gunmen blocked his way. The desks near the center of the room would have to be good enough. Tyler stepped out, unleashed a burst of suppression fire, and ran for the desks as fast as he could. His ears hurt from the barrage of banging steel gaining on him.

Gunshots joined the noise, and a couple bullets whizzed past Tyler. Tyler went into a slide and skidded into the footwell of the nearest desk as racks crashed down around him. He winced at the metallic cacophony. The table shook but held. A frame lay against it at a thirty-degree angle. It trapped Tyler where he was. A moment later, the crashing of another row stopped. Tyler couldn't see much past the wreckage. He didn't want to give away his location by yelling. If they wanted to find him, they could walk closer. He still held the M11. He'd be ready.

No one approached. Tyler waited a few minutes and set his gun down. He lay on his back and tried to push the frame upright, but too much weighed it down. Instead, he nudged the desk askew and slithered out from under it. Tyler wiped the sweat from his brow on his sleeve, picked up his M11, and stood. The two men who came in after the first one were gone. They'd left the corpse. Searching its pockets produced nothing.

The pair of assholes who tried to crush him couldn't have a big head start. Tyler pushed the door open, cleared the front area, and then ran to his car. He slowed on approach. The two rear tires were deflated. He looked at the one on the driver's side and saw a large slash where a blade gouged and pierced the rubber. He only carried a single spare, and replacing even one of his flats would take time he didn't want to spend. "Shit," he muttered. This marked the first time the dark green muscle car wouldn't be drivable since he'd restored it. Lexi would be on campus. Wilkinson might be conferring with the feds by now.

For the first time in his life, Tyler summoned an Uber.

HE'D WALKED a block farther along the road when ordering the car in case the two shooters tried to jam him up by calling the cops. No flashing lights approached. A dark gray SUV pulled up to the curb a couple minutes later. Tyler climbed in the back. His driver was a slender guy, probably in his twenties, who wore a Towson University hoodie and a sideways baseball cap. "If you don't mind, I'm kind of in a hurry," Tyler said as the vehicle took off. "I'll tip well if you floor it."

The driver grinned in the rearview. "You got it, mister." He stepped on the gas and pushed the SUV around a curve. The ride back to Tyler's house should have taken a half-hour. They made it in twenty-two minutes. Tyler left a twenty-dollar tip, thanked the driver, and got out of the SUV. He grabbed some supplies, unlocked the white Tesla Model X, backed it out of the driveway, and drove to the Lord Baltimore Hotel.

In his room, Wilkinson stared at his phone as if willing it to ring. He looked up when Tyler closed the door. "You're alone," he said with a frown.

"I am. I think this was a dead end. There was no truck."

"So it was a phony address?"

"No," Tyler said, "the place was real. It definitely wasn't set up for holding a bunch of kidnapped girls, though. My guess is Durrani used it in case anyone figured out who he was. He might've had a guy watching the place."

"You don't think Alexandra was ever there?" Wilkinson asked.

"I don't think anyone's used the location as anything but a decoy in years."

Wilkinson sagged in his chair. "We're running out of time, Mister Tyler."

"I know."

"How much do you think we have?"

Not much, Tyler thought. Durrani was still in Maryland. There would be no point setting an ambush if he'd already left. He could be ready to leave any minute, however, and Tyler had no further clues as to his whereabouts. "I don't know," he said. "I'm not giving up. With the police looking, too, I think we'll get her back."

"You *think*," Wilkinson said.

"This is a bit outside my expertise," Tyler admitted. "I would say I'd drop it if you wanted me to, but I won't. I'm going to keep looking for your daughter, even if it means I have to get on a plane and chase these assholes down overseas."

"I hope you find her before those measures become necessary."

"Me, too." Tyler wished he could inject his words with confidence, but he couldn't.

~

AHMED RUBBED the bridge of his nose. His uncle shouted at him through the phone. "What do you mean you don't have her?"

"Just what I told you." He set his mobile on the table and popped in a pair of earbuds.

"Why the hell not?"

"We went out," Ahmed said. "I think things were going well." He thought about the kiss but didn't tell his uncle. Confessing how he lost his nerve and needed Lexi to cover for him would only make things worse. "Before I could try to grab her, she needed to leave."

"I gave you one job, Ahmed," his uncle said. "One. You told me you could do it, and I believed you. I need her so I can deal with John Tyler."

"Can't you just send someone to take him out?" Ahmed asked. "If you're so scared of him, you have guys who work for you. What about the blond creep?"

"Don't tell me how to run my business. I have a couple men who told me someone fitting Tyler's description fell for a trap I set. I won't think he's dead until I see his body with my own eyes. Still, if he made it out, this would certainly set him back."

"Why not have them kill him?"

"I can't devote manpower to it right now," Uncle Farzaad said. "When you finish college and run a business, you learn things like resource management. We'll be moving soon, and I need as many men as I can to deal with it. It'd be nice to have you here, too, nephew. Will you see the girl again?"

Ahmed knew he would. Lexi told him she'd be on campus later—in the mainframe lab of all places. He knew where it was. Not many people went there. It would be way less crowded than most buildings on school grounds. The image of Lexi reaching out, grabbing his face, and kissing him flooded his brain again. He touched his lips, remembering how hers felt. He wanted to feel them again. "I can try," he said.

"Make sure you do. You seem a little ambivalent, so I'll make it easy for you. Bring me the girl alive, and I'll pay you twenty grand. Do what you want with her first. I'm not expecting her to be pure."

The money would be a great help to Ahmed's education. He liked Lexi, but he needed to be practical about the situation. Literally thousands of women walked around the Maryland campus every day. There would always be another pretty girl. Still, Ahmed wasn't sure he could do this by himself. He didn't want to falter and let his uncle down. Bringing a friend—and sharing a little of the money—would make things easier. "I'll get someone to help me. Don't worry, I know him. He's trustworthy, and he likes money. We'll bring her to you tonight."

"Can I count on you?" Uncle Farzaad asked.

"Yes," Ahmed said. "We'll get it done."

24

———

Back in his own room, Tyler stared at the laptop screen, wishing he were better at the technology end of things. His phone buzzed on the bed, and he looked at the screen. Smitty called. Tyler ignored it. His fingers hovered over the keys. The address for the rental truck led to nothing, but Durrani and his crew would need some means of moving the girls. A large transport vehicle would be ideal. Load them up and get them to the airport. Smitty phoned again. Tyler rolled his eyes and answered. "Not really a good time."

"I ain't having a lot of fun here, either. You want an update or not?"

Tyler rubbed his temples. "Sure. Hit me."

"All right," Smitty said. "The inspector's still delayed. Something about the contract. When I asked, he told me he'd only talk to you. You want to call him?"

"I might not get to it today," Tyler said.

"Why? What's going on?"

"The easy job I took has gone pear-shaped in a big way. I don't want to get into all of it now. Consider me out for the rest of the day. I'll try to get back on top of things tomorrow if I can. Until then, can you handle whatever comes up?"

"I guess." Smitty sighed. "Why do you always wind up involved in some bad shit?"

"Wish I knew," Tyler said. "If I get a chance to deal with the inspector later, I will." Tyler imagined cracking the man's kneecaps with a wrench would be effective, but he also understood this was his frustration boiling over. He'd talk to the guy and see where the problem lay. Few obstacles remained to opening the shop, but passing an inspection was the first domino which needed to fall. "Thanks, Smitty." Tyler ended the conversation and dialed Sara Morrison.

"This is Sara," she said, and Tyler started to say something before he realized he'd gotten her voicemail. When the greeting ended with a beep, he left a message.

"Hey, it's Tyler. Smitty's running into some issues at the shop. The job I'm on has . . . proven a lot more interesting than I thought. I'll text you Smitty's number. If you can help with a little management or oversight advice, he could probably use it. I could, too. Thanks." He hung up. A few months ago, Tyler asked Sara to assist in dealing with a drug cartel which infiltrated Maryland and murdered a young woman. He didn't want to go back to the well, and despite her many contacts, Sara might not have an expert on Afghan traffickers in her Rolodex.

Tyler returned his attention to the computer. A few minutes later, she called back. "I'm going to send you a text," she said when he picked up. "I did a little research into the name you mentioned. Found some others to go with it."

"Can you email it instead? It's easier for me to pull up on the laptop."

"Sure."

"Thanks. Everything helps at this point."

"Including with the shop?" Sara asked, an amused note in her tone.

"I can't do much there right now." Tyler said. "Smitty might need a hand. I feel bad asking him to basically get things off the ground for me. It's not what he signed up for."

"I'll see what I can do. Go get that girl back."

"I'm working on it. Thanks." Tyler broke the connection. An email popped up in his inbox after a couple minutes. Sara was a great and reliable person, and he probably didn't appreciate her enough. After this was all over, Tyler would work on it.

In the meantime, he intended to rescue Alex Anne like Sara told him.

LEXI ARRIVED home for a snack and a respite before heading back to campus. She immediately saw the Tesla was gone from the driveway. Odd. Her dad would've taken his Olds. He didn't even like driving the electric SUV very much. She parked her Accord and walked inside. As she set her bag down, Lexi texted her dad. *What's up with the Tesla? Do you have it?*

She made a turkey sandwich and carried it upstairs to get some work done. Coffee shops were great, but home was hard to beat for a distraction-free space. If her dad were home, he'd leave her alone. Her phone vibrated with his reply when she sat down. *I have it. The job is off the rails. Will explain later. Love you.*

"What the hell, Dad?" she whispered to the empty room. She knew responding would be pointless. He wasn't much of a talker over any medium, but one requiring the thumbs caused him to be even briefer and more reticent than normal. Lexi took a monster bite of her sandwich while she fired up her computer and checked her grades. All A's except for a B in political science. She rolled her eyes and accepted it. Her GPA would be more than good enough to keep her partial scholarship.

She navigated to her computer class and opened the assignment she'd be working on tonight. Ahmed was right—the idea of using a mainframe anymore seemed really archaic at first. Lexi learned the value they brought, though. Mainframes were great for redundancy, availability, and processing transactions. They were also easy to program for and see results, which was the point of going to the lab tonight. The only access came from terminals onsite.

Lexi devoured the rest of her sandwich and wandered downstairs for chips. Rather than putting some on a plate, she carried the bag back to her room. When she sat, she noticed her phone showed a new text. It was from Ahmed and consisted of a large kissing emoji. Lexi smiled. She got the feeling the young man was nervous. He clearly wanted to lock lips with her but held back. She'd never been especially shy, so she made the move for him. After she finished with her work in the lab later tonight, she hoped Ahmed could muster the courage to make moves on his own. Lexi had no plans to do more than kiss him so soon, but she needed to know he carried some self-confidence.

She sent him the same emoji in reply, put her phone down, and realized she was blushing again.

FINDING THE TRUCK—IF Durrani even rented the specific one Tyler knew about—would be a challenge. He wanted to learn more about the man's organization. Sara provided some data, but he didn't know how current it was. While living in the US, Durrani enjoyed protection from certain forms of intelligence gathering. So far, Tyler stabbed one guy in an abandoned house, shot an American at the industrial park, and saw two more Afghan men with guns there. Durrani would be likely to work with people he knew and trusted, which meant men from his homeland—like the ones Sara found. The American was probably short-term muscle who didn't know a lot.

Barberis mentioned an older guy plus two others who spoke Pashto and waved money around. Tyler would bet the senior member of the trio was Durrani. He wanted to see if the other pair aligned with his new information, however, so he called Barberis. "I was hoping I wouldn't hear from you again," the man said when he came on the line. "No offense."

"None taken. You told me an older guy plus two others visited you about the Alex Anne concert. Can you describe the other duo?"

"They were big. Probably six-three or six-four, and they looked like they spent a lot of time in the gym."

"Afghan?" Tyler asked.

"Definitely," Barberis confirmed.

"Any distinguishing features or details you remember?"

"What's going on here, Tyler? Is Alex Anne still missing?"

"Yes."

"You call the cops?" Barberis asked.

"They're involved," Tyler said. "I feel like this happened on my watch, so I'm not dropping it. I've dealt with money men from Afghanistan before. Don't mind cleaning up another mess."

"All right." He paused, and Tyler heard his rapid breaths hiss in the connection. "One of them had a scar on his face. Under his left eye, I think. They were both ugly. Probably not helpful, but it's true."

"Handsomeness isn't a variable I can search on."

"I don't really remember much else," Barberis said. "The

other guy didn't stand out to me. I was concerned about my sister when they showed me her picture."

"She all right?" Tyler asked.

"Yeah . . . thanks for checking."

"OK. I'll try to run with this." Tyler hung up. He remembered the story of the BMW with the stolen tag. Lexi found the man's name at some point. Tyler scoured his memory and eventually came up with it. Wallace Duncan. He used the laptop to uncover the man's home number and called him.

"I spoke to the police shortly after it happened," the man said in a mousy voice once Tyler told him the reason for his call.

"It's a multi-departmental investigation now," Tyler said. "We think the men who visited you are involved in a lot worse than stealing license plates. What can you tell me about the guys you saw?"

"They were big. I drive a Civic. They probably could have picked it up and carried it away."

"Any other details?"

"I didn't go outside to confront them," Duncan said. "Watching from my window was scary enough."

"You did the right thing," Tyler told him.

"I did get a good look at one of them. I don't think he saw me. He had a scar around his left eye."

Sloppy on Durrani's part to use the same guy for two jobs when his distinguishing feature could be pointed out. "All right. Thanks, Mister Duncan." Tyler broke the connection. Sara's intel mentioned an associate of Durrani's with the scar both Barberis and Duncan mentioned. He could treat his data as reliable. Would it be enough, though? He couldn't count on it. Based on everything he learned, Tyler entered some parameters to set a wide search relating to Durrani, hoped he did it right, and pressed enter.

25

Tyler knew the results would take a while. The laptop was fast and capable, but its wide searches took in a lot of data sources. Tech guys at Patriot called it "scraping," a term Tyler heard Lexi repeat. Every day, computers co-opted some word for their own use. Tyler clenched and unclenched his hands as he waited. He stood up and paced the hotel room behind the desk. Thoughts of dealing with men like Durrani back in Afghanistan played in his mind.

Tyler rummaged through the laptop bag, soon finding a notebook and a pencil. He needed to paint, but the tools he had on hand would have to suffice. Tyler picked up the pencil, sat so he could keep the door in sight, and got to work. He tuned out the background noise of the laptop's hard drive as he lost himself in his art. A cave dominated the left side of the paper, its jagged mouth opening toward the center. Boxes and cases lay strewn about inside.

In front of the opening, three men lay dead. The pencil didn't allow for a lot of detail, but Tyler drew them as he remembered the opium traders looking more than a decade ago. He'd even tried to draw the AK-47s the men and their minions carried. "What the hell are you doing?" a voice roared from his left. Wilkinson glared down at his paper.

"Waiting for the laptop," Tyler said. He looked at the screen. Its progress bar indicated it was close to finishing.

"And you figured you'd just sit here and draw?"

"I have watercolors at home. It's therapeutic for PTSD."

Wilkinson crossed his arms but didn't say anything else about it. "What's the computer doing?"

"A wide search on Durrani and his associates," Tyler said. "I talked to a couple people who got strong-armed by them recently. It all helps footprint the organization." Sara's data would, too, but Tyler didn't want to tell Wilkinson about her. He'd probably overreact and demand Tyler try to get all manners of classified information from a woman who knew better than to provide it. "Even if I can't find the big man directly, I might be able to get a line on someone else."

"You think it'll help you find my daughter?" Wilkinson wanted to know.

"I think it's our best bet right now. Durrani was an opium trader in Afghanistan. He's been doing things like this for years. He's not going to take unnecessary risks. His name's not going to be out there more than it needs to. The other guys in the group may not be as up on OPSEC."

"OPSEC?"

"Operational security," Tyler said. "It's something of an umbrella term but not leaking info about yourself or what you're doing is a big part of it. Durrani might be a pro, but I'm willing to bet not everyone he pays is as good at it."

Wilkinson blew out a deep breath and ran a hand through his hair. The worry lines on his face had only deepened in the last day. Tyler imagined himself in the other man's shoes. While he'd be a lot more active if his own daughter went missing—and had been when Braxton kidnapped her last year—Tyler also knew he'd be constantly on edge. All told, the client handled the situation pretty well, but a bad resolution could push him over the edge. "Time is running out Mister Tyler." Wilkinson inclined his head toward the laptop. "I think your search is done. Let's hope you're right about the other guys." He turned and left the room.

"Here's hoping," Tyler said as he explored the results.

❧

JOSEF DROVE TOWARD DOWNTOWN. His phone vibrated on the passenger's seat, and the car's display identified the caller as Hajira. Durrani's pet recruiter. Josef couldn't deny her effectiveness at getting girls to come willingly. The Nigerian lady had a way of talking to young women—wherever they were from—and convincing them to go with her. She used a few different sob stories and sales pitches she could adapt to the circumstances, and she'd filled a lot of chairs over the years. Josef favored simple abductions, but Durrani was the boss. "What?" he said when he picked up.

"I have three at the bus station."

"We don't need three. Only room for two more in the class."

"These are all good fits for the program," she said, keeping up the facade.

"We can't oversell it," Josef said. "These are firm commitments. Two."

"What do I do with the third?"

"You're going to need to let her down. The easy way is to buy her a ticket and say she can apply again later. The hard way is . . . well, you understand."

Hajira fell silent for a few seconds before answering. "I'm not sure I can pick two."

"I'm sure I can," Josef told her. "Take it from me . . they'd rather you be the one to make the selection."

"How will I—"

"When I get there," he broke in, "you'd better only have two recruits with you. The signing deadline is tonight. You have fifteen minutes." He broke the connection. Blasted woman. She knew where the girls she connived were going. For Hajira to balk at making a hard choice was ridiculous. Josef would be ready to choose for her if she couldn't, and he'd tell Durrani what happened. There was value in having a woman bring naive girls into the fold, but it didn't have to be Hajira time and again.

He was at least fifteen minutes from the bus station with traffic. Additional cars and pedestrians going to the nearby casino would make the last leg take forever, too. Josef snaked his way through the city. At a traffic light, he slipped his 9MM from its holster and screwed a suppressor on. The tinted windows on his SUV wouldn't let anyone see what he did. As he approached the meeting place, he set the pistol on his lap.

Josef drove into the loop in front of the Greyhound station. Hajira waited for him, and two girls stood with her.

ALEX ANNE COULDN'T HELP STARING at the empty chair. A girl sat in it until recently—until their abductors had grown tired of her mouthing off and dragged her away. Alex Anne didn't want to think about what went on next. She could still hear those horrible screams every time she closed her eyes. A few of her fellow captives stared at her as if expecting her to do something. All she could cling to was the hope Mister Tyler still looked for her. No one said a word for hours.

The door opened, and two burly olive-complected men each hauled a protesting girl into the room. One was blonde, too skinny, and looked no older than fourteen. The other also carried too little weight for her frame. She was probably sixteen. Not for the first time, Alex Anne glanced around the room and realized she was the oldest abductee. The thought turned her stomach. If she'd had more to eat, she might've vomited.

"Quiet," one of the men barked as they bound the struggling young women to the final two chairs. Alex Anne gasped. This was it. No seats were empty. Each had a captive tied to it. Whatever sick plan these men were running, they'd completed a major part of it. A few others looked around, and their wide crying eyes told Alex Anne she wasn't alone in her realization.

"What are you going to do with us now?" she asked. Several of the other girls expected her to lead by virtue of age or status. Might as well start acting the part.

"No talking," the same man said.

"It's a fair question," another voice answered. It was the older guy. Other than his hard eyes, his demeanor suggested he just stepped off a used-car lot. The square-jawed blond enforcer walked in with him. "Everyone wants to know what will happen to them. I used to wonder this, as well, in my younger days."

The blond guy shook his head. "Sir, I don't—"

His boss' upraised hand compelled him into silence. "Some of you are new here, so you may not know what will transpire. You may have been recruited to an overseas charity." A few new girls nodded. "Or a school program. There is no charity and no program. . . not in the normal sense, at least. We are an international group, however. Soon, we will leave here and fly to an undisclosed location. There, you will each be auctioned off to the highest bidder." Frightened murmurs went up in the room, and the older guy raised his voice to talk over them. "You will be the property of whoever buys you, and you will do as he says."

"I'm no sex slave!" one of the young women yelled.

"Not yet, my dear," the boss said, "but you will be. We leave tonight. Make peace with your old lives. They're over." He turned and strode from the room, the large blond man with him. The two brawny men remained, and their maniacal stares and beefy fists ensured silence.

26

Tyler looked over the list of Durrani's likely associates. As suspected, almost all were Afghan men. One was his nephew (Turkish on his mother's side), and another was a Serbian mercenary named Josef Mitrovic, the owner of a long and bloody international rap sheet. Sara's report included him, too. She deserved points for being thorough when this ordeal finally ended. He closed the laptop and carried it to Wilkinson's room. The client held an animated conversation with the police, shook his head in Tyler's direction, and turned away. Tyler could take the hint.

He retrieved the Tesla and opened the laptop once he sat in the driver's seat. Its built-in cellular chip established a connection. He knew the people who probably worked for Durrani, and the computer's programs could try and track their movements. Any one person, however, could be hard to find. Considering he was up against the clock, Tyler didn't want to waste time. Even a couple hours to hunt down one man could be too long. He returned his attention to the truck. As expected, the rental receipt included a tag number.

Tyler grabbed his phone and texted Lexi. She knew how to use the machine far better than he did, and he couldn't afford the time it would take to learn on the fly. *Time is short. Can the laptop track a license plate?*

While he waited, Tyler opened some menus and explored the device's capabilities. He wished he understood better how it worked, but his brain processed things like engines, transmissions, and other mechanical parts. Tyler could fix the hardware in a computer, but he could never master the software. His phone buzzed with his daughter's reply. *Caught me just in time. About to go back to campus. Should be able to. Under the tracking menu, look for Real-Time. Be careful.*

Tyler followed the steps she laid out and saw an option marked *Traffic Cameras and Toll Sensors*. He double-clicked it. The only input he needed to enter was the tag number. "It can't be this easy," he whispered to his empty car as he tapped in the letters and numbers. He pressed enter, and the cursor transformed into a spinning circle for about ten seconds.

Then, it displayed recent results. "I guess it can." Tyler looked them over. The van headed down I-95 out of the city. He could be hot on its tail in a couple minutes. He called Wilkinson, who picked up right away. "You'd better have good news."

"I got a line on the transport truck." Tyler fired up the electric SUV and pulled out onto Baltimore Street with screeching tires. "It's on 95 headed south. I'm in pursuit."

"Can you catch it?"

Tyler swung a hard right onto Lombard, gunned it, and made the left onto Howard a couple seconds after the light went red. For a taller vehicle, the Model X handled well. "If not, I'll figure out where it goes."

"Good luck, Mister Tyler," Wilkinson said. "I think our time is short, however. Come back with Alexandra, or don't come back at all." He hung up. Tyler grunted but understood. He sped past the Orioles' and Ravens' stadiums and picked up the highway in short order. The van remained several miles ahead. He would need to zip along at double the posted limit to try and catch up. Tyler pressed the accelerator, and the dual electric motors responded. The speedometer clicked past 80.

Heavy traffic heading out of Baltimore forced Tyler to go slower. He changed lanes as often as he could, keeping an eye on the laptop every few seconds. Past the exit for the Baltimore Beltway, traffic thinned, and Tyler got back on the accelerator again. He eyed the display. His quarry maintained its route. A couple miles later, a camera picked up the van exiting onto Route 100. "Shit," Tyler muttered. Off the highway, he didn't know how many electric eyes and sensors would be able to track the vehicle's movements.

It turned out to be zero. No more data came in. Tyler sped up again and took the exit ramp well above the suggested speed. He didn't see the transport anywhere. Route 100 covered a lot of ground. He needed to narrow its possible locations.

AFTER HELPING her dad figure out how to use his laptop, Lexi climbed into her blue Accord coupe and drove back to College Park. She reduced speed a few times in light traffic, but people driving north hit the worst of it. Lexi swung her car onto Campus Drive and parked in a lot near the computer science building. Close but not too close. It would be a nice walk to and from. Once out of the car, she figured she'd be here a while between doing her actual assignment on the mainframe and hanging out with Ahmed. A coffee couldn't hurt.

It was out of the way, but Lexi hoofed it to the student union building. The line told her she wasn't the only person who decided caffeine would be the best way to power through the rest of the afternoon. Lexi ordered her giant cup, collected it, and walked back outside. The sun hung just above some of the more distant buildings. As she walked away from the union, Lexi saw Ahmed sitting on a bench with another man around his own age. The other guy did the majority of the talking, and his frequent gestures made Ahmed frown.

Lexi waved at him, and he showed a tentative smile. His friend scowled as he looked up at her before returning his attention to Ahmed. Whatever they were discussing, it seemed unpleasant. Lexi hoped he was all right. If she had more time, she would have seen what the argument was about, but she needed to get on with her work. The walk back to the computer science building only took a few minutes.

As she figured, the mainframe lab was in the basement. Couldn't have the rich college donors see old technology on the main floors. Lexi walked past the elevator and took the stairs. She pushed open one side of the heavy double doors and walked in. A few other students sat at terminals already. Lexi picked one with a few spaces between her and the nearest neighbor. A login prompt waited on the monitor. She entered her credentials, pulled her notebook from her backpack, and looked over the assignment.

As she got to work, Lexi wondered about Ahmed and the other guy he talked to. She hoped he was all right.

～

TYLER PULLED to the curb and tried to deduce where the van would have gone. He didn't even know which direction it went from I-95. It still didn't show up on any camera or toll system, so the truck never got back onto the highway or other major artery. It must have taken Route 100 to its destination —which would hopefully be wherever Durrani and his minions kept Alex Anne and the other missing girls.

Going west headed toward Columbia. Howard County. Ritzy. It would be a place Durrani would want to fit in, but maybe not the best location to store a bunch of captives. Too many eyes, and buildings would be expensive to rent. Tyler would pass restaurants, a few other streets, grocery stores, and a shopping center or two before Route 100 terminated at Route 29.

Heading east offered a much longer stretch of road with plenty more places to hide a roomful of girls. Route 1 would have some options. The Baltimore-Washington Parkway would lead to a bunch more, as would I-97. Traffic cameras would acquire the vehicle if it ventured onto either of those major highways. East made more sense. There would be a greater number of options for facilities, and none would attract the attention being in Columbia might bring.

Tyler texted Lexi, thanking her for the tip about the laptop, but he didn't get a response. She was probably on her way back to campus for whatever she had going on tonight. As he pulled away from the curb and turned around, Tyler hoped his daughter made a few friends at Maryland. She'd always been something of a loner, and changing schools when she came to live with him almost two years ago didn't help.

Route 1 represented the first major intersection. Both north and south held plenty of options. Tyler would need to pick one. Maybe he'd even get lucky and find the van he targeted pretty fast in the various nests of lots and industrial parks. It would be nice if something went right.

As he pulled onto Route 1 northbound, Tyler checked the Tesla's range. A hundred and five miles remained. Lexi must not have charged it after she used it last. The Model X was normally good for close to 300, and Tyler figured there to be about double the current figure remaining. If the van led him on a chase, he could have a problem.

He needed to find the girls quickly.

27
___

Ahmed stalked toward the computer science building. He never should have involved Scott in this, but the promise of easy money blinded him, and he spent ten minutes lecturing Ahmed on the best ways to get Lexi to come willingly, then at least as long laying out scenarios if she resisted. The smirk on his face as he talked told Ahmed what he planned to do to Lexi if the chance presented itself. Ahmed wondered if he would intervene. He liked Lexi, and he didn't want to hand her to his uncle, but if he were going to, she'd be intact and unharmed.

It would be better for everyone if she came quietly.

Still, they needed to prepare for the possibility she'd resist. Ahmed intended to lay on the charm. He listened to Scott enough. This was his uncle's operation, and he'd make the first attempt. Lexi liked him. She reached out and kissed him earlier when he got cold feet. Ahmed pushed the door open and walked inside. He diverted into the men's room immediately.

No one else was in there. Ahmed washed his hands, splashed a little water on his face, and dried himself off. He popped a breath mint, crunched it, and ate another. If he were going to woo Lexi and get her to come with him without a fight, he couldn't have bad breath. As he left the facilities, Ahmed tossed a third mint into his mouth. He rode the elevator down to the basement and found the mainframe lab right away.

Lexi sat at a terminal on the left side of the room. Only a few were occupied, and no one took any of the ones near her. If she heard his approach, she didn't look up. Ahmed slid onto a nearby chair and wheeled himself beside Lexi. "Hey, beautiful."

She jolted upright, wheeled her seat away, and formed her hands into fists. Her posture only relaxed when she recognized Ahmed. "Holy crap. Don't sneak up on me like that when I'm working."

"Sorry." He offered a smile. Her reaction dismayed him, though. She wasn't the type to go along quietly. It was one of the things Ahmed liked about her. He covered his reaction by looking at her screen, which she'd crammed full of code. "What are you working on?"

"An assignment," she said as she moved her chair back into place. "Mainframes aren't big anymore, but they paved the way for a lot of what we do today in terms of cloud computing, terminal access . . . those kinds of things. The professor wants us to get hands on with them."

"Looks like you know what you're doing."

She snickered. "Right now, I fake it 'til I make it. The good news is I've learned a few things even in the short time I've been working here. I wasn't looking forward to this assignment when we got it. Now, I don't think it'll be so bad."

"How long do you think you'll be?" Ahmed asked.

"Why?" Lexi grinned. "Got a hot date in one of the residence halls?"

"No." Ahmed shook his head. "Not how I roll. I just . . .

want to see you, and I kind of hoped it didn't involve watching you type for a while."

"I told you I had work to do." Lexi looked at her notebook, checked something on the screen, and keyed another line of code. "I'll try to go quickly, but I also want to get a good grade."

"I get it." Ahmed watched her do the assignment for a couple minutes. He knew how to use his phone, tablet, and laptop, but he didn't really understand what went on under the hood. Some of his friends were good with computers. His thoughts drifted to Scott, and he turned away to cover a scowl. The man would be growing impatient by now. If he were going to coax Lexi from the lab willingly, he needed to get started.

He rolled his chair behind hers, leaned forward, and kissed her neck. Lexi recoiled and put her shoulder against her head. "What are you doing?" she said in a harsh whisper. Another student glanced at them.

"I told you." Ahmed spread his hands. "I want to see you. And I feel a little silly about earlier."

"It's fine." Lexi leaned in and gave him a quick smooch on the lips. "Let me get my work done, though. I'll be happy to hang out with you once I'm finished."

Ahmed nodded and scooted his chair back to where it had been a moment before. While she returned to her project, Ahmed slipped his phone from his pocket and texted Scott. *Plan A is a dud. We need Plan B.*

THE DOOR OPENED AGAIN. Alex Anne looked up as dread knotted her stomach. All the chairs were full. People were still out there looking for her—she hoped. She'd been the target the old guy and his cronies went to great lengths to acquire. They'd need to transport all their captives in the near future. The blond guy and one of the brawny assistants accompanied the boss. "We'll be moving you all soon," the older one said.

"There will be one more chance to use the bathroom," the fair-haired one added. "A truck is on its way. Once it's here, you'll all go inside. You'll walk in an orderly line, or there will be consequences. From here, we're headed to the airport. It's not a long drive."

A voice rose from the back of the room. "What about the girl you dragged out of here?" Alex Anne looked at the new speaker. She'd seen the girl early on in this hellish process. "We need to know what we're dealing with." A tear slid down her cheek. "Is she dead?"

"Of course she is," the boss said. "We know you're all frightened, but we won't put up with open defiance. Our men exercise a lot of restraint in here. If you step out of line, they'll do what they want with you." The burly man put his fore-finger against his head and dropped his thumb onto it. Alex Anne shivered.

"Enough questions," the blond one said. "We'll untie you one at a time so you can walk to the toilet. After, you'll all get into the truck."

"What if I don't want to get on the plane?" the same girl asked. Alex Anne stared at her, trying to compel her to be silent.

"You know your fate," the older man answered. "It will be the same as the other girl's. We won't miss you. It's unlikely anyone will. If you want to go through what she did, then keep mouthing off. Otherwise, be quiet and fall in line."

Thankfully, the girl remained silent. Alex Anne squeezed her eyes shut and cried quietly. If people hoped to rescue her, they were running out of time.

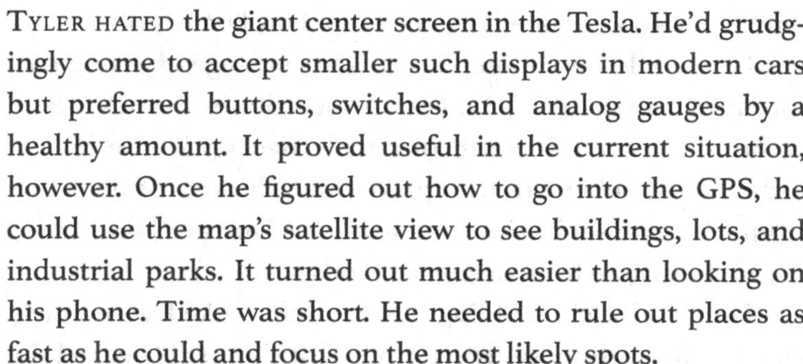

TYLER HATED the giant center screen in the Tesla. He'd grudgingly come to accept smaller such displays in modern cars but preferred buttons, switches, and analog gauges by a healthy amount. It proved useful in the current situation, however. Once he figured out how to go into the GPS, he could use the map's satellite view to see buildings, lots, and industrial parks. It turned out much easier than looking on his phone. Time was short. He needed to rule out places as fast as he could and focus on the most likely spots.

He went north on Route 1 but soon doubted his decision. There were plenty of buildings which could house a couple dozen kidnapping victims, yet none offered the kind of privacy an operation like Durrani's would require. They were all too close to a furniture store, two martial arts studios, a restaurant, a dog park, and more. Tyler made a U-turn and pulled into a small lot to get his bearings.

If the girls were being held along this road, they'd be to the south. The map on the large screen showed Tyler a bunch of possibilities. With a Google Earth view, he could even see things like tree cover and access roads. Past Route 103, a collection of buildings sat off the road on the left side. The map identified a few businesses, but three structures didn't have any name or data associated with them. They were probably empty. Google knew far too much in Tyler's view, and if they didn't know who occupied a place, it was probably vacant.

He pulled back out onto Route 1, crossed over the interchange for 100, and kept going until he made a left onto Cooney Lane. Each side of the road featured several large, squat brick buildings. They were both long and wide with plenty of regular and garage-style doors marking individual businesses and entrances. Signs dotted the exterior of the nearer structures. As he moved farther back in the park, however, signs of occupation grew more sparse. Lots lay empty. Plywood covered the occasional broken window.

This would be a good place to keep hostages. Getting past the front half wouldn't be hard, especially in a truck which could easily hold a bunch of people tied up in the rear. If little foot or vehicle traffic approached, the risk of detection would be minimal. The presence of a Durrani goon could dissuade anyone from nosing around.

The last brick building on the left looked completely empty. The outlines of letters from past signs still marred the exterior. Tyler backed up, stopped the Tesla, and got out carrying a rifle scope. He didn't want a sentry to see an unknown vehicle approach. He crept closer to the front wall. A broken camera barely staying on its mount was the only indication of a security system he saw. Tyler reached the far edge and looked down.

A large truck sat at the end.

A van between him and the truck obscured his view. Smart. Even if someone ventured back here, they wouldn't be able to see anything unusual or illegal happening. Tyler looked through the scope. The long vehicle fit the description of the one Durrani rented. As he watched, a Middle Eastern man emerged from a door and checked something on the truck. He disappeared back inside a moment later.

Tyler ran back to the Model X. He pulled into the lot on the opposite side of the last building. It backed up to woods. There wasn't even a sidewalk to make the short trek to the other side easy. Tyler curbed the Tesla, checked out the map one more time, and climbed out. He slipped a bullet-resistant vest over his head, holstered his M11, and prepared for an assault.

28

The truck would provide a measure of cover. No one sat in it. Tyler could slip in the main entrance and be right in the lion's den. While he kicked in many a door in Afghanistan, he always did so with a team behind him and only after a careful plan. Here, his reconnaissance consisted of looking at a map on a large screen, and he lacked a proper plan. A frontal assault wouldn't be the best choice for success.

Instead, Tyler approached the rear door. He tried the knob and found it locked. His snap gun popped it quickly. Tyler opened the door slowly, his pistol leading the way. He entered into a dim but wide hallway. Racks stuffed with boxes and plastic containers lined the walls on both sides. Most of the light came from under another entrance ahead.

As Tyler slipped past a door on the right side, it opened, and a slender Afghan man stepped out. His eyes found Tyler and widened. Before he could yell, Tyler clamped his left hand over the other man's mouth and steered him back into the small room he'd just left. Inside, Tyler placed the M11 under his left arm and drew a knife. His adversary struggled, but Tyler kept walking and slammed him into the wall. Stunned, the man offered no resistance to the blade driving up between his ribs.

Tyler let the body fall to the floor. He wiped the knife on the dead man's shirt, replaced it in its sheath, and held his M11 before him as he moved from the room. He tried the next door and found it unlocked. Tyler pushed it open. It was a large area full of metal chairs. A few men herded girls from their seats toward the front of the building. Not many young women remained. One of the guys shouted when Tyler walked in. He tracked the front sight up past the man's chest and shot him in the head.

Another scampered away and opened fire with an AK-74. Tyler ducked back into the hallway but not before a bullet clipped his arm. He backed toward the rear door. Clever adversaries would send someone around to catch him in a crossfire. Tyler hoped the men he faced weren't so smart. Machine gun fire forced him farther back, and he took cover in the doorway to the office where he'd killed a man a scant few moments before.

A voice called out from the main room, and the bullets stopped flying. "Is this the great John Tyler?" a man said in an accented voice. It had to be Durrani.

"Let the girls go, and I won't kill you and your men."

"Of course you still would," Durrani said. He was right. They weren't getting out of here alive. As a soldier, Tyler couldn't kill men who surrendered to him, no matter how heinous their crimes. Here, he operated under no such limitations. Tyler inched forward from the doorway. "The girls in here are all very beautiful. You have a beautiful daughter of your own, do you not? What's her name? Alexis?"

The implied threat hardened Tyler's resolve. "If a hair on her head is out of place—"

"My nephew is with her now," Durrani broke in. "She'll

join the rest of these pathetic girls soon." Before Tyler could run into the room, he saw a grenade sliding his way across the smooth floor. He bolted for the rear entrance as it skidded behind him and rattled among the metal. Two steps later, it exploded, driving him into the air and causing everything around him to come crashing down. Tyler landed in a heap, and a bunch of steel, cardboard, and plastic fell atop him. Durrani said something else, but the ringing in Tyler's ears prevented him from understanding.

Durrani's nephew was with Lexi. He needed to get to her. His vision swam, and he gritted his teeth against a rush of pain in his head. It took a moment, but Tyler pushed a shelf off his chest and sat up. He cleared cardboard and plastic debris from his legs, then lifted the rack atop them enough to scamper backward and get out from under it. He almost lost consciousness as he stood. Tyler bent over, took a few deep breaths, and used whatever he could find for support as he picked his way through the blast zone and detritus. Two holes in the ceiling marked where one of the units flew up into it before slamming back down. Ground zero. He staggered into the main room.

It was empty.

Tyler moved to the front door as quickly as he could. The truck was gone, too. "Shit," he muttered as he took out his phone and called his daughter. Lexi was the best thing he'd ever done in this world, and his heart thudded with anxiety at the thought of Durrani harming her. She didn't answer, and the call went to voicemail after the second ring. He needed to leave for reasons besides his daughter. Traffic to this building might have been light, but someone would have heard the gunfire and explosions. The cops would be en route soon, and he couldn't be detained. They couldn't delay him reaching the Maryland campus. Tyler approached the entrance, checked in both directions, and then headed toward the rear of the building. He dashed to the other side and climbed back into the Tesla.

His head felt a little better. Tyler texted Lexi. *You're in danger. Durrani says his nephew is with you. Let me know you're OK.* He guzzled some water and looked at his arm. Only a flesh wound. Tyler glanced at his phone. No reply. He tried calling his daughter again.

It went to voicemail after the second ring.

RICH FERGUSON GLARED at his monitor. He expected someone to have actionable intel by this point. They'd run the name Farzaad Durrani into the ground. He wasn't at his house, which their colleagues in the Harford County Sheriff's Office confirmed. His truck rental resolved to an address which no one used, and the police found no evidence the vehicle even existed. Rich knew the clock was their primary enemy at this point. An operation like Durrani's wouldn't stick around longer than necessary especially with a famous abductee in tow.

He texted Sergeant Paul King and received a colorful negative reply quickly. Next, Rich called Captain Norton. "Tell me you have something," he said when his colleague picked up.

"A collection of stalled leads and dead ends."

"I'm staring at the same."

"These guys are pros, Rich. We came in pretty late. They had time to set up their entire operation before we even knew the first girl was missing. We've been playing catch-up the whole time."

"I know," Rich grumbled.

"Clock's ticking away the fourth quarter, and we're down big. I think we need the big guns at this point."

"I agree. Let me know if you uncover anything."

"Sure," Norton said. "You do the same." Rich confirmed he would and hung up. Sharpe didn't want him going to the FBI. They tended to dominate cases and minimize the locals' involvement. At this point, Rich didn't care who did the work or got the credit for it. They needed as much coverage as possible. He called an acquaintance at the local field office.

"I hear you're a lieutenant now," Special Agent Jason Hess said.

"Save the congratulations. We have a problem."

"Must be bad if you're calling me."

"It is," Rich said. "Flesh traffickers. We know they've grabbed a few girls already, and we have almost nothing. A few names, but they don't turn into anything."

"How long do you think you have?" Hess asked.

"Not long. We're working with the state folks, but no one's making any headway." Rich wondered if John Tyler figured anything out. He gave Sharpe Durrani's name in the first place. It probably constituted the last piece of information he'd share. "We think they've been at it a couple days, and they've already kidnapped someone famous."

"Jesus Christ. You should've called me yesterday."

"Probably," Rich said. "You know how these things go. Politics and all. I'm reaching out now. I'm happy to send you what we know. Can you mobilize a team to start working this as soon as possible?"

"It sucks, Rich," Hess said. "I wouldn't drop a pile of crap in your lap like this."

"The price you pay for being a fed."

"Yeah, yeah." Hess sighed. "I'm in. Send me what you have. I don't know if we can make a difference at this rate, but I hate traffickers. We'll do what we can."

"Thanks." Rich opened an email to Hess and dropped in

the latest compilation of notes as a PDF. "It's on its way to you."

"All right," Hess said. "I'll stay in touch. Make sure you do the same."

"I will. Thanks." Rich hung up. Sharpe might be unhappy, but so be it. He'd deal with the captain if he needed to. In the meantime, he wanted to be out in the field chasing down leads with his officers. Rich grabbed his holster from a desk drawer, slipped the leather paddle over his belt, and headed for the parking lot.

ALEX ANNE CRIED when the blond guy untied her. "Quiet," he said in his harsh accented voice. She sniffed once but tried her best to be silent. After seeing what these men did when a girl stepped out of line, she didn't want to be subjected to the same fate. Earlier, she thought being their famous quarry might give her an exemption. She'd entertained the idea of being a leader for the younger girls forced into captivity here with her.

Now, she simply wanted to survive. Hell likely awaited her, but if she remained alive, she'd have a chance to escape. Or for someone to find her. Despite her grim surroundings for the past however many days, Alex Anne still clung to the hope she'd be rescued. Mister Tyler would find her. Maybe Donnell was still alive. They'd have the police with them, and every horrible man who came in and out of the room would get shot.

"In the truck," another man ordered, snapping Alex Anne from her brief but satisfying reverie. The men had already loaded a dozen girls in. All of them were chained at the wrists to the interior wall of what looked like a large moving van. Despite the chill in the air, it felt warm and stale as Alex

Anne stepped onto the bare metal floor. She felt the other girls eyeing her with disappointment through their tears. She was older. She was famous.

She'd failed them all.

From somewhere behind her, Alex Anne heard a gunshot.

She dropped into a crouch. Donnell hammered it into her over the years. At the same time, she turned. One of the horrible men lay dead, and the boss shouted at Mister Tyler before gunfire chased him into hiding. He'd found her. She smiled, and even the scowl of the guy herding her farther into the truck couldn't deter her. He proved hard to see around, and Alex Anne couldn't follow what happened.

Then, she heard an explosion, and the building vibrated. She gasped even as the olive-skinned man bound her to the wall. Panicked voices came from inside. The blond guy and the boss herded the last few girls out. "Tie them up quickly," the older man said. "We need to go." Alex Anne looked inside the building until they closed the door.

Mister Tyler didn't come out.

The engine burbled to life as one of the men finished lashing the final girl into place. He banged on the wall to the front part of the truck and sat on a small bench. They lurched forward. Alex Anne couldn't see anything out of the rear. She felt the vehicle make a right turn, then another, and then it picked up speed.

They were headed to the airport. No more rescuers would come. Her life as she knew it was over, and she'd cried so much, no more tears would come.

29

En route to their destination, Durrani slipped his phone out of his front pocket. Over the years, he'd tried to keep in touch with many of his fellow traffickers from Afghanistan. Once he left his home and began moving other goods, he added to his network. Some of his associates were no longer among the living, victims of the American military's constant campaign of aggression. Some of them remained, however, and he wanted to get the word out to them.

Durrani opened an email and added the group entry for his associates. He composed the message as best he could while the vehicle sped and bumped along the roads.

MY FRIENDS,

I believe some of you remember the American soldier John Tyler. He and his fellow aggressors disrupted our operations years ago. You may not know him by name, but I promise you'd recognize his face.

We haven't seen the last of him.

Tyler is snooping around my operation. He's already done the kinds of things you would expect a man like him to do. I'm about to complete a major transaction, and he's threatening it. In the event I don't make it out alive, I'm going to share his information with you. Do with it what you will.

Best,

Durrani

DESPITE PREFERRING HARD COPIES, Durrani knew Josef emailed him everything, also. Sometimes, they needed to review details on the go, and it was easier on a phone or tablet. He found the file Josef prepared about Tyler, attached it to his email, and sent the message. He didn't know how many of his potential recipients were still alive, if they'd remember Tyler, or if they'd have the means or motivation to do anything about him if they did.

It was an attempt to get revenge down the line. A shot in the dark. Durrani knew from experience they sometimes hit their marks.

~

LEXI SETTLED INTO HER WORK. Ahmed remained nearby but left her alone. As she finished the first part of her homework, she wondered how her dad fared. At least the police were involved, and he didn't need to try and take on a band of kidnappers by himself. She looked at her phone, saw no signal carried into the lab, and frowned. She'd check in with him later.

As she struggled with a new batch of instructions for the mainframe, Lexi heard someone else approach. She looked up and was surprised to see the young man Ahmed argued with earlier slide into a chair and join him. For his part,

Ahmed didn't look thrilled by the new arrival, either. "Who's your friend?" she asked in a quiet voice.

"This is Scott."

"Nice to meet you," Scott said in a tone suggesting he found the experience quite unpleasant. Lexi wondered what he was doing here as the two men held a whispered conversation. Something weird was going on. Maybe Ahmed was in trouble. Lexi couldn't fight his battles for him, but perhaps she could help behind the scenes. She grabbed her phone while neither of them looked at her, set it to record, and then slid it face down closer to the pair.

They kept their quiet chat going for a few minutes. Neither got animated like before. Lexi didn't like this whole situation. She wanted to hang out with Ahmed, not meet his barely social friend. Was he going to give Scott the boot at some point? She wondered exactly what they'd been talking about before, if it involved her, and whether they were into something weird. As she rushed through her assignment, they finished their conversation.

Lexi picked up her phone and stopped the recording. "You about ready?" Ahmed asked. He forced a smile. Something was definitely up with him, and his friend didn't help the situation. Lexi put her mobile to her ear and pressed play with her thumb. She turned up the volume and heard their hushed chat.

"Dude, what are we waiting for?" Scott asked.

"I told you, I don't like this."

"It was your idea."

"I know," Ahmed said. "My uncle's, really. He's asked me to help out."

"So let's help him. We just need to bring her alive, right?"

"Yeah."

"Means we can have some fun with her first," Scott said,

and Lexi's stomach lurched. She held up her finger as Ahmed shot her a questioning look.

"I don't know," Ahmed's recorded whispers told his friend.

"I brought knives," Scott said. "You know I come prepared. She'll go along with whatever we want."

Lexi stopped the playback. These two planned to abduct her and hand her to Ahmed's uncle—after sexually assaulting her at knifepoint, of course. What the hell did she wander into? Was this simply bad luck, or did Ahmed target her? He approached her for help with an assignment originally. She kept a pistol in her car. It might be the only way out. "Ready?" she asked, hoping her nerves didn't spill over into her voice.

"Yeah, let's go," Ahmed said.

Once they left the confines of the lab, cell signal returned. Lexi saw two missed calls and three texts from her father advising her she was in danger from Durrani's nephew. Ahmed. Her dad was headed to campus. She didn't want him solving this problem for her. Getting rid of them without killing them would be ideal, but a solution like that wasn't in her father's wheelhouse. Besides, Alex Anne needed him more right now. She fired off a quick reply. *I'm fine, Dad. He wasn't a problem. Take care of everyone else.*

Lexi hoped she knew what she'd gotten herself into. The three of them walked down the hall toward the elevator. No one else lingered in the area. Scott surged ahead of her and blocked the path. He lifted his jacket to show a large knife in a leather sheath. "You should come quietly."

~

THE TESLA WAS plenty fast and surprisingly nimble for an SUV. Tyler pushed it over 100 as he sped down the highway toward College Park. Alex Anne and the other girls would have to wait. Lexi needed him, and he wasn't about to let anyone associated with Durrani lay a hand on her. The man must have done this to get back at him for Afghanistan. No matter. Tyler would send him a few pictures of his dead nephew soon enough.

His phone vibrated, and the large center screen displayed Lexi's text. *I'm fine, Dad. He wasn't a problem. Take care of everyone else.* Tyler breathed a huge sigh of relief. He saw a place for emergency vehicles to turn around. The current situation certainly constituted an emergency. He pulled to the shoulder, slowed, and swung the Model X around. Tyler stopped on the shoulder heading northbound. His manic driving left the vehicle's range at 30 miles.

He cut the engine and fired up his laptop. Thanks to his jaunt toward the University of Maryland, Durrani's truck would have a head start on him. They needed to be going someplace major to move the girls, though. Probably an airport. They'd be visible on traffic cameras and toll sensors. The program reacquired the van. It passed a traffic camera on I-195.

They were headed to BWI.

The destination alone wasn't enough. BWI was a massive place. Other airports Tyler had flown in and out of dwarfed it, but finding one truck there would prove impossible. Tyler needed to narrow the search. They were taking a plane, but it couldn't be a commercial airline. They'd be way too exposed. A charter, then. They were expensive. Good thing Durrani could use Amanda Painter's credit cards to pay for whatever he needed. Tyler ran the account.

No hits.

He frowned at the screen. Backdating it showed the truck rental, so he queried the right account. He ran the search again anyway and got the the same result. They must have used a different card. Tyler ran some more queries. Amanda Wilkinson. Amanda P. Wilkinson. Amanda Painter Wilkinson. No hits on any of them. Durrani wouldn't risk paying for the transport himself, but Tyler punched in the man's name anyway.

Nothing.

Another account had to be in play. His fingers drummed the steering wheel as he tried to recall the conversation with Wilkinson about Alex Anne's mother. They'd been split up for years. The woman was barely involved and ran the fan club like a business. Tyler remembered thinking the name was terrible. He closed his eyes and concentrated. What was it?

The Double-A Songbirds.

He entered the name into the search and got a result. Alex Anne's fan club chartered a flight from BWI. The charge told him the name of the charter company but not which runway the plane would use. No matter. He could find out. The most important detail: it left in under an hour. Tyler started the Tesla and took off, merging into traffic. His destination was well within its remaining charge, but he needed to hurry, and fast driving would deplete the battery. Tyler hoped it lasted long enough to get him there.

30

Lexi eyed Scott's knife. He kept it sheathed, but she could tell the blade was long enough to get the job done. She wished they'd encounter more foot traffic, but the basement of the computer science building wasn't exactly a hangout hotspot on a Friday night. No, she was on her own, especially after telling her dad to take care of Alex Anne. Lexi felt Ahmed approach from behind. Scott took a step forward. They could overpower her if they grabbed her. She needed to retain the advantage.

Her car was in a parking lot about three hundred yards from the door. She ran track in high school and still kept in shape. Covering the distance wouldn't be a problem. Doing so while keeping these two behind her would be. Lexi thought about the orientation of the campus. The staircase next to the elevator would lead to an exit but not in the right direction. She needed the steps at her six.

Scott flashed a wicked grin. Lexi raised her foot and stomped down on Ahmed's. He yelped, and she turned and kneed him in the groin. It folded him in half, and she pushed him over as she sprinted past. Lexi glanced back long enough to see Scott helping Ahmed back to his feet. They took off after her. She came to the end of the hallway and pushed the door for the stairs.

Locked.

"Shit!" Lexi dodged to the right. There was another set of steps down there. She wished any of the doors she passed were open. None were, and they were all dark. Footsteps gained on her. A hand clutched her jacket, and she grabbed it and ripped it away. Lexi turned enough to see Scott seize her arm. He forced her face-first into the wall.

Lexi snapped her head back, hitting him flush on the nose. He cursed and let her go. Ahmed ran to them and tried another grab. She avoided his hand and gave him a solid right in the solar plexus. The confined space of the corridor favored the men, however. Lexi was faster and quicker, but the current venue nullified her advantages. She needed to get somewhere else. With both of them stunned, she took off again. This time, the door to the stairs opened when she pushed the bar. She sprinted up the steps two at a time.

Despite keeping her fitness up, Lexi was breathing hard when she reached the main floor. She dashed through the exit, got her bearings, and sprinted toward her car. Behind her, she heard two sets of hurried footsteps. While few people were in the building, she hoped to see more in the parking lots. Someone would wonder why two men chased a woman. She glanced back. Scott tried to keep his knife out of sight. She lowered her head, tried to ignore her pulse pounding in her ears, and kept running.

～

TYLER CALLED the main number for BWI chartered flights as he drove. "I need some more information," he said when a woman answered. "I don't know which hangar my party's plane is using."

"Of course, sir. Do you have the name on the reservation?"

"My contact's last name is Durrani, but I think he made it under a business account called the Double-A Songbirds."

Tyler heard the tap-tapping of computer keys as she looked up the data. "I have it here," she said a moment later. "They're using hangar Cee-Six, and they're scheduled to leave in about forty-five minutes. You should hurry."

"I am," he said. "Thank you." Tyler sped around a semi and took the exit for 195. The Tesla's range displayed ten miles left. Its responsiveness grew duller as zero neared. Tyler looked at the center display as he merged, figured out where he needed to go, and turned it off. Maybe it would buy him an extra mile when it counted. Traffic was light on a Friday night, and he made it to the airport exits quickly. Staying straight led to arrivals and departures for commercial flights. Hotels, parking, and charters took the last exit onto Route 170.

Five miles showed on the display as Tyler navigated the curving ramp. He headed away from the accommodations toward the back half of BWI. A narrow road led to the hangars. For a while, the only things Tyler saw were bushes and fences. About a half-mile later, hangars appeared in the distance. The first one he came to was logically numbered C1 on a sign near the street. The structure itself lay about a quarter-mile from the asphalt.

As Tyler neared the fifth building, the Model X slowed down. The batteries gave out. He pulled it off the road before it died completely, leaving it behind an azalea bush. The hangars weren't far away. Each featured its own parking lot, though the one for number five looked emptier than most. Durrani's rented truck and the van which accompanied it both sat in the lot for C6. Tyler would be exposed walking across the dirt and grass to the buildings. There was little cover to be found. Carrying a big gun would attract attention.

He checked the straps on his vest, made sure he carried spare magazines for the M11, and opened the door. He dropped to a crouch right away and closed up the SUV as quietly as he could. Tyler remained at the rear bumper. A man walked a patrol around the hangar Durrani used. When he disappeared around the far edge of the building, Tyler stood and walked. He cursed under his breath when another man came into view. Two on guard, and he knew the second fellow spotted him.

Change of plans. He headed for C5 instead. The runways lay beyond the front of the buildings, but they were only about a hundred yards apart. Small planes didn't need as much room to pull out or in. Tyler kept his head down, waved to the guy walking the beat around number six, and rolled new tactics through his mind.

31

The two guys patrolled a steady beat. If these hangars weren't so remote, they would've attracted attention by now. Maybe someone would see them and figure they were guarding a celebrity who booked a charter. When the first man Tyler saw reached the back of the building, he touched his finger to his ear and took up a post. He remained there. The other guy must have remained near the front.

It meant things were going down.

Tyler edged from behind the fifth building. He used the small rifle scope to surveil the situation. The sentry at the back took a pack of cigarettes from his pocket, shook one out, and lit it. From the front of the building, an engine grew louder. Tyler couldn't get a good look from where he was, so he sprinted to the front of number five. A plane stopped at the sixth hangar and prepared to enter. He used the scope to peer through a window and saw a bunch of girls standing around, including Alex Anne. All of them looked a little dirty, and most cried.

A quick count revealed eighteen girls in total. He also

noticed three men not including Durrani or the two outside. A dozen and a half captives. These monsters worked quickly. Tyler took out his phone and texted the details of where he was and what he saw to Leon Sharpe. He pasted the first part of the message to Sara Morrison so she knew the results of her intel. The matter would fall outside of the captain's jurisdiction, but he'd know who to call. Sara might, too. If the worst happened and Tyler failed, having a fallback made it more likely Alex Anne and the other girls would be rescued.

With the plane about to enter the hangar, Tyler didn't have a wealth of time. He dashed toward his original spot and then paused when he came to a door. The snap gun was stuck in his 442. If this entrance were locked, he'd need to move on. Tyler tried the handle.

It opened.

He heard a muffled voice as he slipped inside, like someone talking from behind a door. Could have been a man in an office. Tyler spotted what he wanted quickly on a workbench and ducked back out. He walked around the rear of the building and approached C6. The Afghan guard with the AK-74 eyed him as he approached.

Tyler held up the pack of Marlboros he'd swiped from next door and lifted one free of the pack. He'd never smoked more than a handful of these things in social situations, but he'd seen enough people doing it in the army to mimic the motions. "Got a light?"

The other fellow grunted and offered a curt nod. The nearby plane's engine revved. The guard took his hands off his gun and fished around in his pockets. Tyler drew his M11 and shot him in the midsection. The guy crumpled to the concrete. He tried to lift the automatic weapon, but Tyler kicked it from his grip. "How many men?" he asked as he stood over the wounded sentry.

No reply. Tyler repeated the question in Pashto. "Too many . . . for you," the guy said.

"Doubt it. I see eighteen girls. I know your boss is Durrani. I'm going to ask one more time. How. Many. Men?"

"You must be Tyler," he said in English before spitting out a mouthful of bright crimson blood. "Durrani told us . . . you might come."

"Here I am. Answer the question."

"Piss off," he said. He tried to hock more blood at Tyler, but it rolled down his chin.

"It's up to you how easy your final minutes are," Tyler said. He stepped on the bullet wound. The guy grunted in pain. This wasn't Tyler's favorite tactic, but he couldn't afford to waste time. "How many?"

"You're dead. There are seven . . . counting me."

"You poor idiot," Tyler said. "I wasn't counting you." With the plane's engine still roaring, Tyler shot the fallen man in the head.

Leon Sharpe drummed his fingers on his desk. His best men were working on the abductions. The state police had troopers on the case, too. The feds were even involved, which Sharpe expected even if he didn't relish the idea. Still, if they could crack the case, he'd be happy. Saving the girls was the important part. Who got the credit only mattered for people's CVs, and Sharpe didn't need to pad his. He wasn't going anywhere.

His cell phone chirped, and Sharpe read the text from John Tyler. *Found the girls. 18 total. BWI charters. They're in C6 and leaving soon. I'm about to go in.* "Of course you are," he grumbled. He'd known Tyler a long time. The man was probably the best at coming up with a plan, kicking down a door, and dealing with hostiles. Still, he didn't have a team with him this time. BWI sat in Anne Arundel County. Sharpe picked up the phone and dialed the deputy chief. "Good thing I still work long hours, Leon," Ben Hammond said. "What can I do for you?"

"I have reliable intel there's a sex trafficking operation leaving BWI with a dozen and a half kidnapped girls soon."

Silence was the only reply for a few seconds. "I want to be sure I heard you right. You're telling me traffickers are going to be wheels up at my airport soon?"

"I am," Sharpe said.

"What's the source of this intel?"

"A reliable person who's on the scene. He's . . . a consultant for us. Working with the security team of one of the victims."

"Jesus Christ," Hammond said. "I need to put together a huge response for something like this. It's not going to be immediate."

"I know," Sharpe said, "but it needs to be as fast as you can make it. I can send some people, too, if you want."

"We got it. I'll have units there within fifteen minutes, and a SWAT team on scene within a half-hour. You think I have enough time?"

"I hope so."

"Me, too," Hammond said. "Tell your consultant to stand down and leave the rescue to the professionals."

Sharpe laughed. "Tell him yourself. And good luck when you try."

LEXI DASHED across the asphalt lots toward her car. A million thoughts danced through her head, racing as quickly as her legs. She felt like an idiot for telling her dad she didn't need his help. He'd mentioned some sex traders in connection with Alex Anne, and Lexi wondered if the same man sent Ahmed and Scott after her. It sounded like a tactic that would be squarely in the playbook of a monster.

Her Accord coupe sat apart from other cars almost two hundred yards away. A few men in Terps baseball caps congregated about a hundred feet ahead. They looked up as they saw Lexi sprinting in their direction. "Call the police!" she hollered as she neared them.

"Go on, girl!" one of the men said.

"Oooh, playing hard to get," another offered.

These men weren't going to help her. "You guys are assholes," she yelled as she ran past them.

"Get her, boys!" one of them said to encourage her pursuers. "I think she likes the chase."

Lexi shook her head at the ridiculous attitudes of college men. She was on her own here. Ahmed looked to be in decent shape. Scott carried more weight on his frame. With her track experience, Lexi figured she could outrun them. She just needed to reach her car and get the Glock 19 in her glove compartment. Lexi sucked in a deep breath, blew it out, and envisioned herself running a race in high school. She hit another gear as her arms and legs pumped.

The car sat fifty yards away now. She glanced back over her shoulder. Scott had moved a couple paces ahead of Ahmed. She enjoyed a good lead on both of them. Now, it needed to hold up. She'd lose valuable time opening the car door and the glove box, then bringing her pistol to bear. If the men behind her ran ten miles per hour, she might have about three seconds. Lexi had been to the range a bunch of times. She was a good shot especially from within fifty yards.

She'd never done it under such a crushing deadline, however.

Lexi pulled her key fob from her pocket and unlocked the

car. It would save her a little time. She grunted, and her hamstrings burned as she sprinted the final fifteen yards faster than she ever remembered running. Like her dad, Lexi preferred to back into spots. It made a quick getaway easier. She threw open the passenger's side door, popped the glove compartment, and drew the Glock from its holster in one clean motion like she'd practiced.

Scott stopped about ten yards shy of her, his eyes narrowed on the gun in her grip. Lexi's heart still pounded. Her hands shook holding the weapon as she spread her feet into a proper stance. She wasn't sure she could hit a target at even this short range under the circumstances. Scott held up his knife and showed a wicked smile. "Put the gun down now, girl. If you come quietly, it'll be easier." Ahmed halted and stood a couple yards behind his friend.

"I have a better idea," Lexi said. "You drop the knife, and I won't shoot." She blew out the remaining breath in her lungs.

"You're not going to shoot, anyway." Scott held the blade out toward her and advanced.

Lexi fired once. Twice. Three times. Each shot blasted into Scott's torso. His face took on a confused look as he pitched forward in mid-stride. The knife clattered from his hand as his body hit the asphalt. All the idiots standing nearby turned heel and ran away. The gunshots rang in her ears. Ranges required protection. Here, Lexi had to shoot or be taken. She turned to Ahmed, lining iron sights onto his chest. "You, too. Drop it."

"You shot him!" Ahmed looked between his fallen friend and Lexi. "You really shot him."

"I'll do the same to you, Ahmed." Lexi's pulse still drummed in her ears, though her hands no longer shook. "Put the knife down."

"Lexi, we can talk about this."

"I'm done talking to you," she said. "Drop the knife, or I'll drop you."

Ahmed stood rooted in place. He glanced at Scott's corpse. Lexi remembered meeting Ahmed. The awkward smiles as he introduced himself and asked for help. His hesitancy to make a move, forcing her to go for the kiss. Was it all a ruse? Did he just want to abduct her this whole time? Did it even matter? No, Lexi decided. It didn't matter. He would comply or suffer the consequences. "I need you to come with me," he said.

"Not happening."

"I made a promise to my uncle." Ahmed stepped forward.

Lexi fired twice more.

32

Alex Anne stood in the hangar and cried. She and most of the other girls were in tears. There was nothing left to do. Ropes bound their wrists and ankles, so fighting back and running were impossible. Even if someone managed to try, a bunch of armed men walked around. Two outside made sure no help would arrive. Alex Anne wondered about Mister Tyler. She'd caught a brief glimpse of him where they'd all been held. But a grenade chased him toward the back, and then he never emerged after the explosion.

He was probably dead. Just like Donnell. These kidnappers snuffed any hope the captives had. In some ways, it was even worse than the abductions. What looked like a giant garage door slid up at the front of the building as a plane neared. The chilly evening air spilled in, and Alex Anne wrapped her arms around herself to keep warm. No one offered any of the girls a coat. They were afterthoughts until they flew to their destination.

The blond guy and the boss held a whispered conversation nearby. Alex Anne took slow steps to her rear to try and catch what they talked about. ". . . Might be one more coming," the older man said.

"I thought we were full."

"We are, but there's room on the plane. My nephew's working on it. Part personal favor and partly a way to keep John Tyler off our backs." Alex Anne suppressed a gasp. Was he still alive? In their conversations, he'd mentioned having a daughter. Were the kidnappers going after her now, too?

"He's dead," the blond said. "The hallway blew up on him."

"I'm not counting on it until I see a body," the boss replied. "You didn't deal with him and his unit in Afghanistan, Josef. I did. Unless I see a corpse, I'm going to assume he's still coming for us."

"You said your nephew's working her. You trust him?"

"More or less. He'll bring her if he can."

"Are you prepared to leave without her if everyone else is on board?" the lackey asked.

"Of course," the man in charge said. "Our cargo isn't going to wait for one more American whore. We have a plane full of them."

Alex Anne bit her tongue as the blond took a walkie-talkie off his belt. "I'll check in with the guys outside." The radio crackled to life. "Pazir, do you copy?" He waited, but no response came. "Pazir, do you copy?"

"I told you," the boss said in a weary tone.

"It could be nothing. His radio might be out."

"And John Tyler might have killed him," the older guy said.

"Tabish, come in," Josef barked into his handheld radio. "Do you copy?"

"I'm here," came a moderately-accented reply.

"You see anything out front?"

"Just the plane, but you should be able to see it, too." The hangar was long but narrow, so the pilot backed the small aircraft inside.

"You seen anyone who shouldn't be there?" Josef asked.

Over the sound of the quieting engine, Alex Anne heard a loud bang. Was it a gunshot? She dropped to a crouch as several of the girls screamed. One of the men yelled at them to stay calm. The long door began its descent. Alex Anne wondered about the noise. Was someone here to save her? Before the door slid shut completely, Mister Tyler slipped inside and hugged the wall behind a forklift. He'd found them again.

For the first time in days, Alex Anne allowed herself to be hopeful.

RICH FERGUSON RETURNED his holstered gun to his desk drawer. He slung his jacket over the back of his chair and spiked his keys onto the desktop. Nothing. He'd run into challenging investigations before, but the police always found a lead. They always had an angle. Here, nothing presented itself. If John Tyler didn't hand them the name of Farzaad Durrani, they probably wouldn't have found it on their own. Rich sank into his chair and sighed.

Worse, Tyler succeeded in finding the traffickers. Rich felt glad someone did—he wanted the girls rescued regardless of who got the credit for it. Part of him wanted it to be an actual law enforcement agency, however. Worst of all, Captain Sharpe farmed the operation out to Anne Arundel County. BWI lay in their jurisdiction, and the BPD would only serve in a backup capacity. He thought about calling Norton or Hess and quickly changed his mind. Going around Sharpe— even if Rich wasn't one of his direct reports—would only damage his career. The best thing to do was be ready if needed.

Rich's cell phone rang. He didn't recognize the number, which proved common in his job, and he picked it up while still in an unpleasant mood. "Ferguson," he barked.

"Lieutenant," a woman's voice said, "I'm hoping you can help me. I just talked to Leon Sharpe, and he directed me to you."

Of course he did, Rich thought. "How can I help you, Miss . . .?"

"Morrison. Sara Morrison. I work for the US Department of Defense."

"I'm not sure what I can do for you, then."

"You're familiar with a man named John Tyler, I presume?" Rich frowned and didn't answer. "I'll presume your silence means yes. Apparently, he texted two people from wherever he is—Leon Sharpe and me. The message I got didn't come with a lot of details, however, and I was hoping you could supply them."

"Your friend's a loose cannon," Rich said.

"You're probably right," Sara Morrison said. "I tend to call him a knight-errant, but then again, I love him, and it sounds like you think he's a pain in the ass."

"He is."

"There are times I won't argue the point with you, Lieutenant. This isn't one of them, though. I feel a little responsible because I gave Tyler some information he might have used to find a group abducting young women to sell abroad."

"Miss Morrison, I don't think—"

"You can tell me yourself," she said, "or Captain Sharpe can order you to. You didn't sound like you were in a good mood when you answered the phone. I'm giving you a chance to not make it worse."

Rich sighed. If she'd talked to Sharpe first, he would have

given her Rich's desk number. "How did you get my cell number, anyway?"

"I work for the Pentagon. I can get anyone's phone number."

During his time in active duty, Rich didn't harbor much affection for Pentagon civilians. Talking to Sara Morrison, he saw no reason to revise his opinion. Still, he didn't need Sharpe browbeating him into compliance. "Fine. They're at BWI . . . the chartered area. Sharpe didn't tell me which hangar, but local cops are en route, so I'll presume it's the one with the commotion outside."

"Thank you, Lieutenant," Sara Morrison said. "I hope your night gets better." She hung up.

Rich set his phone down. Durrani and his men going down—no matter who made it happen—would help.

TYLER DIDN'T WANT to shoot the guard along the side of the building. The jet engine grew quieter, so the shot would stand out more. It cost him the element of surprise. He was going to lose it at some point soon, anyway, but he wanted to drop at least one more guy before it happened.

No matter. He'd done work like this before. With his Special Operations unit in Afghanistan, Tyler breached many multi-purpose Taliban compounds. Guns. Vehicles. Drugs. Many of them were larger and defended by more men than this hangar. He liked his odds, but he wanted to size up the situation.

The plane stopped near the rear wall. All the girls were inside, and Tyler spotted Alex Anne right away. He also saw Durrani, who ducked behind any available cover along with his men. The cowards left the young women out in the open. They possessed enough sense to drop down low. Tyler wondered how many would become human shields. He couldn't let it escalate so far.

The interior was more long than wide, and the square footage was ample. Apart from a stack of tires and some mechanical equipment, the hangar consisted of mostly bare floor and walls, with catwalks down the left and right sides, and a forklift resting under the raised platforms against each wall. An office sat in the back left corner. Metal support beams ran across the domed ceiling, along with the rails and mechanisms to open and close the large door, which was currently down.

Nowhere for anyone to go.

One of Durrani's men fired from behind the wall of rubber. The rounds all hit the industrial equipment Tyler stood behind. If they were clever, they could catch him in a crossfire. It would be difficult to defend against shooters behind the tires and the other forklift. Instead, another man fired randomly in Tyler's direction. He wasn't a threat. Tyler focused on the one behind cover as shouts went up among Durrani and his lackeys.

Using the AK-74 he took from the first guard he killed, Tyler pumped a burst of bullets into the top tire. It popped, and a bunch of black shrapnel sprayed backward. The guy behind the stack stepped out, and Tyler put three rounds into his chest. The others were spread out and smart enough not to hide behind something so easily removed. Occasional bursts of gunfire came in Tyler's direction. He'd chosen this spot for the protection it offered, but if he wanted to get the girls out of here, he needed to move.

It would be a long sprint to the other forklift. The hangar could hold a football field, and even with some suppressing fire before he moved, Tyler didn't think he'd make it all the way over there. The center of the room remained clear so planes could move in and out. If he wanted to get closer, he'd need to do it along this wall. Tyler looked through the front windshield of the forklift. Cases of aircraft parts sat in a large pile on the floor just beyond it. It wouldn't offer as much cover as his current spot, but he'd be closer to the action.

Tyler edged out along the industrial vehicle. He set the AK on full auto and laid down a hail of bullets as he stepped out. No one returned fire as he dashed behind the boxes. Rounds thunked into the metallic parts, but the makeshift structure held. Tyler peeked out to see where everyone stood. Durrani and a tall blond man held an animated conversation. If the guy behind the building told him the truth, there should be two more men somewhere. Tyler spotted one camped behind the forklift on the other side. The last one remained hidden.

More bullets slammed into Tyler's cover. They came from directly ahead. He glanced over the boxes and spied a man hoofing it back into the office. A logical place to hide. Tyler pressed his back against the wall. The man on the opposite side wouldn't have an angle to shoot him. He readied the AK and peered over the boxes. No movement. He waited, checking to make sure the threats didn't change. A gun barrel poked out from the office door. A head followed it a second later. Tyler adjusted his aim a little and fired, bursting his opponent's skull with two shots.

An engine started, and Tyler thought it was the plane at first. Maybe the pilot realized he wasn't being paid enough to deal with a shootout on top of flying trafficked girls to parts unknown. The forklift surged forward, and the lackey driving it was smart enough to raise the grabber. Tyler didn't have a good shot. Durrani and the blond still talked, though they pointed between the remaining girls and the plane they stood behind. Was the guy in the Bobcat keeping Tyler busy while everyone else herded the young women onboard for a quick getaway?

Tyler backed up a few steps. Operating the vehicle and the lift took two hands, so the driver couldn't shoot at him. Shots from the proper angle would make it past the raised metal arms and blast through the windshield. Tyler thumbed the AK into burst mode and moved to his right toward the center of the floor plan. The driver followed suit. Tyler took a step to the left, lined up the head as best he could, and fired a trio of three-round bursts. A couple ricocheted off metal, but most found the mark, shattering the glass. The driver jumped down. He'd avoided all the bullets, but he sustained a bunch of cuts when the windshield imploded. Before he could ready his gun, Tyler drilled him in the chest.

Tyler moved behind the vehicle in case anyone else brought a weapon to bear. All quiet. He could hear Durrani barking an order in a foreign language. Not Pashto. The man clearly didn't want Tyler to know what instructions he gave. Choices were few, however, and most of the men Durrani brought with him lay dead in or around the building.

Tyler edged out from behind cover. Most of the girls were already on the plane. This was his only real chance to rescue them.

33

Durrani watched as Shahu stuck his head out of the office only to get it shot apart. He wouldn't lose another operation and all its profits to John Tyler. The man cost him too much already. "We need to finish," he said to Josef in the latter's native language.

"What about him?"

"He won't shoot over here." Jabroot climbed into the forklift and drove it toward Tyler. Durrani hoped it would work even though he figured he'd only be adding another corpse to his ledger. He hollered into the plane for the pilot to help. "I'm paying you well enough, dammit. Get them on. We'll buckle them in later."

The Bobcat moved toward Tyler. Durrani didn't like doing work he paid others to do, but he didn't have time to be particular. He grabbed a random girl, hauled her to her feet, and ordered her onto the plane. She took halting steps into the cabin. Another followed her. Once a few more climbed on, Durrani picked up Alex Anne by the shoulders. "Time to begin your new life, my dear."

"Mister Tyler will stop you," she said. She tried to plant

her feet and resist, but Durrani got her moving, and Josef made sure she stayed in motion.

"He'll be dead before we take off." Bullets blew the fork-lift's windshield apart. Jabroot stepped down, shaking glass from himself as gashes already dotted his body. Durrani knew how it would play out. Before his man could bring his weapon to bear, Tyler cut him down. "Hurry," he ordered as he shoved another girl toward the plane. Tyler stayed behind the Bobcat. They finished loading all their captives. Durrani shut the door. Tyler moved next to the industrial vehicle.

"Am I taking off?" the pilot asked.

"Yes! Yes. Run him over if you need to." The plane taxied forward. Tyler stepped out of the way, the AK held in front of his face. If he found a good angle for a shot, they could quickly be without a pilot, and then they'd be in real trouble.

'Swing closer to him," Josef ordered.

Durrani frowned. "What are you doing?"

"Making sure you get to your destination with all the cargo. I'll take care of Tyler." He strode to the door and looked out the window. One hand closed on the handle, and the other held his Glock. "I'll meet up with you when I can. You don't need me for the flight."

It was true enough. The girls were bound at the wrists and ankles. If he experienced any trouble, the pilot could help once the plane was at altitude and flew itself. Plenty of men would be waiting for them when they landed. "Good luck." Durrani clapped Josef on the back. "This man has been a thorn in my side for over a decade. I only wish I could stick around to watch you kill him."

"I'll send you a picture of his corpse," Josef said. He twisted the handle and jerked the door open. Before he jumped down, he fired a shot.

～

Lexi sat on the hood of her Accord and stared at its blue metallic paint. She focused on her breathing. Inhale. Exhale. She'd fired plenty of shots before but only at paper or wooden targets. The closest she came to taking aim at a person would be the vaguely human-shaped outlines on targets some of the ranges used. A few moments ago, she'd pumped rounds into Scott and then Ahmed. When the idiots nearby scattered, Lexi realized she was alone, so she called 9-1-1 herself.

Three campus police cars rolled up with lights flashing. Red and blue reflected off Lexi's windows. Two plainclothes officers got out first, hands on their weapons. A pair of detectives joined them next. Lexi remained in place. She left her gun on the asphalt near the left front tire. The first plainclothes officer, a slender black man, looked down at the weapon as he approached. Another siren howled closer as an ambulance entered the lot. It wouldn't be in time for Scott or Ahmed.

"I'm Sergeant Means," he said. He kept his tone soft. Non-provocative. "My partner is Detective Akin. What's your name?"

"Lexi . . . Alexis Tyler."

"You a student here, Miss Tyler?"

"Yes," she said. This marked Lexi's first real encounter with the police. She'd never been in trouble with the law before—including not getting any speeding tickets despite her lead foot. During his time in private security, her dad dealt with the cops several times. He'd never officially offered her advice on it, but she remembered his editorials bleeding into the storytelling. *Only answer the question they ask. The cops are trying to solve a crime, not be your friend. The less you say, the better.* It all sounded prescient in her current situation.

"This your gun?" Means asked. Akin, a shorter, stockier,

and younger white man, stood nearby and crossed his beefy arms. Lexi nodded. "You fire it?" She nodded again. "Want to tell me what happened?"

"Those two chased me." She jerked her head toward the two corpses. "They have knives. I'm not sure what they wanted. I ran out here, got to my car, and grabbed my gun."

"It's registered?" Akin said.

"Yes."

"You know guns aren't allowed in campus buildings."

"It was in my glove box," Lexi said, fighting the urge to roll her eyes.

"We'd rather you not have one here at all," Means added.

"Your policies should come out and say it, then. I have a concealed carry permit. It's all in my purse."

"You're a young college student, and you have a concealed carry permit?"

Lexi shrugged. "It's all in order."

Means slipped on a pair of gloves and picked up her Glock. He dropped it into an evidence bag, sealed it, and handed it to one of the officers. The two held a brief conversation with Means doing most of the talking and all of the pointing and gesturing. "Akin, check the handbag." He looked at Lexi. "Do we have permission to search your car?"

She didn't think they needed to ask in the circumstances. "You have permission to open the car and get my purse," she said.

Akin's face looked like he'd been sucking a lemon for an hour, but he opened the passenger door and retrieved the bag from the floor. He found Lexi's wallet and flipped through it. "She's got the C-C. We'll have to check the gun in the database."

"You know these two?" Means asked, the sweep of his hand taking in the bodies of Ahmed and Scott.

"Just the one. Ahmed. I only met his friend today. It

looked like they were arguing a while ago, so I was surprised to see him join us."

Means took out a small notebook and clicked the end of his ballpoint pen. "You and Ahmed dating?"

"I wouldn't call it that," Lexi said. "We went out once, I guess."

"You liked him?" Akin asked.

"Sure . . . until he and his friend chased me at knifepoint."

A few uniformed cops walked toward them herding the guys who ran off. If nothing else, they could corroborate the fact Scott and Ahmed chased her. "Looks like we have some witness statements to gather," Means said. "We'll also check security cameras and see if anything turned up. You mind hanging around, Miss Tyler?"

"Do I have a choice?"

Means shook his head. "No."

TYLER DIDN'T HAVE a good shot at the pilot. He moved to the side of the plane when the door suddenly opened, and a gun barrel preceded a blond man just inside the opening. The pistol fired, and a round slammed into Tyler's midsection. His vest soaked up the worst of it, but the force still blasted the breath from his lungs, and it probably snapped a rib or two in the process. Tyler stumbled back a step and landed on his butt. The blond man jumped down to the floor.

He didn't have time to line it up, but Tyler took a shot with the AK. He got lucky and hit the man's right hand, knocking the pistol from his grip. Before he could get off a more accurate shot, however, the guy was on top of him, swatting the Kalashnikov from his grip. Tyler rolled away from a kick and winced as his ribs protested. He looked at where he shot his opponent. Part of a finger was gone. It probably hurt like hell, but he could still use the hand in combat.

Tyler got to his feet. "You must be Josef," he said. The twin-engine jet stopped behind them. Was Durrani waiting for his main lackey to finish the fight?

"Durrani is tired of you," he answered in a voice carrying an eastern European accent. "Has been for years. I've only been sick of you a couple days." He drew a serrated knife from his belt and held it in his left hand. Tyler unsheathed his, a conventional blade. He didn't care for knife fights, but Josef was a soldier turned mercenary. He'd been trained. He would be more predictable.

Josef feinted a slash, but Tyler recognized the lack of a weight shift and didn't fall for it. He wanted to end the fight quickly, both to rescue the girls and because of his throbbing ribs. This time, the Serb came forward. Tyler moved to the side and countered with a short cut which found the mark along his foe's hip. Josef grunted in pain and turned to face Tyler. Fury twisted his slender face into a deep scowl.

The mercenary reversed his grip and made a few quick slashes at Tyler's face. He was able to avoid them all, but the speed of the attacks kept him on the defensive. He felt himself breathing hard, too. Rib injuries were awful. He needed to end this. Josef spun quickly. Tyler ducked under the cruel cut and rolled away, but he was slow to get back to his feet. Josef capitalized with a cut along his left side under the vest. Tyler covered the wound with his arm and backed away a step.

The engine revved higher, and the plane started forward. Josef didn't even turn. "Your boss is leaving you," Tyler said.

"All part of the plan," Josef said. "I know where to meet up with him when you're dead."

"Get on with it, then." Josef liked to attack high with long swipes. He stood a few inches taller than Tyler, so he was basically slashing at shoulder height. It was hard to play defense in a knife fight, however, and Tyler thought he'd found an opening. Sure enough, Josef drew his arm back for another cut. Tyler ducked as his adversary brought the blade forward, thrusting out and burying his knife in Josef's solar plexus. Blood burbled out of the mercenary's mouth. His weapon fell from his hand and clattered on the concrete. Tyler pulled his blade out and Josef sagged to the floor.

The plane reached the end of the hangar. It still moved slowly and needed to make a left turn to get to the runway. Tyler picked up his fallen AK-74, sighted an engine, and fired. He hit his target, but the plane kept going and began its turn. He couldn't let it take off. Alex Anne and every other young woman on board would be gone forever if it did. Tyler lined up another shot but no longer had one as the plane angled toward the runway. The pitch of the engines changed as it accelerated. Once it straightened out on the tarmac, it would gain speed quickly.

Tyler sprinted after it as quickly as his injured ribs would allow.

34

Tyler had never been blessed with a great deal of foot speed. He did well at distance running, but short sprints were not in his wheelhouse even with uninjured ribs. Today, he felt slower than normal as he dashed after the jet. He ran outside the hangar. The aircraft was finishing its turn onto the runway. Tyler took aim at the same engine he hit a few seconds ago as the plane straightened out.

He exhaled and fired.

Again, the bullet didn't have any visible effect. Maybe they weren't powerful enough. Perhaps the speed of the turbines made the engine a poor target. Tyler took another shot and stared glumly as it also did nothing. Three shots, three hits, zero results. These weren't the ratios he was used to.

The jet gained speed. If Tyler couldn't figure out how to stop it, it would take off, and Alex Anne and every girl onboard would be gone. He'd texted Sara in the hopes she and her people at the Pentagon could do something if he failed. Foreign intelligence operations might be able to track the jet in the air. If nothing else, they should be able to find Durrani no matter where he landed.

But would they be in time?

Tyler feared the answer. He needed to change tactics. Shooting an engine did nothing. He ran a few yards down the tarmac and moved to the side. The jet grew louder. It would be airborne in a few seconds. Tyler dropped to one knee, flipped the AK to burst mode, and peered through the sights. This would be his last attempt to stop the plane. It was something of a desperate gambit, but the little he knew of aircraft made him think it would work.

Over the growing roar, Tyler blew out all his breath and sighted ahead of the front tire. He gauged the plane's speed, moved the barrel a bit, and fired. Three bullets ripped the tire to pieces. The plane lurched as the rubber fell away. Sparks went up a second later, and the landing gear snapped in half. The jet fell onto its nose and skidded down the tarmac. Tyler ran after it. It slid toward the grass as the pilot tried to stop it. He did a good job controlling the skid, and the aircraft came to a stop along the right side of the runway.

Breathing hard from the pain in his ribs, Tyler approached. He tossed the spent AK-74 to the ground and drew his trusty M11. Nothing happened. Tyler stopped about twenty yards from the plane, keeping the door in his sights. He waited. Patience was indeed a virtue, and it had saved his life several times during his active duty days. Maybe it would save Alex Anne today. Durrani's entire operation rode on getting a nice payday for the famous singer.

He couldn't kill her, but he might use her as a bargaining chip.

The door opened a few seconds later. A pair of slender bound arms appeared in the opening. Alex Anne walked awkwardly down the steps as Durrani pushed her to the fore at gunpoint. Her ankles were tied together, also. The Afghan used his precious quarry as a human shield. He wasn't very tall, so Alex Anne completely blocked any shot Tyler could take.

~

MEANS AND AKIN drove Lexi to the nearest campus police station. They made sure to tell her she wasn't under arrest each time she asked. It was to better coordinate the intelligence they'd been able to gather about the incident, or so they claimed. It sounded like bullshit, but she went along. They tried to slip in a few not-so-casual questions in the car, but she ignored them. At the station, they parked her in an interview room.

She waited. Her dad preached the value of patience. If the cops conducted a competent investigation, they would know Ahmed and Scott chased her. They would talk to the guys who whooped and hollered as she ran and then scattered when the shooting started. If they couldn't manage it, she would lawyer up.

They kept her isolated a while. There was no clock on the wall, and Lexi's phone remained with the desk officer in an envelope. She didn't know how much time passed. Eventually, Means and Akin opened the door, pulled out their cheap chairs, and sat opposite her. "The registration for your gun checks out," Means said.

"Same with your concealed carry," Akin added. "I still don't know how you managed to get one, but it's legit."

Lexi didn't say anything. She knew all the paperwork would come back good. They were probably fishing for something, and she wasn't going to oblige them. Means opened a file folder, tilted it upward so she couldn't see the contents, and whispered something to his partner. She didn't take the bait. "You seem very calm, Miss Tyler," Means said, breaking the silence.

"If I don't say anything," Lexi said, "you tell me I'm calm as if there's something wrong with it. If I sat here and ran my mouth, you'd say I was nervous and try to use whatever I told you against me." She shrugged. "This seems like the lesser of two evils."

"You don't think we're on your side?"

"I think you're on the side of whoever signs your chief's paycheck."

Neither man uttered a word for a few seconds. Then, Akin said, "We recovered a bunch of security footage. Got cameras all over the campus now. It looks like they first confronted you in the computer science building. We saw you running out of a stairwell and them following a few seconds behind."

Lexi nodded. "I was in the mainframe lab doing an assignment. Ahmed came down. His friend joined us a few minutes later. I didn't like him. I'm not sure whose idea it was to try and kidnap me, but they were both in on it."

"It seems like it was Ahmed's," Means said. "We looked at his phone. He reached out to . . ." he glanced at a paper. " . . . Scott Barton with the idea. Offered him five thousand to help."

"Wow." Lexi let out a mirthless chuckle. "I hoped I'd be worth more."

"You were. Ahmed was getting twenty grand from his uncle, a man we've been able to identify . . . with some help . . . as Farzaad Durrani." Lexi remembered hearing her dad mention the name, and she felt herself frown. Durrani was an old drug trafficker from Afghanistan who moved on to girls. What did he want with her, and why involve his nephew?

"I see you recognize the name," Akin said.

Lexi nodded, silently cursing her reaction. She didn't offer any information about where she'd learned of Durrani.

"Want to tell us where you heard it?" Means asked.

"No."

"No?"

"It's not relevant," Lexi said. "You told me this Durrani would pay Ahmed twenty thousand for me. I think that's more important."

"He wanted you alive," Means said, "though he didn't care if Ahmed . . . well, you know."

"I can figure it out." Lexi crossed her arms. Did Ahmed only introduce himself to her to weasel his way into her life at his uncle's behest? The whole situation made her feel sick. Lexi frowned at the sour taste in her mouth.

Means closed the manila folder. "In light of everything we've found, the chief says we're not going to charge you with anything tonight."

"Tonight?"

"Investigations are fluid."

"I'm sure they are." Lexi stood. "Can I go?"

"We're not going to keep you," Means said. "You want a ride back to your car?"

Lexi shook her head. "I'll walk. The fresh air will do me some good." She left the room, collected her things from the desk officer, and exited the station. If her knowledge of the College Park campus were correct, she had about a mile to cover before making it back to her car. The chilly night air felt good after being in the room. Lexi couldn't shake the images of Scott and Ahmed as they advanced on her. She'd liked Ahmed, and it turned out he only acted like he was interested in her for his uncle.

The sour taste returned. Lexi sprinted into the trees just off the sidewalk, bent at the waist, and vomited all over the ground.

35

Durrani kept the muzzle of his gun against Alex Anne's temple. His other hand held her in a loose headlock. Tyler kept his own pistol trained on the pair. He didn't have a shot at the moment, but the instant he did, he would take it. "Put your gun down," Durrani said.

"Not happening."

"I'll kill this whore."

"Pretty dumb claim," Tyler said. "She's worth more than everyone else on the plane combined. If you wanted a real standoff, you should've grabbed someone else. You're not stupid enough to shoot your meal ticket."

"Let me take her, then. You can have the rest."

"I think you know my answer."

Durrani scowled. He kept his weapon pointed at Alex Anne's head. "I hate you, John Tyler."

"Good for you. I barely remember you at all. You were just another asshole who handed opium profits to the Taliban. You weren't special then, and you're not now." Tyler meant every word, but he also hoped his taunts would get Durrani to turn the gun toward him.

"I'm not taking your bait," Durrani said. "I'm too smart for you."

Tyler ignored the comment and focused on Alex Anne. Tears ran down her face. He stared at her until she turned her eyes to him. He wagged his left elbow, recalling their conversation about dealing with the idiot who hopped the barrier at her mall appearance. It seemed like ages ago, but it had only been a few days. She frowned as if she didn't understand, so he made the gesture again. "What are you doing?" Durrani demanded.

"My arm hurts," Tyler said. "I guess I elbowed your blond lackey a few too many times before I gutted him. He thought he was a tough guy, but he turned out to be fake."

Alex Anne's eyes widened. It was hard to tell in the evening light, but Tyler swore the left corner of her mouth turned up. Durrani's arm drifted over her chin. She locked eyes with Tyler and offered a tiny bob of her head.

Then, she bit her captor's forearm.

Durrani howled in pain. His arm slipped from around her, and Alex Anne drove an elbow into his chest. She ducked and scampered away as Durrani stumbled back a step. Tyler capitalized on the opening, pumping five rounds into him. The old trafficker landed on the tarmac with an inglorious thud. Tyler walked to the crumpled form, kicked the gun away from him, and checked for a pulse. He was dead.

"I knew you'd come," Alex Anne said as fresh tears ran from her eyes. She started toward Tyler.

He held up his hand. "Stay here. Get behind the plane. Is there only one pilot?"

"Yes." Alex Anne headed for the tail section. "He's armed."

Tyler nodded and climbed the stairs. He stopped on the top step, ducked into a crouch, and moved into the cabin. A tall, lanky man with a thin mustache and sandy blond hair trained a pistol on a cabin full of scared girls. They stared in silence as Tyler stood and kept his sights on the other man. "Flight's grounded," he said. "Put it down."

The pilot looked between the young women and Tyler. "I wanna walk out of here."

"Should've thought about it before you agreed to fly a plane load of scared girls halfway across the world." The pilot said nothing. "How much did Durrani pay you?"

"Fifty grand," he said and lowered the gun.

A voice from one of the far seats spoke up. "Sir, he bragged he could do whatever he wanted with us."

"H-He already started," a girl in the front row stammered through sobs, and Tyler wondered what the coward had done while alone in the cabin.

"You're disgusting," Tyler said.

"I'm dropping my gun." He did, and it drummed off the carpeted floor. "You going to let me leave?"

Tyler took a couple steps forward to improve his field of fire. "Fifty grand, huh?"

"Yeah," the cornered man said. "I'll split it with you if you let me go."

Tyler emptied the magazine into the other's torso.

The girls gasped as the pilot slumped over dead, and a few of them cried. Tyler holstered his spent gun. "Hello, ladies. I'm sorry for what you've been through. How about we get off the plane?" He took out his knife and cut the closest captive free even though she tried to squirm away as he did. Considering what all these girls had been through, he could hardly blame her. Tyler handed her the knife. "Cut each other free . . . then come down." He heard sirens approaching. Finally. "If any of you need medical help, I think it's on the way."

Tyler descended the steps. His primary knife remained

on the plane, but he used a pocket model to cut Alex Anne's ropes. She wrapped him in a tight hug. "You have no idea how grateful I am," she said, her voice cracking.

"I'm glad you're all right," Tyler said. He sat on the runway, and Alex Anne dropped down beside him. A phalanx of emergency vehicles sped closer.

A DOZEN COPS approached with their pistols drawn. Tyler provided them an extremely condensed version of what happened and stressed the girls needed medical attention. Four paramedics came forward. Two stopped to tend to Alex Anne, and the other pair boarded the plane. One of them, a stocky blonde woman, popped her head back out a moment later. "Got one in here, too. Probably the pilot."

Once Alex Anne checked out all right, the paramedics turned their attentions to Tyler while the police worked the scene. A few plainclothes officers appeared. The SWAT van rolled up a few minutes after the initial crush of vehicles, but they'd stayed out of the action once it became clear the county didn't need to provide an armed response. Their armored vehicle drove away as one of the EMTs checked out the cut on Tyler's side. "Ever had stitches before?" he asked as he cleaned the slash wound.

"Quite a few times," Tyler said.

"You all right otherwise? You look a little pale."

"Vest caught a round. Probably a cracked rib or two."

The wiry paramedic shrugged. "Not much you can do for those except rest."

"It'd be nice," Tyler said. Maybe he could open the shop in peace now. If Anne Arundel County's finest didn't throw him in jail first, of course. Tyler winced as the needle pierced his skin. A few minutes later, his side was stitched up. It would be another scar he wouldn't want to talk about. As the paramedics moved toward the plane, two waiting cops approached. They were a tall, beefy Latino man and a short Asian guy of average build. Their blue suits almost matched.

"I'm Sergeant Ramirez," the larger man said. "My partner is Detective Wong. Who are you?"

"John Tyler."

"Normally, when I hear about a problem at the airport, it's a drunk passenger hassling the flight crew. Tonight, there's a broken plane on the side of the runway, and eight men are dead. What the hell happened?"

"Would you believe me if I told you they all shot themselves?" Tyler asked.

Ramirez gestured in the direction of Durrani's corpse. "I've never seen a guy plug himself five times in the chest. Try again."

"I happened to arrive and see what looked like an international trafficking operation trying to get a bunch of young women out of the country. I took swift and decisive action."

"Why didn't you call the police?" Wong said.

"Note how long it took you to get here." Tyler held up a hand when it looked like Wong wanted to rebut. "I know. You had to get the SWAT team together. Send a bunch of people. It takes time to coordinate the response." He jabbed his finger toward the jet. "The broken plane you mentioned was a couple seconds from taking off with a dozen and a half kidnapped girls on board. Does the county have a jet to chase it down?"

Ramirez crossed his burly arms. "And you just happened to be driving by the charter area of BWI?"

"I work for one of the girls," Tyler said. "Her father hired me to join her security detail."

"She got kidnapped anyway?"

"Unfortunately, yes."

"Sounds like you're not very good at your job," Ramirez said.

Tyler swept his hand around the scene, covering the hangar, runway, and plane. "I'll let the evidence speak for me, Sergeant."

"The evidence says you should've called us." Tyler remained silent. He'd addressed the point when Wong made it, and answering it a second time seemed non-productive. "You look ex-military," Ramirez continued. "Am I right?"

"Army. Retired about nine years now."

"Trying to relive your glory days?" Wong asked.

"Definitely not," Tyler said.

"Could've fooled me."

Tyler didn't respond with the obvious barb, and Ramirez filled in the conversational gap. "I got eight men dead here."

"And eighteen missing girls saved." Tyler shrugged. "The math is pretty simple."

"Eight men dead. You rolled up and did it. No judge. No trial. No jury. Those were human beings."

"Biologically, I'm sure you're right," Tyler said.

"How many people you killed?" Ramirez asked.

"Eight, according to you."

"No, no." Ramirez's face turned red. If he were an older man, Tyler might have been concerned for his blood pressure. "You did a spell in the army. I'm sure you saw your share of combat. How many?"

"I didn't keep track," Tyler said. "Snipers like to know their kill count, but I think it's ghoulish."

"Who'd you kill?"

"The Taliban, mostly. Other insurgents and terrorists. People who propped up their networks. They all deserved it."

"You ever kill anyone who didn't deserve it?" Tyler didn't

say anything, and Ramirez pounced on the silence. "You did, didn't you?"

He recalled the family of four he'd gunned down under illegitimate orders and a falsified intelligence report. Even the court martial of his former commander couldn't erase the memory or make it any less unpleasant. "It's a long story, Sergeant. It has a lot to do with why I retired."

Both officers frowned and fell silent like they didn't expect the answer. They probably thought Tyler to be an adrenaline junkie who couldn't let his past time in the service go. He knew those types. Over the years, he served with some and even met a few in therapy at the VA. Wong pointed around at the various scenes of carnage. "Like my partner pointed out, eight men are dead. You regret any of those?"

"You're very black-and-white, Detective," Tyler said. "I'm sure it's useful . . . at least in basic police work. Someone is either speeding or not. The man threw a brick through the window, or he didn't. Where it's not useful is in the gray you can't see. A lot of the world lives there."

"This isn't about shades of gray," Ramirez said. "I want to know what happened. Specifics this time. Run me through it from when you arrived."

"I drove my daughter's Tesla." Tyler inclined his head toward the area where the vehicle's battery died. "It's dead out there. There was one guy behind the hangar and another in front. I took them out, slipped inside, and dealt with four more. The plane taxied out to the runway. I only had my pistol plus an AK I took from the first asshole. Shooting the lead tire seemed like the best bet. I hit it, and the landing gear collapsed. Once the plane stopped, I took out the ringleader and the pilot."

"All these men were armed?" Wong wanted to know.

"They were," Tyler said.

"I still think you should've called the police."

"We've been over this, Detective. If I called, and you rolled up when you did, we would've watched the jet disappear from view . . . maybe never to be seen again."

Ramirez was about to add something when his phone buzzed. He looked at the screen, frowned, and walked away to answer the call. Wong leaned in once his partner was out of earshot. "I know he plays it close to the vest. Probably why he's a sergeant, and I'm not. I think you did good work here tonight. If it were my call, you'd be getting a medal."

"I have enough medals," Tyler said. "You want to do something for me, let me go home."

"Not up to me."

"You charging me with anything?"

"Ramirez might want to charge you with being a prick," Wong said.

Tyler shrugged. "Been guilty of it most of my life, Detective. I'm glad it's not illegal."

Ramirez, his back to Tyler and Wong, pulled his cell away from his ear. He held it in a tight fist for a few seconds, and Tyler wondered if he would spike it off the runway. He wore a scowl and pursed lips as he approached. "I just got off the phone with my boss's boss—who's the deputy chief of police, I might add. Apparently, he talked to a Captain Sharpe in Baltimore." Ramirez turned toward Wong. "It seems Mister Tyler here is a consultant on a trafficking task force, and he's authorized to act if he sees something going down." His expression soured even more as he talked. "Turns out we're supposed to thank Mister Tyler for his heroic actions and let him go."

"What the hell?" Wong said, dropping the pretense of being on Tyler's side.

Another car rolled up. This one was a classic dark federal SUV. A man about Tyler's age stepped out and approached. "Good evening, gentlemen. I presume my client is free to go?"

"Your client?" Ramirez asked.

"Kevin Lowery. I'm representing John Tyler. I'm sure the county doesn't want the bad publicity of detaining a hero."

"Look here, Mister Lowery—"

"It's Major," he said, flashing an ID. "I might be in my civvies at this late hour, but I work for the Judge Advocate General on Fort Meade."

Ramirez and Wong conferred for a few seconds before the sergeant said, "Fine. He's free to go."

"Have a good night, guys." Tyler stood, ignoring the ache in his ribs.

Ramirez stopped him with a hand to the chest. "One more thing. I don't know what strings you pulled, but I know bullshit when I smell it."

"The army and the police are similar in one significant way," Tyler said. "A lot of following orders."

"The next time you're at our county's airport," Ramirez said, "I hope you're here to catch a flight."

Tyler offered a single nod. "Me, too, Sergeant. You'll forgive me for not flying charter, I hope." He walked back toward the SUV with Lowery. "I'm going to guess you got a phone call recently."

He nodded. "When Sara Morrison calls, I answer. Seems like you didn't really need me tonight." He handed Tyler an unadorned business card. "Keep me in mind if these guys hassle you again."

"I will," Tyler said. "Thanks for coming."

"You want a lift?"

"No." Tyler looked at Alex Anne. "I still need to make sure the young lady over there gets home safely. We'll find a way out of here."

"All right." Lowery climbed back into the Yukon, fired it up, and drove away. Tyler walked back toward the plane. Ramirez and Wong glared at him the whole way.

36

Lexi made it back to her car. She opened the door, sat down, and grabbed a water bottle from the passenger's side door. Her hands shook twisting off the cap off, and it took her a few attempts to get it. She tried deep breaths to calm herself, but the adrenaline needed to work its way through her body. It felt like coming down after a long run at a cross-country meet. Lexi managed not to spill any water as she drank.

She fired up the Accord and stalled it on her first attempt to leave the lot. "Get it together, Lexi," she chided herself. She got the gas and clutch working in sync the second time, and she soon left campus and zoomed down Route 1. Despite cold temperatures, Lexi lowered the windows. The air buffeting her as she drove felt good in an oddly therapeutic way. She put them up some as she merged onto the highway and picked up speed.

Even through narrowed openings, the wind noise thudded into the cabin. Lexi turned up the radio to compensate. When no station played a song she liked, she flipped to Bluetooth connectivity, and the latest Alex Anne album blared through the speakers. She smiled at the song before worry overtook her. Was her dad OK? He'd mentioned wrapping things up. Lexi always worried about him, but he was on his own this time. His friend Rollins wasn't around to help. She needed to check in with her father.

Flouting Maryland mobile device laws, Lexi sent a text while driving up I-95. *Haven't heard from you in a while. Hope you're OK. Let me know. Love you.* She pushed harder on the gas, and the Accord's V6 urged the coupe north of 100 miles per hour. This enabled a pretty short drive home. Lexi left her car in the driveway and walked into the house. Her phone buzzed with a reply from her dad. *All good. Alex Anne is safe. Talk soon. Love you too.*

In the dining room, Lexi stared at her dad's liquor cabinet. He wasn't a big drinker, but he kept a decent stash on hand. The events of the evening replayed in her mind. Lexi enjoyed beer, and her dad didn't mind her drinking a couple here and there despite her being underage. Dipping into the hard stuff might be pushing it. Even if he didn't care, she'd never tried whiskey before, and getting her first taste when trying to drive down the memory of shooting two people seemed like a poor idea.

Lexi opened the fridge, popped the top on a longneck, and enjoyed a healthy pull. She replied to her dad. *Long night for me, too. I'm sure I'll be up when you get back.* In reality, she wanted to talk to him. Of all the people who could understand what she went through, her dad would top the list. Last year, he shared his story about killing an Afghan family while under illegal orders. Lexi knew her situation was different, but she wished she hadn't needed to pull the trigger.

A response came. *Things went pear-shaped for a while here, but we're good. Leaving soon. Glad to chat when I get home.* Lexi smiled. It took a little while for her and her dad to warm up to each other when she first came to live with him. He'd been deployed a lot when she was younger, and her mother took every opportunity to demonize him for it. In the intervening years, her opinions of both parents did a one-eighty. Lexi had barely spoken to the woman in months after her mother and uncle conspired to go after her dad's pension. Rachel would be in prison several more years, and not for the first time, Lexi wondered what kind of relationship they'd have when her mom got out.

She finished the first beer, cracked a second, and started in on it.

TYLER LET Alex Anne use his phone to call her dad. He gave her some space to have the conversation. While he couldn't hear what they said, she cried, laughed, and looked happy for what had to be the first time in days. "He's sending a car for us," she said as she handed his mobile back. "Thirty minutes."

"I hate to be an imposition." Tyler jerked his head toward the Model X, visible now with the mass of emergency vehicles gone. "I drove the Tesla here, and the battery died. My other car has two flat tires thanks to Durrani's men."

"We'll take care of it all." She grinned. "How could we not after what you did?" She wrapped him in a hug, and Tyler winced. "Are you all right?" Alex Anne asked as she pulled back. "Did I hit your stitches?"

"No," Tyler said. "I got shot by the blond asshole. Vest soaked it up, but Kevlar spreads out the impact. I probably have a couple cracked ribs."

"Should we take you to the hospital?"

Tyler shook his head. "They don't really do anything for this type of injury. Hell, they don't even tape ribs anymore.

Some brand-new doctor would just tell me to take it easy for a couple weeks."

"You should."

"Maybe I will." Tyler remembered his laptop remained in the Tesla. "I need to get something. Want to walk with me?"

Alex Anne fell in step beside him. "I'm not sure I'm ready to be alone quite yet, even if it's just for a couple minutes." They arrived at the Model X. "Nice car."

"Thanks," Tyler said. "It belonged to the chief lackey of my former commanding officer. I killed him when they came after me and Lexi. Technically, it's hers now." Tyler opened the door and retrieved his laptop bag from the passenger's seat.

"It's electric, right?"

"Yes. Takes some getting used to for certain."

"How can you open the door if the battery is dead?" Alex Anne asked.

"There's a twelve-volt which keeps the basics running even if the main one dies." He smiled. "I'm a mechanic. I probably couldn't fix a lot of things on this SUV without some training, but I understand the basics of how it works."

Alex Anne walked around, opened the driver's side door, and sat in the seat. She was a few inches shorter than Tyler, so it took some effort for her feet to reach the pedals. She felt the leather steering wheel. "I think I need to get one of these."

"I'm sure you can afford to," Tyler said.

"My dad's pretty cheap." Alex Anne smirked. "He has a Suburban, but he always tells me I don't need a car." She gripped the wheel with both hands and acted like she made sharp turns in a race. "He's wrong. I think I need one of these."

Tyler looked across the cabin at her. Alex Anne reminded him a lot of Lexi in some ways. She looked relieved to be safe, of course, but the trauma of the last couple days would linger for a while. "You going to be all right?"

"I *am* all right," she said. "Thanks to you."

"Not what I mean," Tyler said. "You probably know I was in the army for a long time. I did four deployments to Afghanistan. Saw a lot of combat. It . . . wears on you after a while no matter how tough you are or how you're wired." He paused. "I ended up with PTSD. Probably unavoidable, but it wasn't something I ever thought I'd need to deal with. I got into a really good therapy program at the VA. Even now, I still do parts of it to manage everything."

A single tear slid down Alex Anne's cheek. "You think I'm going to have PTSD?"

"How could you not after what you just went through? I'd do another combat tour right now before I endured what you did."

"I guess you're right." Alex Anne wiped her face on her sleeve.

"Talk to someone. A professional. You're going to need to deal with this, or it'll eat you alive." Tyler frowned. He never thought he'd be an evangelist for a shrink, but here he was. The right doctor and program mattered. "I served with a few guys who thought they were too macho for therapy. It was for sissies."

"What happened?"

"One or two of them made it." He thought of his buddy Musa who found his way back to the life he used to lead. "A few lost themselves in bottles . . . either booze or pills." Tyler patted the M11 on his hip. "One put his gun in his mouth and ate a bullet." Alex Anne paled. "I'm not trying to scare you. Honest. This kind of talk isn't something I'm good at, as I'm sure my daughter would tell you. I just want you to take it seriously."

Her head bobbed slightly. "I will," Alex Anne said in a small voice. "Thanks."

They lapsed into silence and waited inside the Model X. The reserve battery kept the cabin lights on until the hired car arrived. It was a late-model Lincoln Continental. Tyler opened a door for Alex Anne and then let himself in on the opposite side. He kept the computer bag with him. "You know the destination?" he asked the driver, a Latino man around his age.

"Yes, sir."

They left the airport. Alex Anne let out a deep breath once the car turned onto a real road. The driver soon got them back on the highway headed toward Baltimore. Tyler wondered if this were actually Durrani's last trick. A fail-safe to ensure they nabbed their primary target in case the main mission went off the rails. He slipped his hand into his jacket under the guise of cradling his ribs. Donnell called him paranoid. Maybe he was, but a little extra vigilance didn't hurt right now. Tyler only relaxed when the car neared the Lord Baltimore hotel, and he saw Wilkinson standing out front.

Alex Anne got out first. She ran to her dad and hugged him. Both of them shed a few tears. Tyler stayed by the car to give them some space. "Thanks for the lift," he said to the driver as he tapped the roof. The Continental soon pulled into an available space, and Tyler approached Alex Anne and her dad. Wilkinson opened his arms for a hug. Tyler put up a hand. "Cracked ribs. I'll take a handshake."

"You got it." Wilkinson grabbed Tyler's hand with surprising strength and shook it. "Thank you." His red eyes rimmed. "Thank you for bringing her back."

"Glad I could do it."

"Come inside with us."

"I guess I still have a room here," Tyler said. He maneuvered his way in front of father and daughter so he could go in first. At this late hour, the lobby was empty of everyone except the lone desk clerk. Tyler walked into the elevator ahead of them and then checked the hallway when they reached their floor. No problems anywhere. Durrani's operation really was over.

Inside the suite, Wilkinson asked, "Is there anything else we can do for you, Mister Tyler?"

"Actually, yes. I have two vehicles needing to be towed. A Tesla near the hangar, and my 442 from the place on the truck registration."

"We'll make sure it's done," Wilkinson said. "You look a little tired. Can I have the car take you home?"

Tyler still had a room here. He remembered Lexi texting and saying she'd still be up when he got home. She'd never been prone to late nights. Maybe she needed something. "Sounds good," he said. "It's been a long couple days."

"All right. Just tell him your address when you get there. I'll be in touch in a day or two. I'm sure we'll want to see you again."

"And meet your daughter," Alex Anne added. She walked to Tyler and hugged him around the neck to avoid his ribs.

He patted her on the back. "I'm sure she'll be thrilled. Will you two be OK here alone?"

"I think the threat is over," Wilkinson said. "Don't you?"

"Probably, but you're paying me to be paranoid." Tyler unholstered his M11, popped in a fresh magazine, and handed the pistol to Wilkinson. "Know how to use one?"

The larger man frowned but accepted the gun. "I've been shooting a few times."

"Good. I hope you don't need it. If you do, pull the slide back and let it go to rack in a cartridge. It'll be ready to fire. Give it back to me when I see you again."

"What about you?" Alex Anne asked.

Tyler grinned. "I'm paranoid. I have plenty more."

37

The Continental dropped Tyler off at his house. Lexi's Accord Coupe sat in the driveway, and a couple interior lights shone through the front window. She was keeping late hours. "Thanks for the lift . . . again."

"Have a good night, sir," the driver said as Tyler climbed out.

Tyler unlocked the front door and walked in. The kitchen and dining room lights were on. Lexi occupied a chair at the small table. Three empty beer bottles sat atop it, and her hand encircled a fourth with some liquid still in it. Her eyes looked red and a little puffy. Tyler grabbed a longneck from the fridge and took a seat beside her. "Long night."

Her head turned toward him. "Alex Anne is safe?"

"Yes. She and all the other girls. Eighteen of them on the plane. I managed to stop it before it took off."

"Durrani is dead?" Lexi asked, and Tyler swore he heard a hard edge in her question.

"Along with everyone in his organization," he said.

Lexi picked up her beer and took a long drink. "And his nephew," she said in a voice just above a whisper.

Tyler's jaw went slack. It took him a few seconds to recover. "What? You told me you were good. He wasn't a problem."

"I know." She closed her eyes, and fresh tears spilled over and ran down her cheeks. "He was with me when I answered you . . . he and a friend I wasn't expecting to be there." She paused for another draught. "It was just supposed to be Ahmed. We were going to hang out after I finished in the lab."

Tyler scooted his chair closer and put his arm around his daughter. She leaned into him and rested her head on his shoulder. For a couple minutes, neither of them spoke. Lexi cried a little. Tyler figured she'd gotten a lot of it out before he arrived. He wanted to ask her why she didn't tell him what was really going on. It was hard to craft the question without sounding like he was blaming her, though. He chose a different tactic. "When you're ready, tell me what happened."

"Ahmed and I went on a lunch date earlier." Tyler stewed at hearing this. Durrani probably sent him to woo Lexi. It made sense. If the man himself spent months running an op on Amanda Painter, he could ask his nephew to try and pick up one girl. It meant Durrani knew a lot about Alex Anne, including the fact Tyler recently joined the security detail. Kidnapping Lexi would keep him busy and unable to prevent the plane from taking off. "It was nice," Lexi continued after a moment. "I needed to go back to do some work at the mainframe lab. I told him we could meet afterwards."

"Sounds like he dropped in on you."

She nodded against his shoulder. "I'd seen him arguing with someone before I went in. That was the guy he brought. Scott . . . a creep he was paying to help him kidnap me."

"I was on my way to campus when I couldn't reach you," Tyler said. "I could have dealt with them for you."

"You had eighteen other girls to save."

"None as important as you."

They lapsed into silence again, which Lexi broke by continuing the story. "They were both there, but I didn't think they'd actually go through with it. I figured if I resisted, they'd see I wasn't an easy mark, and they'd back off."

"Makes sense," Tyler said. "Criminals love low-hanging fruit."

"I fought them off at first," Lexi said. "They carried knives. They were . . . more serious than I thought. So I ran. My car wasn't super close, but I knew I'd be faster than them. I bolted across the parking lot, opened my car, and grabbed the Glock from the glove compartment. I gave them a chance, Dad. I did." Her voice cracked. "They wouldn't take it."

"You did the right thing. Who knows what they'd've done to you if you hadn't?"

Lexi lifted her head and wiped her eyes with her left sleeve. "How old were you?"

"What do you mean?"

"When you . . . you know."

First killed someone, Tyler finished in his mind. "Twenty-three," he said. "My first tour of Afghanistan. I wasn't even in Special Forces yet. Just like you, I gave him a chance. He wouldn't take it." Tyler recalled the young Afghan man defiantly cursing at him before raising his rifle. "When it's them or you, be decisive. Sounds like you were."

"Yeah." Her voice was small.

"You're four years younger than I was, and I think you were faced with an even worse choice. You did the right thing. I know it stings now, but you did."

"I hauled ass across that parking lot." Lexi stared into the distance as she recounted what happened. "I don't think I've ever run so fast in my life . . . even at a cross-country meet. I just knew I wanted to get to my car. I made it ahead of them. Scott was closer to me. He wouldn't drop the knife." Her eyes closed. "I gave Ahmed the same choice. He'd already seen what I did. Why didn't he put it down?"

"Money," Tyler said. "One of the oldest motivations in the world. He was probably committed to helping his uncle, too."

"I was all right after Braxton," Lexi said.

"So was I . . . thanks to you." It was true. Tyler hadn't gotten the better of the fight with his former commander, and Lexi hitting the man with the Tesla turned the tide.

"You know what I mean. He kidnapped me, and he was trying to kill you. I didn't kill him, but I was fine to watch you shoot him. This's different."

"Sure," Tyler said. "You were a lot more threatened and more involved."

Lexi sat in silence for a moment, and Tyler gave her time to process everything. Eventually, she asked, "How do you get past it?"

"Tough question. It's going to be different for everyone. Some people can never get over even the good shoots like yours. Others shrug it off and sight down the rifle at someone else."

"Is that where you fall?"

The question stung even though Tyler knew Lexi didn't add any venom to it. "More or less. I've always been able to see what needs to be done and how to make it happen. Maybe it's what makes me a good mechanic. It also means I'm practical when it comes to . . . dealing with people. You know about the time Braxton gave me false orders, and I took out a family who'd done nothing wrong." He felt her nod against his shoulder. "It sticks with me. Now, I make sure. Either a good person is in danger, or a bad person is living up to their reputation. Sometimes both. People love to wait for the cops or think they'll save them, but it's a fantasy. The police can't be everywhere, and they can't stop everyone. There are times people need to take decisive action to save themselves or someone else. You did it. A lot of others might have faltered, but you were strong. Don't beat yourself up for it. I know it sucks right now, but you did the right thing, and on some level, you know it."

"Yeah." Lexi sat up and wiped her eyes. "I know. Your therapy program helped, right?"

"It did," Tyler said. "I went for a lot more than shooting two people, though. I'd seen a lot of time in combat, and there was the whole . . . Braxton situation. Unprocessed guilt, or whatever they call it." He sighed. "This is another thing which is different for everyone. My shrink won't be yours, and my program almost certainly wouldn't be. But if you think you need to talk to someone other than me, go ahead."

"It's nothing personal, Dad."

"I know. I'm not exactly the warm and fuzzy type." Lexi grinned, and Tyler chuckled. "I gave Alex Anne a similar talk a little while ago. She's been through quite a lot in the last couple days, too. A few years ago, I never would've thought I'd be an evangelist for therapy, but here we are."

"Here we are." Lexi leaned in again and hugged Tyler.

"Watch the ribs," he said, and she raised her arms to embrace him around the neck. "I'll have to tell you how my night went sometime."

"Tell me tomorrow." She yawned. "I'm going to bed. Thanks for the talk, Dad. I think it helped."

"Sure, kiddo. Get some rest."

Lexi left the kitchen and walked upstairs. Tyler grabbed the empty bottles, rinsed them, and dumped them in the recycling. His talk of therapy made him think he needed to paint. He would. Like Lexi, however, he could wait until tomorrow.

38

The next morning, Lexi yawned as she padded downstairs slightly after ten-thirty. She hadn't slept so late in months, and she needed it after the events of yesterday. Coffee was the first priority. She filled her mug and looked around the kitchen for something to eat. Her dad left a pan of scrambled eggs covered on the stove. Lexi smiled, heated them, made some toast, and enjoyed a quiet breakfast at the table. Her dad must've gone to work. She wondered how he got there. Their only working car was her coupe, and it sat in the driveway.

She filled her water bottle and walked back upstairs. Despite showering before bed last night, Lexi took another. She felt she still needed to wash something off herself. Once she dried her hair and put on fresh clothes again, Lexi sat at her computer. It was the weekend. Whatever homework waited for her could keep right on waiting. She checked her email, found nothing of interest, and then opened a new message.

. . .

Dear Mom,

I know it's been a while since we talked. Honestly, I'm still pissed at you and Uncle George, and I probably will be for a while. Let's just not discuss it.

Dad and I are still doing well. College has been interesting recently, but my grades are strong, and I'm making a few new friends.

LEXI PAUSED and wiped a stray tear from her cheek. Despite what went down with Ahmed and Scott, her experience at the University of Maryland had been positive. Classes were good and appropriately challenging, she liked the campus, her teachers were mostly solid, and she'd found a couple new friends after struggling to make them toward the end of high school. In time, she might even be able to talk to them about things like the Ahmed mess. Not yet, though. Her dad would be a good sounding board, and her mom could get the news in generalities. She continued typing.

When I first came here to live with him, I was angry. Mostly at you for getting arrested and going to jail, but also at him for not being around more beforehand. It was a rocky first couple weeks, but we made strides and ended up in a good place. No offense, but I wish I'd come to live with him sooner, even with having to change schools and everything.

For the first time, I think I understand Dad. I know you loved him, but you two are very different people, and I'm not sure you ever understood him. I didn't, either, until recently. I'm sure we'll still have our moments of disagreement here and there, but we're in a great place.

It'll take a while until I want to see you after what you and Uncle George tried to do. I would say I hope he's doing well wher-

ever he landed, but I don't care anymore. Let's try to keep in touch through email, at least.

Love,
　Lexi

SHE SENT THE EMAIL, dabbed at her eyes with a tissue, and closed her laptop.

TYLER ARRIVED at his shop early. After the chaos of the last couple days, it felt good to be in a more relaxed environment. The place looked ready to open. All the equipment gleamed in the overhead lights. The main area smelled faintly of the paint job Smitty said wrapped up yesterday. It beat the paneling on the walls at many garages. Tyler's new business was almost ready to open.

The inspector, however, still hadn't arrived.

"I'm telling you this guy's a prick," Smitty opined over a cup of coffee.

"I agree." Tyler opened his bag and took out the old Patriot laptop. The inspector's business card sat atop his uncluttered desk. Once the computer came online, Tyler searched for whatever he could find about the man.

Smitty jutted his chin toward the laptop. "You gonna blackmail the guy with whatever this thing tells you?"

"If I have to." Tyler picked up the phone and set it back down again. "I know I've been gone for a few days. Thanks for everything you did covering for me. I'll tell you the details sometime, but let's just say the job went sideways."

"Usually means people are dead when you're involved."

Tyler remained silent. "It's your shop now. You kill someone here, you get to clean it up."

"No," Tyler said. "I'd delegate it to you." He grinned. "Experience has made you good at it."

"Well, shit," Smitty said. "I knew I should've half-assed it."

"You're like me. We both have to whole-ass the things we work on. I'm gonna call this guy now." Tyler pushed the speaker button and dialed the number on the inspector's business card. When the man answered, Tyler said, "You're overdue for an inspection at my car repair shop, Mister Talley. When can I expect you?"

"I've had a few scheduling problems."

"Maybe you'd like to resolve them and give me a time and date. Say . . . today or tomorrow. Anytime."

Talley offered a theatrical sigh. "Don't think I can fit you in. If you'd like to pay for priority service, maybe I could."

Now, they'd reached the heart of the matter. As Tyler suspected, the guy wanted more money. "We have a contract with a rate we both agreed to. I expect you to honor it."

"I've got a specialized skill set," Talley said. "I'm kind of in demand."

Tyler glanced at his laptop. "Kent Talley. Resident of Hamilton. Husband of Marcia and father to Kent Junior and Kelly."

"So you looked me up." A tremor in Talley's voice belied the calm he tried to project over the phone line.

"Let me tell you something, Mister Talley. I didn't settle on the name Special Operations Classic Car Repair because I liked the way it looked on a sign. It's because I was a green beret. I did four combat tours of Afghanistan. Among the many things my time in the service gave me a is a low tolerance for bullshit and the people who peddle it. Unless you'd like to see me demonstrate *my* specialized skill set at your house, I suggest you come to my shop and fulfill your contract as soon as you can."

"You'd come to my house?" Talley said, panic in his tone. Tyler remained silent. "I got a wife and kids. You'd really do something to me with them around?" Again, Tyler didn't offer anything. He'd long ago learned the value of silence in situations like these. People disliked quiet. They would talk to cover the gap, or they'd respond to what they expected the other person might say. "You're messed up, man." Talley sighed. "Fine. I'll be there in two hours. Be ready." He hung up before Tyler could answer.

"There." Tyler made sure the speaker went off when the call ended. "Problem solved."

"Would you really gut the man at his house?" Smitty asked.

Tyler stood and winked on his way to getting more coffee.

39

Four days later, Tyler let Lexi drive the Tesla to Alex Anne's house. Both the electric SUV and his 442 got dropped off the evening after everything went down. The Olds sported two new tires, and while the Model X still needed a full charge, it had been meticulously detailed. The Wilkinsons lived in a posh area of Cockeysville on Pot Spring Road. The house proved easy to miss as neither Tyler nor Lexi saw it until they'd been around the cul-de-sac twice. The mailbox carried no markings—not even a house number— and the pines and firs lining the driveway hid the impressive home from the road.

More evergreens covered the front yard. Manicured hedges waiting for spring popped up near the walkway and front door. Tyler dreaded the landscaping bill, but he figured Wilkinson could afford it. Twin double garage doors marked the end of the driveway. Lexi parked the Tesla in front of the left one. "Good thing we didn't bring my car," Tyler said as he got out. "The neighborhood watch would already be beating us with sticks."

Lexi grinned. "Made from a hundred percent recycled

wood." She rang the bell when they arrived at the front door. Donnell, sitting in a wheelchair, answered a moment later.

"Great," he said. "Now, you know where we live." A smile slowly spread across his face. "I'm just hassling you. Come in."

"Good to see you," Tyler said, and the two men shook hands. "Did you ever get to a hospital?"

"Yeah. Once the traffickers were dead, Mister Wilkinson insisted I go. The police had to question me because I got shot, but it was easy. Tied into a closed case."

Tyler introduced Lexi and Donnell and then said, "You got discharged in record time."

"Just made it back here today," Donnell said. "The deacon really did a good job."

A door opened somewhere, and Tyler caught a whiff of Italian food coming from the kitchen. It ramped his hunger up a level or two. "Christ, they'll let anyone in here." Cliff rounded the corner.

"Explains how you got in," Tyler said as he and his former boss bumped fists. "I guess I forgot to send you a report on the job."

"It all right. The local news did it for me. I'm filling in here until Donnell is back on his feet." He handed Tyler a folded check. "The company got a bonus. I'm passing some of it on to you."

"Some?"

"I'm saving up to buy a chunk of Patriot back from Danny," Cliff said. "I want to be the majority partner again. I think he's done some damage, and I want to fix it."

"I could shoot him for you," Tyler offered. Lexi elbowed him in the side, which still hurt.

Cliff shrugged. "I'll let you know if he takes my offer."

A few minutes later, Jeff Wilkinson and Alex Anne joined everyone else. Wilkinson brought in a chef to prepare an

Italian feast. Fresh mozzarella with capers and breadsticks formed the first course, the best lasagna Tyler ever ate was the entree, and the chef brought out a huge plate of cannolis for dessert. Finishing even one was a struggle. Tyler pushed his dessert plate away and sucked up the pain in his ribs to let out a deep breath. "Thanks for dinner."

"It's a small gesture compared to what you did," Wilkinson said.

"I think the men want to drink port and talk," Alex Anne said to Lexi. "Want to see my room?"

She beamed. "Sure." The two girls went upstairs.

"I do have a few bottles of port," Wilkinson said.

Donnell held up a hand. "I don't mean to cut off the celebration, but I have to say something." He paused and frowned. "I think I should resign."

Wilkinson did a double take. "What? Why would you?"

"It's all my fault." His voice cracked. "What happened to Alexandra. I should've waited." He bobbed his head toward Tyler. "I should've waited for you to finish so we could do the transport like we'd planned."

"As much as I'd love to say I would've taken out all three men," Tyler said, "we'll never know. They got the drop on you. They could've gotten it on me, too. Then, we'd both be dead, and no one would've been available for an airport shootout."

"I should've waited," Donnell repeated.

"Yes. I hope you will if you're ever in a similar spot again . . . but we don't know how things would've gone down. I think you should stop beating yourself up over it."

"I'm not asking for your resignation," Wilkinson said.

"Maybe you should," Donnell muttered.

"We were up against a professional operation. It's my job as manager to be prepared for things. I could've told you to stick around. I could've told the Arena guy to piss off. We can all do a little better. When the next tour comes around, we will. Maybe we'll even ask Mister Tyler to consult again."

"I'd be happy to," he said. "Even happier without giving up part of my check."

"Yeah, yeah," Cliff said.

"All right." Donnell's eyes welled, and he paused to collect himself. "I appreciate it. I might still be rough on myself for a bit, but I'll stick around as long as you want me."

"Good." Wilkinson nodded. "Now, how about some port?"

LEXI'S BEDROOM at her dad's house was about average in size. Maybe twelve feet by fourteen. Pretty much the same at her mom's. Some of her friends' rooms were much larger. Alex Anne's was on a completely different level. It must have been twenty by thirty. Lexi had seen smaller apartments. A king bed and three dressers dominated the floor space, and a huge walk-in closet held a ton of outfits and clothes for all seasons. "This is incredible."

Alex Anne shrugged and looked down. She smoothed her hoodie even though it didn't have a wrinkle on it. "I'm really not trying to show off."

"I get it. Well, I guess I don't *really* get it, but ... uh ... you know."

"It's fine." Alex Anne offered a small smile. "I'm really outgoing on stage, but it's easy. There are thousands of people, but they're all at a distance. I'm a little more introverted one-on-one."

"Me, too." Lexi saw a lot of similarities between herself and Alex Anne. The singer was a couple inches shorter, but they were close in age, had a nearly identical hair color, and both favored hoodies and jeans. "You know why I first listened to your music?" Alex Anne shook her head. "Your name. I saw an Alex who was a girl. I'm Alexis. I go by Lexi, but boys used to tease me and call me Alex." She let out a dry chuckle at the memory. "I went to school with a lot of Kayleighs and Madisons and Mackenzies. It was nice to see someone whose name looked like mine."

"Alexandra and Alexis aren't so different." Alex Anne walked to the door. "Want to see the studio? It's down the hall."

"Yes!" Lexi shot to her feet, inwardly chiding herself for being such a fangirl. What was she, fourteen again? It was nice to know someone she admired turned out to be a good person. She told herself to dial it back a notch, and that notion flew away as Alex Anne opened the studio. It took up the majority of the second floor and was even bigger than her bedroom. Polished wood floors held a rack of guitars. A drum kit and microphone sat near the back of a small raised stage. Another door led to a control room with a large window and a ton of recording equipment.

"This is awesome," Lexi said. She thought about the weight of all the equipment and whatever it took to make the studio soundproof. "Why isn't it on the ground floor?"

Alex Anne giggled. "That's your first question?"

"I guess I inherited my dad's sense of logistics." Lexi felt herself blush.

"At least half of this space is an addition over the garage. We reinforced everything under it. The heavy stuff is mostly in the new half." Lexi noticed this once Alex Anne mentioned it. The front part of the studio held a table, four chairs, a bookcase, and a few instruments. "You play anything?"

"I played sax in middle school and my first two years of high school," Lexi said. "I'm out of practice, though."

"Who cares?" Alex Anne smiled. "Pick it up. I'll get a guitar." She returned a moment later with a plain brown acoustic model and sat in one of the chairs. She plucked the strings and tuned it while Lexi grabbed the sax. "Let's do one of my earlier songs. I think it's appropriate." Alex Anne strummed the guitar, and Lexi recognized the song right away. She waited for her smile to fade before she added the accompaniment.

A few seconds later, Alex Anne sang the opening verse to "Smile Through the Pain." She played the bridge without missing a note, and Lexi joined her in singing the chorus.

"You gotta smile through the pain.

"Run through the rain.

"Go through all this shit and know you'll never be the same.

"Won't get off the train.

"Can't erase the stain.

"Smile through the pain."

Alex Anne finished with a guitar flourish. "I was fourteen when I wrote that song." Her fingers plucked random strings. "My first boyfriend dumped me. It all seems silly and dramatic now, but six months is a big chunk of your life when you're young."

"You should play on stage," Lexi said.

"Thanks." Alex Anne smiled and ran a hand through her hair. "I've thought about doing a stripped-down album. Less overproduced and more acoustic." She patted her instrument, her hand making hollow thunks against the thin wood. "It's hard. Everyone sees me as some sort of pop princess." She affected a catty tone for the last two words. "I'm a creator. I want to write songs. These last few years, I think I've gone along with what people expected of me. Now, I'm going to make the music I want to make."

Lexi nodded. "Good for you. It worked for Taylor Swift."

"I guess it did." Alex Anne paused and set her guitar back on a stand. "I overheard my dad talking to a cop a couple days ago. Durrani went after you, too?"

Lexi's head bobbed slightly. "Through his nephew. When

endearing himself to me didn't work quickly enough, he and a friend tried to grab me at knifepoint."

"I'm glad you got away," Alex Anne said.

"I'm my father's daughter."

"He talked to me about therapy." Alex Anne rocked slightly in the chair. "Told me it helped him, and I should do it, too, after what I went through."

"I think I got the same chat," Lexi said. "It definitely worked for him. He's still . . . well, you've met him, but he's a lot better than he was seven or eight years ago."

"I'm going to do it," Alex Anne said with a clear-eyed nod. "I'll probably catch heat for it in some circles, but whatever. You should, too."

"I think I will."

"We can be therapy BFFs."

Lexi grinned. "Maybe we can even write a song together about it."

"Deal." Alex Anne held up a finger. "But no sax."

Lexi nodded in agreement. "No sax."

40

Three days later, a ribbon stretched across the entrance of Special Operations Classic Car Repair. Tyler didn't want all the fanfare and formality, but Sara hatched the plan, and Lexi agreed. Outnumbered again, Tyler went along with it. He eschewed scissors, flipped open his lock-blade knife, and cut through the ribbon in a quick swipe.

Lexi hugged him first, and then Sara followed. Tyler's ribs felt far less sore now. He looked at the sign, the last piece of the puzzle—and among the most costly—to be finished. It would be large and visible to motorists driving by. The location—a former gas station near the intersection of Northern Parkway and Harford Road—was convenient to Baltimore, the county, and the surrounding area. It would also save Tyler about ten minutes each way on his commute compared to Smitty's. Lexi promised to manage the business' social media, which Tyler both appreciated and dreaded at the same time. She'd already set up the Facebook page and gotten some likes.

The inspection had gone well—perhaps because Talley

feared for his life—and the business opened on schedule. The familiar lifts from Smitty's sat ready to use in the four work bays. With the doors officially open, Tyler celebrated by brewing a fresh pot of coffee. Everyone held a mug and stood outside to enjoy the fresh air. The weather even cooperated by being warmer than normal for a late winter morning.

Tyler sipped his black coffee. "I couldn't have done this without you. All of you."

"Few people open a place like this by themselves," Smitty said. "Speaking of which, we're gonna need employees at some point. Your girlfriend told me I should remind you."

"What can I say?" Sara asked. "I like hiring people."

Smitty raised his paper cup toward her. "I was glad to have your help a few times along the way."

"Someone needed to hold down the fort while the knight-errant was busy elsewhere," Sara said.

Tyler put his arm around her. "I'm just glad you work for free. No way I can afford the hourly rate of a senior Pentagon executive."

Sara looked up at Tyler and winked. "We'll discuss payment later."

"Get a room," Lexi said.

Tyler wondered when her outreach would pay off. They'd gone the old-school route and put flyers up. Tyler even offered to use recycled paper and quell Lexi's objection to being wasteful. She'd handled the more modern methods, including posting in classic car forums and asking a few bloggers to talk about it.

Fifteen minutes later, a vintage Mustang made the turn from Harford Road into the lot. A man in his sixties walked inside. Smitty and Tyler both talked to him about the maintenance for his car. They'd start with brakes and all the engine filters and then see what else the classic ride needed. After the man left, Smitty stayed behind the counter. Lexi and Sara sat on the couch in the waiting area. Conspiring on something, no doubt. It was good to see them getting along, even if them putting their heads together often created more work for Tyler.

He sat at his desk in his small office. From the top drawer, he pulled out a watercolor painting he'd been working on the last couple nights. It served as both a revision and rebuttal to an earlier piece. A man stood with his back to the frame. A squat building sat on the left, and a few dead men with guns lay on the right side. Earlier, Tyler painted a fork in the road, and the man presumably needed to choose which path to walk.

This time, both scenes were on different sides of the same street.

Later, Sara kissed Tyler goodbye, and Smitty worked on the Mustang. Lexi stood outside enjoying the fresh air. Tyler joined her. "I saw your painting," she said after a moment. "The earlier one, too."

"What do you think?"

"A few days ago, I mentioned Sara telling me she thought you were a little lost."

"I remember," Tyler said.

"I think you're well on the way to finding yourself, Dad."

"Good. I'd always wanted to before I turned fifty-one."

Lexi rolled her eyes. "You know what I mean. I'm still not convinced sitting behind a desk and opening Excel is really your thing. It looks like you're coming to terms with it, though. Maybe I shouldn't read too much into what you paint, but that's my impression."

"I think it's a smart one," Tyler said. "Seeing you and Sara sitting on the couch and plotting my demise made me realize you both inspire me in different ways. For you, I want to be the stable dad. To her, I'll always be a knight-errant."

"You don't have to park yourself behind a desk for me,

you know," Lexi said. "That's not the kind of stability you can do."

"I know it now. It's what the painting means. They're not two separate paths I have to choose between. I guess it took me a while to figure it all out."

Lexi grinned. "I thought you were supposed to get wiser as you got older and grayer."

"I wish I'd had your smarts when I was nineteen," Tyler said.

"It's a gift," Lexi said with an absent flip of her hair.

Tyler smiled. "Never mind. I take it back."

END of Novel #3

Hi there,

I hope you enjoyed *Lost Highway*. Tyler does another favor—this one for Lexi and her friend Stacy—and it leads to four dead bodies and going on the run from an unknown enemy with an endless supply of killers.

You can preorder *Four on the Floor* today!

THE END

AFTERWORD

Thanks for checking out this novel! I hope you enjoyed reading the book as much as I enjoyed writing it.

I write mysteries and thrillers with snark and flawed heroes. If this sounds like something you like, you can check out my catalog below.

The John Tyler Thrillers

1. The Mechanic
2. White Lines
3. Lost Highway
4. Four on the Floor (Spring 2022)

The C.T. Ferguson Crime Novels:

1. The Reluctant Detective
2. The Unknown Devil
3. The Workers of Iniquity
4. Already Guilty

5. Daughters and Sons
6. A March from Innocence
7. Inside Cut
8. The Next Girl
9. In the Blood
10. Right as Rain
11. Dead Cat Bounce (December 2021)

(Note: C.T. Ferguson appears in *White Lines*.)

While these are the suggested reading sequences, each novel is a standalone thriller or mystery, and the books can be enjoyed in whatever order you happen upon them.

For the most current listing of books, please visit https://www.tomfowlerwrites.com/mybooks.

Connect with me:

For the many ways of finding and reaching me online, please visit https://tomfowlerwrites.com/contact. I'm always happy to talk to readers.

This is a work of fiction. Characters and places are either fictitious or used in a fictitious manner.

"Self-publishing" is something of a misnomer. This book would not have been possible without the contributions of many people.

- The great cover design team at 100 Covers.
- My editor extraordinaire, Chase Nottingham.
- My wonderful advance reader team, the Fell Street Irregulars.